Mafia Games
Vi Carter

Copyright © 2021 by Vi carter

All rights reserved.

No portion of this book may be reproduced in any form without written permission from the publisher or author, except as permitted by U.S. copyright law.

WARNING

This book is a dark romance. This book contains scenes that may be triggering to some readers and should be read by those only 18 or older.

NEWSLETTER

Join my newsletter and never miss a new release or giveaway by scanning the QR code below:

PROLOGUE

O'REAGAN
AN CHLANN

CLAIRE

"I have this recurring dream."

I lie down on the leather couch, placing my hands over my stomach that tightens and squirms beneath my fingertips. I'm afraid each time I speak of the fire. But I know how important it is to talk about it, or so my therapist, Rose, tells me. My lashes flutter closed as I continue to speak.

"I'm back in my bedroom. I'm lying on my bed. The canopy that floats above me hangs down. The small ballerinas that my mother stitched into the fabric are gone, and the rest is going fast with each lick of the flames."

I shift on the couch, hoping to cool down my burning skin and slow my racing heart.

"You are safe, Claire. This is your safe place." Rose's voice is gentle.

I don't open my eyes but nod and exhale a shaky breath. "I'm frozen, yet I know I should move, but I'm transfixed on the destruction before me. I'm entranced by how the red waves move. It's not until heat sears me and my nose twitches that I look away from the flames. It's the smell of burning hair that has my stomach roiling."

I swallow a lungful of fresh air.

"You're doing great." Rose's voice is closer to me now, and I don't like that she moved, and I hadn't even noticed. "This is your safe place, Claire." Her voice is soft as she speaks, and I picture her wearing her half-smile with her head tilted to the side; it's her encouraging look.

I should open my eyes and remind myself that I'm not there anymore. That I am safe. That I am not back in my bed. That I am not fifteen again.

"I keep telling myself that I need to move. I need to get out of bed, but my broken legs won't permit it, and the room is growing hotter." My eyes snap open. My mind has taken enough for one day. I sit upright on the couch.

Rose is disappointed that I stopped. She tries to recover quickly, but I see how her eyes tighten in the corners, creating lines that showcase her fifty years of age. She taps her pen three times on the page. "You did great."

I run my tongue along my teeth, trying to find my balance as I reach for the glass of water that sits alone on a small white table. Rose doesn't speak as I take a large swallow. Then placing the glass back down, I run my hands down my yellow sundress until my fingers glide across my knees.

"Why did you stop?" Rose speaks again while dipping her head so she can see me as I try to hide from her questioning gaze.

"I'm tired." I won't meet her stare; instead, I glance behind her at the rows of white bookshelves that coat the wall from ceiling to floor.

"Tired, how?"

My gaze snaps to Rose, and I want to tell her to mind her own business. My sharp thoughts have guilt turning my cheeks pink, and I look away from her before she can read the anger on my face.

"I had a late night," I lie.

Her pen glides across the page. I have often wondered what she is writing, but no matter what angle I tilt my head, I can't read what's on the paper.

The diamond-shaped clock on the wall ticks slowly, like the batteries are dying or time is about to stop altogether.

"In your dream, do you get out of bed?" Rose asks.

I wrap my arms around my waist. My belly aches. "No."

Rose nods and scribbles more words.

I still have thirty minutes left in this session. I know holding back won't benefit me. I focus on the scar on my knee. My fingertips trail along the puckered skin as I speak.

"He comes for me." I don't peer at Rose but focus straight ahead. "He walks through the flames. They don't even burn him. They actually part for him." A smile haunts my lips. I have no idea why. The image is terrifying.

I take a peek at Rose, who gives me an encouraging nod.

"He sits on my bed that is burning, and all the flames go away." I grind my teeth to try to keep my emotions in check. "He leans in close to me, and I think for a moment he's going to say something." My heart starts to race. Fear tightens my throat, cutting off any further words.

Rose waits a beat. Maybe she sees the fear in my eyes; maybe she doesn't want this to stop. It's the most I've ever willingly said. I want to say it all, but it's too much.

Silence swallows us, and the clock ticks louder for a while.

"And does Leonard say anything?"

"No." I sputter out. "No, he laughs."

He laughs while my parents burn in the next room. While they scream as the flesh falls from their bones.

"He laughs," I repeat.

CHAPTER ONE

O'REAGAN
AN CHLANN

RICHARD

The tennis ball bounces back to me like it has done a million fucking times before. Staying sane in a place like this isn't easy.

At first, I screamed that I wasn't mad. When a lunatic, aka mad dog, screamed that he wasn't mad either, I knew I was rightfully fucked as they dragged me to the back of the asylum. The nurse on duty enjoyed sticking a syringe into my neck a little too much. "This area is reserved for the real fuck ups." His words were warm on my cheek, and I grinned, even as my body failed me.

The moment they dropped me into a wheelchair, my legs were strapped down. As the nurse strapped my arms to the chair, I opened my sluggish eyes and forced a steady voice. "I'll remember you." And I would. Like a sketch artist, my mind took in everything about him, down to the mole under his left eye.

He pulled back instantly, and fear latched onto him like a starving person to a hot meal. I stared at his face as long as I could before whatever the fuck was in the syringe did its job.

I tried to stay aware as they wheeled me down a half-lit corridor.

"You're as white as a sheet. Lighten up." A male voice behind me broke through my foggy state.

*"He didn't tell **you**; he'd remember you."*

"He'll be secured in a glass box for his duration here. So relax."

"He's on suicide watch?" Shock laced mole man's words, his fear erased as this knowledge settled in.

"Yep. Director said we have to keep a close watch on this one."

Light moved across my lids, and I half opened my eyes as the wheelchair was spun fully around, the nurse moving backwards through a set of double doors.

Mole man stumbles when he sees my eyes open.

"He's still awake."

The man steering my wheelchair laughs. "I put enough in the syringe to knock out an elephant."

I grinned, or I hoped I did. That's the signal I sent to my lips as I stared at the nurse.

"I'm telling you, Gerard. He's fucking smiling at me."

We stop moving, and I wished I was more alert. I relaxed my face and let my eyes close. The squeak of shoes halted in front of me.

Gerard tuts. "This is going to be a really long shift if you keep this up."

"He was smiling at me a minute ago."

"He's out cold. So stop fucking around."

We are moving again. I am tempted to open my eyes, but the drugs that raced through my veins have taken over. My will to stay awake is no match for the shit in my veins.

The tennis ball hits the glass wall before coming back to me. Rodger, in the next room, is screaming. His mouth agape as he tears at his hair. I throw the ball again, and he goes wild, frothing at the mouth. My lip twitches as he throws himself against the glass wall that divides us. His large body that has been deprived of anything healthy has no impact on the glass. These glass boxes were built to keep us in. I know this already. I have tried every single thing to escape in the three years I have been here, but this place is tighter than a nun's gee.

My tennis ball hits the glass again, and he loses his shit. I should really stop, but this is my only entertainment. This is what I have been reduced to. Torn black hair floats to the ground as Rodger continues to have a psychotic breakdown. His room turns red from the swirling light over his door. On instinct, I glance at mine. I've only ever seen it lit up once before.

After stuffing the tennis ball down between my bed and the only stone wall, I get up and walk to the far wall that's made of glass, too.

My glass coffin holds a single bed, a piss pot, and a small locker with no door.

Three nurses, all wearing protective clothing, line up outside Rodgers' room. They look like they are ready to enter into a violent crowd. Rodger backs away and starts pointing at me. When he glances at me, I wink at him, setting him off again. He launches himself against the wall just as the door opens. My gaze flickers to the nurses who are entering. I don't want Rodger to get sedated too quickly. What was the fun in that?

He follows my gaze and dives away from them. He's quick; I have to give the fat fucker that much. He races to his bed and stands on it; the mattress dips with his weight. They try to pull him down, but he's kicking his short fat legs and screaming. I'm grateful as I watch the madness that there's no sound. The red light stops swirling, catching my attention. When I look back, Rodger is restrained on his bed as a sedative is injected into his ass.

Shows over, folks.

I turn my head and come face to face with Lenny, the piece of shit. I salute him, and he juts out his chin while wearing a toothy smile. He holds his fist to the glass, and I mirror the action. We fist bump as if we were friends. Not in my world, but in this morons world, we are friends.

There is nothing memorable about Lenny. He looks like a regular guy. I'd even go to the extreme and say a happy regular guy. That is the furthest from the truth. Lenny is the type of man you think of when places like this are built. Some of us don't deserve to be here, but he does—every single ounce of him.

He's all my anger and hate stuffed into an overgrown body. Sometimes when I look at him, I start to drown in my hate, and I have to remind myself that my revenge will be the sweetest thing I have ever tasted.

I let my lip drag up. He nods his head as his gaze moves past me. I turn as Rodger is carried from his room. The door closes behind the three nurses as they wheel him somewhere deeper and more fucked up in this building.

My body is tight, and I don't want to turn to Lenny. I don't want him to see a snippet of my truth, so I walk away and sink to my bed. I throw my arm across my eyes. It's a do-not-disturb sign or an out-of-service sign. I lay still for a while and picture her.

She's smiling, but I can tell the emotion isn't real. Her long piano fingers shake as she lowers them to the table; it's her tic. She clutches her hands together to stop the tremble, but the tremor never really leaves her fingers, and yet he never sees it. I do. I see everything.

The buzz is subtle, but I know what it is. I don't move even as my door opens. I don't shift my body, but every cell in me is alert and awake.

"Richard, you got yourself a visitor."

Hope surges, but it's stamped into the ground by anger that I don't display as I sit up. William keeps his hand on the door. His mop of red curls obstructs his vision. He blows hair out of his eye only to have it fall back. I glance behind him to where two more nurses stand. One steps in, holding a pair of chained cuffs. I'm tempted to smile at Gerard. His gaze narrows, his stance stoic, as he steps to the left of my room.

I rise off the bed and hold my head high. At six foot four inches, I tower over most of these men. Holding out my arms in front of me, I spread my legs slightly and wait as they circle me. I want Gerard to use the cuffs he holds. His left-hand keeps touching the baton that's strapped to his side.

William takes the cuffs from Gerald's hands, much to my disappointment. The third nurse has moved to my right. A drop of sweat makes a pathway down the side of his face.

"Hold your arms still," William states as he approaches.

I don't blink as he clasps the cuffs on me.

"Aren't you going to ask who your visitor is?" He asks once I'm cuffed and deemed non-threatening.

My gut clenches, but I refuse to allow any emotions to enter my features. "Who is it?" I ask. William smirks at me with bravery that he shouldn't own. "You'll have to wait and see."

I ignore his laughter as I glance at Gerald. He's watching me. There is no laughter or amusement on his face. His fingers still rest against his baton. He knew chains wouldn't hold me back if I really wanted to hurt someone. A lesson he learned the hard way.

Right now, I didn't want to hurt anyone. They had me curious about the visitor.

We leave my glass box, and the air is different. It's poisoned by the smell of shit.

"What the fuck is that smell?" It's Gerald who asks. William clutches my chains and moves me along like I'm a dog on a leash.

"It's Derek. He covered his room with feces again to prevent us from seeing him." This tactic I had seen used before. It wasn't the smartest thing to do, considering you were stuck in a glass box with the smell of your own shit.

I know the moment we are coming to the front of the building. The floor under my feet is tiled, the walls painted and not flaky.

They steer me right, and we move down another hallway that I have been down only once before. "Is this where visitors are taken?" I ask, knowing full well they aren't. There is only one room down here.

"Yes." William's voice carries humor, and when I glance at Gerard behind me, he's watching me. I turn back around as William stops at the door and knocks.

"Come in."

William brings me in and reaches for my cuffed hands.

"Leave the cuffs on."

I should have a million feelings right now, but I have none as William steps aside and my father, Liam O'Reagan, head of the Irish Mafia, comes into view.

He's seated behind the director's desk, sipping a cup of tea.

"Sit down." He puts his cup down on the desk as he speaks to me.

It's been three years since I've seen him and not even a "how are you?" Or an explanation as to why my mother or siblings never came to see me, I keep it all in I move to the desk.

"You can leave." My father speaks as I sit down.

"Are you sure?" Gerard speaks up.

"Yes." My father still watches the men over my shoulder. It takes twelve seconds for the room to empty and the door to close.

His dark gaze swings to me. "Son. You look good."

He looks slightly older. His dark hair peppered lightly at the front. His suit sits perfectly on his straight frame. My father gives away nothing as he waits for me to speak.

"What do you want?"

Disappointment flashes in his gaze, and it pisses me off.

"You show your hand too quickly." He picks up his tea.

I slam my cuffed hands on the table. "You came all this way to teach me a lesson?"

"No. But it is a lesson you clearly haven't learned. Contain that anger, Richard, before it consumes you."

Contain. I am barely breathing because of how fast the anger is pumping through my veins.

"Why are you here?" I ask, gritting my teeth.

"I'm here to take you home."

His words should have me smiling. I've fought to get home for three years, but right now, at this second, I want to be taken back to my glass box where I plot against them all. Leaving here would put everything into motion. It would have me spilling all the blood that deserves to be spilled.

"Let's go." I raise my chained hands in the air, testing him.

"Your freedom has a price."

I control the darkness that threatens to blanket my mind. Let me introduce you to my fucking hateful father. Everything has a price, most of what he has given me has cost me way too much, and I am pretty sure this time will be no different.

Working with my father had already cost me my freedom and landed me in this madhouse.

CHAPTER TWO

O'REAGAN
AN CHLANN

RICHARD

I drink in the taste of freedom as my father and I leave the asylum. I rub my wrists like a weight has been removed from them. It's a false sense of security. An even heavier weight has been placed on my shoulders at my father's words.

I am to be a King on a panel of four for the Irish Mafia. This is my father's first condition. I am like a placemat for a drink or a pawn in his wicked game.

"So, you just want me to look pretty?" I ask him as I rub my wrists again as though the cuffs have been on them for the full three years and not just minutes. Before I left the asylum, I was handed the clothes I arrived in. Everything is too tight from spending all of my time working out. Exercising kept me sane, or so I hope.

"Exactly." My father stops at his Bentley and glances at me over the shiny roof. Everything about him is pristine, from his perfectly brushed dark hair to the tip of his shoes that you can see your reflection in.

I glance away from his dark eyes, the same as mine, and at Mullingar's madhouse, my home for the last three years.

"Leave the past in the past, son."

I grin at my father, but my expression holds not one ounce of amusement. "Wouldn't that suit you?" I say and climb in to the car. I'm sure I hear my shirt tear along the side with the quick movement I make. A part of me wants to shame him for putting me, his son, in an asylum. I glance at him again. I hate that everyone says I am his double. In looks, yes, I have his dark features, but under the flesh and bones, I have a heart. It might be black, but it still beats, unlike his. I glance back up at the drab building with its endless sea of windows looking down on me. I can feel their judgment as a reminder of all the things they see and hear. I want to leave now, but my father takes his time unbuttoning his tailored suit jacket before climbing into the car. "A lot has happened while you've been gone. You arriving back with an attitude won't serve anyone well."

I turn in my seat and face him. My anger unleashes itself, its inky fingers reaching out, but my rage doesn't sink into my father's flesh. No, my father is made of unyielding steel that I've never been able to penetrate. He tried to mold me into a mirror image of him.

I'm sure I'm a fucking disappointment.

My own anger and armor dissolve, and exhaustion that I have hidden for so long takes root and drags me lower. "Why?" I'm breathing heavily. The smell of leather, car polish and my father's cologne fills my lungs.

My father doesn't start the Bentley; he's setting up his phone and putting on his seat belt. I don't think he's heard my question. My weak attempt at trying to understand why he took me to this building three years ago. When I walked through the old front doors, I had no idea that I wouldn't see the light of day for a long time. My gaze is dragged up to the sky. The sun blinks in and out behind a mass of dark clouds that promise a shower shortly.

"Emotions are dangerous in our line of work. Most times, they are unnecessary. You reacted to your emotions twice, and that is a weakness that I wanted to remove from you." My father draws my attention away from the looming bad weather. His eyes hold the truth of his words. Or what he believes to be the truth. "Jack will never rule. You will."

My gut tightens. "So you locked me up in an asylum for three years?" Rage starts to grow, jump-starting my hunger for blood that I want to feed.

"First, I put you there so you could see how damaging emotions really are. Every single person in that place drowned in their own emotions, and look where it landed them."

"I reacted to a hysterical mother!" I grit my teeth. My defense sounds feeble. I had taken the life of one of our men to stop him from killing a woman. Yes, she was part of the problem but killing her wasn't a solution. The woman still died that day at my father's orders leaving behind three orphans. He made sure I watched. I thought that was the lesson. Obviously, I was wrong. I lick my lips, my mouth dry from resentment and lack of water.

"It doesn't matter what form they come in. If they are a problem, we take care of it. It's not always pretty. Women, men, and even at unfortunate times a child may be the sacrifice." My father turns to me. "Secondly, I didn't place you there for three years. You killed a nurse, and that's what kept you there."

I want to argue if he hadn't placed me in the asylum, I wouldn't have killed the nurse. I wouldn't have nearly died. I wouldn't have almost lost my mind. I'd like to say my stay at the asylum didn't break me, but I'm not sure how much truth is in that statement.

"I'm not looking for a replacement, Richard. I'm looking for a leader who will carry the O'Reagan name."

My father starts the Bentley. Our father/son chat over. Or so I thought.

"A lot has happened while you've been gone."

The thought of my siblings and mother is there again in my mind. My father will see it as a weakness if I ask about them. He's right. I bury my questions under my rage that barks at me, demanding a lump of meat in the form of my attention.

"We have a panel of four Kings. Jack, Shay, You and me."

Fucking great. "Shay?" I question, and I get a kick out of seeing the slight tightness in my father's jaw. His half-brother Connor is a thorn in his side, so to hear Connor's son Shay is a King is a surprise.

"He helped cover up Jack's mess."

I'm sitting up now. This is interesting. My shirt stretches even further at the movement, and I feel it split at my spine. I'll be shirtless by the time we get home. "What did Jack do?" Jack is three years older than me, but I always look at him as my little brother. I'm taller, bigger, and my father favors me and told me that I would rule, and Jack will be my right-hand man–my crutch- that I honestly don't need. He will be a crutch I will kick out from under my feet. I have my own men. I know the path I want to go down, and it doesn't include Jack or Shay.

"His girlfriend killed Cian." My father says the words with no emotion attached to them.

I'm caught between looking out the window at the passing world I get to re-join and trying to hold on to the lessons my father taught me. Jack has a girlfriend, and she had the balls to kill Cian. I already like her.

Silence filters in, and I'm used to seeing the world with no sound. Looking out the window, I watch the gray buildings fall away, and greenery slowly starts to spring up until it swallows all the gray. Trees line either side of the road, some arch over us canopying the road. That's when I know I'm going home when fields roll out either side of us.

The boy in me wants to cry that we made it home— that we survived.

"Also, your uncle Finn was shot."

I glance at my father to gauge his reaction to this; he doesn't give anything away until his next sentence.

"He's in a wheelchair." Irritation clings to his words, along with a hint of disappointment. As if Finn is a fuck up for getting himself shot.

As my father continues to fill me in, I wonder, did anyone ask where I was during all of these family tragedies?

"He's not happy, and neither am I." My father states.

Finn getting himself shot is such an inconvenience on my father, clearly.

"I need you to kill him." My father says the words matter of factly as he pulls up to my house. The large black iron gates dominating the entryway start to open slowly. Large, black, marble eagles sit either side of the gates, resting on pillars with outstretched wings as though they might take flight at any second. Their sharp eyes and long beaks make them look threatening. That's why I fell in love with them. I had them transported from the Czech Republic and restored over here. My mind wants to focus on the eagles, but my father is waiting for an answer.

"What did he do to deserve your wrath, besides being in a wheelchair?"

My father doesn't like being questioned. He's watching the large gates open. My stomach tightens. I'm home.

"He's an inconvenience, and it's cruel to leave him as he is."

I laugh. I shouldn't. "So you are putting him out of his misery. How noble, father."

My father glances at me, his smile like a shark circling blood. "No, son. You are going to put him out of his misery." My father refocuses on driving as we make our way up the long, swirling driveway.

I want to ask him, is he sure? Has he thought this through? But I already know my father thinks everything through. That's why he's in the position he is in.

There is no more talk of Finn as my father stops the car at my front door.

"All your staff have been notified of your return." My father doesn't remove his seat belt.

I won't thank him. I know the staff is here from the lights that shine from random rooms on all three floors. They never left. I always had communication with my men. I'm sure my father is aware of that fact.

I remove my seatbelt.

"Your mother believes you have been in the Czech Republic the last three years."

I clench my jaw.

"So do Jack and Dana."

So he had made up a story about my whereabouts. No wonder no one visited me. But, did they not try to contact me and find it odd when I didn't respond. I want to ask, but I don't.

"You will have to make your travels believable, son."

I nod without looking at my father. "Is that it?"

"Yes." His word releases me, and I'm out of the car.

The cold iron handle under my fingers ignites more of a loss in me. I don't linger as I open my front door and let it close on my father.

I might have to bend to his will, but he isn't welcome in my home.

Mario greets me in the entry hall with a bow of his head. He's glancing behind me. "Your luggage, Sir?" He asks.

"I don't have any." I walk past him, my eyes sweeping across every inch of the space. It feels foreign but familiar to me. Dark paintings line the walls. The oak flooring echoes my steps as I pull off the jacket.

"I need a fresh t-shirt." I fire over my shoulder at Mario.

"Yes, Sir." His dainty steps annoy me as he dashes up the stairs. He isn't privy to where I was. I keep him around. I know he is one of my father's many spies.

I enter the living space, where I saw the light on from outside. The minute I step in, Davy stands up. The leather on the couch behind him remains dented, making me wonder how long he has been waiting. His army green knee-length shorts allow me to see his tattooed legs. A Nazi symbol consumes the front of his thigh, and I know if he turns, I'd come face to face with Adolf Hitler. He adores the man. I don't give a shit who he looks up to, as long as he is loyal to me, which he is.

His small frame and bald head make him appear non-threatening. That's why I picked Davy. A black belt in martial arts. He is a weapon, and I gathered many over my time.

He grips my outstretched hand and pulls me towards him. We don't hug, but we stand close. There is such respect in his eyes; my own respect for him shines back.

"Welcome back." Davy grins.

"Is it ready?" That's all I've really been thinking about. It's consumed my mind for the last year, and now that I'm finally home, I get to actually see the final product.

Davy's smile leaves his face. He still holds my hand and gives it a shake. "Yes. It's ready." I release him, and he fixes the glasses on his nose before leaving the room that I take a quick look at it as if it might disappear. Once again, the feeling that none of this is mine has me peeling off my shirt to distract myself.

Mario is lingering in the hall, holding a white t-shirt. He looks stiff and half afraid as I take the top and pull it on. The t-shirt is tight, but I don't fear it tearing at any second.

"Anything I can get for you, Sir?"

"I want a meal prepared and ready in one hour. Also, call my tailor I need all new suits." I speak while walking.

"Yes, Sir." Mario's words reach me as I move under the large arch that takes us into a second hallway.

Davy's steps are quick, and he almost skips. He's excited. Not about the glass box, but about completing the assignment that he's been overseeing for the last year. He opens a door, and we move down the steps into the basement that has now been transformed.

Davy flicks on the lights, and one after the other, they come to life, allowing the room to expand, eradicating the darkness.

"You really built it." I move off the final step and into the basement.

"I always follow your orders."

Davy moves in front of me. Pride has his shoulders back, his chest out, and a slight smile on his face. "It's beautiful."

I didn't see beauty in the construction. I step up to the wall of glass and touch the cold, thick wall.

They had done exactly what I had requested. They built a glass box, complete with a glass ceiling. Inside the box is a king-size bed and a wardrobe filled with clothes; I know this because I asked for it to be filled with white dresses, all size six

A tub sits in the center, with a toilet and sink to the left. A small table and chairs with a circular rug under them are close to the opening, which I walk around to.

"This is the only way in or out. It's exactly as you asked for." Davy reaches out, and I take the key card.

Everything inside the box is white, just like I requested.

"I'm impressed." I glance at Davy. The box takes up half the basement. They had to build it in this room, and that would have been no easy feat.

"Now, are you going to tell me what it's for? I'm assuming it's some form of torture?"

"Torture is a good word for it." I step away from the glass box. Three years in one, and now I will place someone else in mine. I almost feel sorry for them, but that small bit of pity crumbles, and in its place, excitement blossoms. My father really had taught me one lesson in particular very well. Never strike an enemy. You befriend them and find their weakness. That's exactly what I am doing. I think of Claire in her white summer dress, looking like an angel.

"Our guest will be arriving tomorrow." I walk around the glass box. The large King size bed is made up. Everything is ready.

"A female, I can assume from the clothes."

I place the key card in my pocket and turn to Davy. I trust him with my life, but I don't have to explain myself to him.

He knows I'm done talking. He points to the left of the room. "The glass coffin." As he says it, the glint in his eyes looks like he holds a question mark over my sanity.

I walk over to the other item I had instructed him to have built. The coffin is sitting on large wooden planks held up by concrete blocks. "I wasn't sure where to place it."

I kneel down and run my hand along the top of the coffin. The material is so familiar to my flesh. My fingers turn the small knob, and I slide back a small slot of glass, like a tiny window.

"It's perfect. Great job." I slide the small window closed and stand up. "The crew who built all this?" I ask.

"Dealt with," Davy responds. Meaning they are dead.

"All the men will be ready for duty tomorrow." Davy continues.

I have twenty men who are trained with the defense forces but have never seen any combat, so I put all their skills to use.

"Good." I return to the glass box that will be occupied tomorrow. "Her name is Claire," I speak to Davy while staring at the clawfoot tub. The legs are gold, the only color in the box. "The feet are gold," I state.

Davy doesn't answer, and I glance at him. "The legs of the tub are gold. I want them white, and I want it done by tomorrow."

"It will be ready." Disappointment has Davy pushing up his glasses.

I don't leave but pat him on the back. "I know it will." *Or heads will roll.* I don't have to threaten him; he's watched enough of his comrades fall for their deficiencies.

CHAPTER THREE

O'REAGAN
AN CHLANN

CLAIRE

"We welcome you here today..." I turn away from the mirror and stop myself before running my hands down the front of my dress.

I feel so small but force myself to look back into the mirror. Wide blue eyes stare back at me. I appear dazed.

I look stupid. I can't do this.

I scrape my long blonde hair off the back of my neck and hold it up to try to cool my body down. I've been asked to be a keynote speaker at a school tomorrow. The idea that I could give a child advice makes my insides crumble, leaving a puddle of ruins around my feet.

Worst. Idea. Ever.

I tried to say no, but the word yes took its place. I want to be a normal nineteen-year-old. I want to be confident. I want to stop being so afraid of everything. I release my hair, and it falls down, stopping at the small of my back. I try out a smile and roll my eyes at myself. I look deranged.

I leave the mirror with a bad taste of defeat in my mouth. Picking up my phone, I scroll until Rebecca's name appears, and I hit the text message button.

I'm sorry. I won't be able to attend tomorrow. My apologies for the short notice.

My finger hovers over the send button. I glance up at my fridge. A magnet of the Eiffel tower holds up a picture of the pyramids in Egypt. To the left, four alphabet magnets that were on my fridge when I rented this place hold a multitude of pictures of places, like the Great Wall of China, the Statue of Liberty, all the way to the plains of Africa.

Anyone who comes here would think I am well traveled. That's two lies in one thought. No one ever comes here, and I have never left Ireland.

Glancing back at my screen, I hit send and throw my phone on the counter.

I want to scream at the thief who's taken my courage, my backbone; all that I am left with is something that is broken, and like the sands of time, it's pouring rapidly through my fingers. I thought time heals all wounds, but mine are gaping.

A knock at my door drives me out of my state of self-pity that I slip into far too often. The knock comes again, and a new fear knots my stomach. Could it be Rebecca? Irrational thoughts plague me as I stare at the front door.

Rebecca doesn't know where I live, and even if she did, I had just sent the message. She couldn't have gotten here that fast. Maybe she's in the area?

But what would she want to talk about in person that she couldn't speak about over the phone?

I'm questioning things while looking around the small space. Two heart-shaped cushions sit neatly on the brown couch. A red throw lies across the back of it. The couch is positioned across from a small unit that holds my TV. The coffee table is old and doesn't match the rest of the furniture, but it was here when I moved in. My laptop sits on the coffee table, half-open. I should close it.

Another knock drags my attention back to the door. Rebecca doesn't know my address repeats in my mind.

The knock comes again, and I swallow my wild thoughts and open the door.

I blink up at the tall man whose shoulders are suitable for a rugby pitch. His dark gaze burns over me, and I feel unbalanced as I reach for the doorframe. He doesn't speak. A normal person would ask him his name or ask him what he wanted? Not me.

"I didn't eat, so I'm a bit dizzy." I try to explain my reason for clutching the door frame without looking like a nut.

His gaze slices through me. I don't want to keep looking up at him. Craning my neck isn't helping my dizziness. I try to ignore a buzz that races along my bare arms.

He still hasn't spoken. My brain is telling me something isn't right.

"I'm sorry. How can I help you?" I put on my receptionist's voice. I reach for it like a lifeline. My voice sounds more stable, giving me some false bravado.

"You can't." His deep, gravelly voice has me dragging my brows down.

I've heard that voice before.

My heart had been pitter patting only moments ago and is now in full throttle mode.

"Do I know you?" I already know I don't. I wouldn't ever forget a face like his. Someone had carved it; his features strong and bold. He has no right to look so good. He carries himself with the same boldness that his perfect face holds.

His large frame moves closer, forcing me slightly back and making me release the door frame.

"No, you don't, Claire."

His voice washes over me, leaving a path of confusion and fear that seeps into my bones, making me useless at this very moment.

He moves, and the smell of his cologne and something stronger assaults my nostrils. The smell grows heavier until it's cutting the back of my throat, making me want to cough. I try to step away and ask him to leave.

His hand covers my mouth with a cloth, and I go into full panic mode way too late. My senses start to shut down as I claw at the air, missing the mark, which is his face. My stomach roils, and I turn my head on instinct, thinking I'm going to be sick. He doesn't remove his hand from my mouth or allow me to move my head much. I feel like I'm falling as my body loses the ability to keep me upright, but his arm is like a vice around my waist, pulling me tightly against him. I blink up into his hard face, and my mind grows more frantic before it slowly shuts down and the world turns black.

My mouth is dry like someone stuffed it with wool soaking up every drop of liquid from my mouth. I swallow as I push up on the bed. The soft fabric under my hands has me pausing. Pain sparks behind my half-open eyes, and I close them. My other senses come to life. I don't smell my lavender fabric softener. I crack one eye open. I take in the white sheets on my bed that appears larger than it should.

Since when did I put on a white bedspread? I sit up further, my eyes absorbing everything my brain refuses to acknowledge. My wall is gone. A sheet of glass rises before me. I slam my eyes shut as my heart stalls in my chest. My bare arms take the onslaught of my fear as each hair rises.

I duck my head into my chest. I can smell him.

I start to stand and nearly fall off the bed. A fist slams into my stomach as I spin in a full circle. This can't be real. What is this?

This isn't real.

My legs carry me to the glass wall. I want to touch it to prove to myself that the box isn't real. I don't want to touch the glass in case it is real. Bile claws its way up my throat, leaving a burning path of fire in its wake. I touch the cold glass, and a scream that I didn't know was there spills from my lips as I dance back away from the glass. I spin to the other wall.

Shaking my head, I stumble to it and touch the glass wall. It's real. Another scream pours from my mouth, and I run to the next wall.

"What is this?"

My heart thrashes against my chest, and the room shifts under my feet. But I can't accept what I'm seeing. I touch the glass again, and my mind bounces so fast that I can't keep up with one thought. My body overheats before it grows cold.

The world stills when I notice him watching me.

"No."

He smiles as he walks toward me. But his smile isn't normal. It's hard and arrogant, almost gleeful, yet angry. That smile would make you want to run while your feet stayed rooted to the spot. That smile is reserved for people who are close to meeting their maker.

"No," I whisper again. My neck feels tight, like all the small bones in it might snap at any second.

"Welcome, Claire." His deep voice is like a match being run along a flint.

His voice sets a fire in my veins that has me slamming my hand against the glass that doesn't even rattle. "Let me out."

He stalks even closer. His black eyes dance with a darkness that I want no part in.

"Let me out now. My family will report me missing to the authorities." My voice shakes and rattles.

He tilts his head slightly to the left. "No one will ever find you, Claire."

I flounder, my chest ready to cave in. I hit the wall again like I can break through the glass and remove the cruel smirk from his striking face. "Let me out!" I scream until my throat is hoarse.

My fists are no match for the solid wall of glass. They fall to my side, and I clutch my white dress.

White dress? I stop touching the material and raise my hands in the air. I'm backing away from him. These aren't my clothes. The walls spin, and I'm drowning in terror.

I can't breathe. I clutch my throat like I might be able to fight whatever is cutting off my air, but there is nothing I can do as I struggle for oxygen. My legs buckle, and he stands, watching me crumble. My heart slows, and black spots sprout in front of my vision. I hit the floor. His feet move along the wall, and I don't want to close my eyes. *What will happen?* My heart slows even further, and pain squeezes my chest. A tear runs from my eye as my body gives out on me.

I open my eyes. I'm on the floor. It's not my apartment floor. The memory of his dark eyes has me sitting up. My head is spinning as I glance around the glass box. I'm alone. There is nowhere for him to hide. That tiny bit of knowledge calms me for a split second before I start to panic again.

I am in a glass box.

I get up and try not to notice the tub, toilet, or sink. Like this isn't built for the long term. A wardrobe behind me has me tempted to walk to it, open the doors and see what's inside.

No need. You won't be staying.

The voice of reason has me gliding to the wall again, and I touch it. That single touch has me biting my cheek until I taste blood. This is real.

I run my hand along the glass, trying to feel for a crack, but I don't feel anything. The pulse beats in my fingertips that are slippery from beads of sweat.

I step away and close my eyes. A sob I keep swallowing demands its release, but I tell it soon. First, I need to get out of here. I swallow the sob, but tears still escape. I blink them away and wipe my hands on the white dress that I want to take off. I try not to think about how it got on my body or who took off my clothes, or what happened to me when I wasn't lucid. Trepidation triples and weighs down my feet, making my movements sluggish.

I need to get out of here.

I run my hand along the glass again and keep walking. Nothing obstructs my movements. Everything in the room stands away from the glass. I pass a small table with two chairs. My stomach curls in on itself. Two chairs. Why two? Why chairs? Why a glass box? Panic starts to claw its way up, and I force the sense of dread down unsuccessfully. My fingers hit a small bump, and three seconds later, another. I stare at the area and follow the outline of a door.

There is no handle or anything that would allow me to open it. I push the door at first, but nothing happens. I slam both hands against it, but the glass doesn't budge.

I turn around and pick up a chair. I picture the chair hitting the wall and glass shattering on top of me. My mind paints a vivid picture of a wave of jagged glass crashing down on me. There is no time to reconsider what I'm about to do. All I know is that I can't stay here for one more second. I charge at the outline of a door like a warrior who's gripped with fear but determination and slam the chair against the glass. The wood cracks and splinters with the impact, and coldness seeps into my shaking hands as I drop the broken chair.

A scream pours from my mouth as I fall to my knees amongst the broken chair and my fractured mind.

I don't want this to be real. But I know it is.

CHAPTER FOUR

O'REAGAN
AN CHLANN

RICHARD

I carry her from her apartment. She's cradled into my chest like she is something precious. A sense of protection has me pulling her closer until I have to force myself to loosen my grip, so I don't hurt her. She feels right in my arms and that, I hadn't expected. She weighs nothing, no more than a feather which suits her somehow. Her angelic features and long blonde hair make me think of an angel. An angel was the first thought I had the day she stepped into the asylum.

We were all dark devils, and here was a pure angel amongst us. If I believed in them, which I don't, she would be one. Her eyes are closed as I carry her to my car, but the memory of how striking her blue eyes are have me wanting to wake her just so I can see them again. Being this close to her stirs a primal instinct inside me. I want her.

Placing her carefully in the back seat of the car, I take my time positioning her hands across her flat stomach. My hands glide down her sides, I allow myself to trace her curves; my fingers greedily race across fabric until they touch the flesh of her leg. Her head rolls to the side as I glance back up at her. I should leave before anyone sees me. My fingers trail all the way down to her bare feet before I stand up and reluctantly close the door. Having her body isn't part of the plan.

Taking her to my home and keeping her locked up is. I get into the car and start the engine. Pulling away from the curb, I do a quick sweep of the area to see if anyone is watching. The building windows are empty, and no movement along the walkways gives me a sense of confidence that no one saw me take her.

Her scent lingers on me. The urge to see her has me moving the rear-view mirror until her hands and stomach come into view. I push my foot to the floor, needing my car to move faster. She is a temptation that I am fighting hard to resist. I don't know why I've been with plenty of beautiful women. I have no problem attracting them. I just never keep them around. Maybe it's being locked up so long and not having a woman under me. Either way, I know I need to get her into her cage and out of my car.

The gates are slow to open, and the moment there is enough space for my car to drive through, I push my foot on the gas. My house appears, and I drive around back. Mario is out on errands. I gave him enough to keep him busy for a while.

Claire is still asleep as I carry her from the car and into the house. I cradle her to my chest again, knowing this will be the last time I hold her. Taking her down into the basement, I linger at the door of her new home. A moan escapes her slightly parted lips. I slide open the glass door and carry her to her bed. Laying her down, her blonde hair falls across her face. My gaze drags down her long legs, and I reach out and touch her calf, running my hand all the way up to her knee. Another moan falls from her lips. I leave her and take a white dress out of the wardrobe.

I thought this part would be easy or even fun, but it's torture to my rock-hard cock. She moans several times as I undress her. Coincidentally, she's wearing white panties and a white bra that she fills nicely. She's flawless, her body pure perfection. I wonder if she's as fragile as she looks. I like my sex rough. I think I'd break her. I move her several times to get her into the white dress. It's a simple, plain summer dress that falls to her knees. I stand back and admire my work.

She stirs this time, and I know time is running out as the sedative is wearing off. I want to stand here and watch her open her eyes. I want to drink in every moment of her waking up. But that isn't part of the plan. Once I leave the box, I won't enter it again.

It takes an army of whispers at my back to make me leave the box. The whispers are echoes of my father's words.

"If you want to hurt someone, you befriend them, find out everything about them, and then you take the most precious thing away from them, all the while you make them watch as you destroy what they love before you destroy them. That way, you will be remembered, and no one will cross you."

The door slides shut behind me, and I turn, facing the glass. My heart starts to race and thrash against my chest. This moment I have fantasized about over and over again. I touch the glass to allow the truth to sink in. I have really built the glass box, and she is really inside it.

I walk around the cube and stop at the bed that she still lies on. She starts to stir, and I know it's showtime, so I slowly step deeper into the basement and watch as she fully wakes up. I'm waiting for the guilt to churn heavily in my stomach as she spins around, shaking her head while muttering to herself. But the guilt doesn't come. She's touching the glass, and that's when her gaze finally settles on me. Her face grows whiter, and her mouth opens. "No."

Her lips tug down, and pure fear is etched into her angelic features. She's like a biblical image. An angel captured by the devil.

I can't stop the smile that spreads across my face as I walk toward her. I want a front-row seat. An excitement I've never felt before bubbles through my veins.

"No."

"Welcome, Claire."

My words halt her for a second before she races to the glass and slams her small fists against it. "Let me out."

I move closer, soaking up her hysteria, her fear. This is a side I never saw of her. All I saw was her good manners, great punctuality, and frequent smiles.

"Let me out now. My family will report me missing to the authorities." Her voice shakes along with her small balled-up fists.

"No one will ever find you, Claire." That is a promise. Everyone who worked on this is dead. The only living people who know about the box are three people whom I trust with my life. She will never leave this box.

Her small fists hit the wall again. "Let me out!" Her scream is hysterical, and it widens her stunning blue eyes. They are electric with fear.

I growl as my cock grows hard.

She starts to lose control, and I watch her spiral into a frenzy before she fizzles out on the floor. I stay long after she's passed out. My breathing is heavy, and I know if I stay here for one more second, I'll enter the box and ravish her. I take the steps two at a time to put as much distance between us as quickly as possible.

I lock the basement door behind me and pocket the key. I pat my other pocket that holds the key card.

"Everything you requested is in the kitchen." Mario's voice snakes up behind me.

Composing myself, I turn to him. "Thank you. You can finish up now, Mario." He glances at the basement door. But once he finally looks at me, he dips his head and scurries away like a frightened child. But he's clever, sneaky. He is, after all, one of my father's men.

I wait until he leaves before entering the kitchen to find two bags on the kitchen table. I open them and take out the random items: A rope, masking tape, along with coffee that I don't drink, some razors, a bottle of brandy that I take out of the bag and hold up. I'm tempted to open the bottle, but I don't.

I don't need to give myself a reason to lose control. My resolve is already slipping, and she has only been here a few minutes.

I leave the kitchen, and I'm tempted to go back down, but instead, I go up to my room, where I take a shower.

It's a habit to reach in and check the water. The showers were never warm in the asylum, and oftentimes the ice-cold water would freeze your balls off. My hand parts the warm water, and I step into the gushing stream. I know I'm not in the asylum anymore, but that doesn't stop me from showering at record speed. My senses are on high alert for footsteps, any movement at all.

My first shower in the asylum, I hadn't expected anyone to come for me, but they had. Letting my guard down was an error in judgment that I would never allow to happen again.

My skin is red from the rough quick drying I give it. I get dressed and wonder, will this feeling ever leave me. Will every shower result in me relieving what the fuckers did to me?

Anger pumps heavy and fast in my veins, and I'm seeking out my phone to find my calm. The thought that seeing her face will calm me has me fumbling with the device until the cameras I had installed in the basement blink to life, and I see she's awake, staring at the door. Instantly my anger dissolves, and I'm ready to sit down so I can watch her for a while, but she moves, turns around, and picks up a chair. She races to the door and smashes the chair against the glass.

Fuck.

CHAPTER FIVE

O'REAGAN
AN CHLANN

RICHARD

She's sobbing on the floor. A broken chair scattered around her. My gaze roams her bare legs, looking for cuts or marks that might have been inflicted by her attempt to escape. I clear the last step into the basement, but she's too distraught to notice me. That's okay. I like watching her. I like being on this side of the glass.

She appears unscratched. She swallows a sob, and her head jolts up. She's scurrying away from the wall like she can hide from me.

"The glass is unbreakable." I remind her.

Her blue eyes swirl and widen at my words. She's still on her knees, and I kneel down, too, so we are at eye level. Her chest rises and falls, reminding me how perfectly her breasts filled the white bra.

"Let me out!" Her voice is hoarse but still sweet. "Why are you doing this?" Her lip trembles, her pale face drawn.

Why am I doing this?

I rise slowly. The time for questions isn't right now. For now, I will allow her time to settle into her new surroundings.

"I'll have food sent down to you soon."

My words are like strings that tug her off the ground. "I don't want food. I want to go home!" Her voice is tinged with hysteria, and instead of leaving like I had intended to, I stay a little longer.

"You aren't going home." My words are calm and clear.

A trembling hand covers her mouth. She's shaking her head. "Why are you doing this?" She turns away from me and spins like she's searching for someone or something. I have no idea why, but I use the moment to analyze how I feel.

I feel aroused. I'm aroused by her beauty, maybe even by her fear.

As she spins back toward me, she's frazzled, and I wonder if she will pass out again. The fight in her blue eyes doesn't die for one second.

My arousal grows as she stumbles away from me, but she doesn't even blink.

"Why am I here? Why me?"

"Why not you?" I ask her and step closer to the glass.

She takes a step back, blinking rapidly. "What are you going to do with me?"

"That's up to you, Claire."

A sob falls from her lips. "How do you know my name?"

I can't stop the smile. It's a smile that a cat might give to a mouse when he knows he's winning. "In time, I will tell you. Just not right now."

I glance down at my watch. My tailor is due any minute, and I have spent longer down here than I had intended.

So I decide to take my leave and give Claire the space she clearly needs to settle in.

"How do you know my name?" Her shouts follow me as I turn away from the glass and make my way out of the basement and up the stairs. Davy's bald head greets me as I step into the hallway. He stuffs the phone that he had been staring at into his pocket.

"I want Eamon and Marcus to guard this door at all times." I give the order as the doorbell rings.

Mario appears out of the kitchen wearing a fucking apron around his waist. Davy's gaze narrows as Mario greets me and answers the door, allowing my tailor entry.

"Why can't you get some eye candy to cook our food instead of that?" Davy asks.

Davy hates anyone that is different, and Mario gets under his skin.

I pat Davy on the back. "Because if the eye candy caused trouble, I'd have to kill them."

"I'd do it for you." Davy fires back, wearing a grin that I don't quite buy. He isn't joking. He would kill a woman if I asked him to.

"Mario is your eye candy for now. Get him to cook a meal for my guest. Eamon can take it down."

Davy stands a bit straighter at my request. "I'll have it done."

Mario closes the front door as my tailor waits in the hallway, and I walk towards him.

"Mr. O'Reagan." He holds out his hand that I take as I scramble for his name. "You have grown quite large." He says while shaking my hand.

"He's a late bloomer," Davy interjects as he heads for the kitchen.

I release John's hand. I think it's John and lead him upstairs. When I glance back down, Mario is standing in the hallway, watching me. I raise a brow, asking him silently what-the-fuck-he's-standing-around-for.

He bristles before marching into the kitchen where he belongs.

I spend the next thirty minutes being measured by John, who thankfully doesn't attempt to make small talk.

"How long will it take?" I ask, stepping away from John as he gathers up his notes and measuring tape.

"I should have your tailored suits ready in three weeks."

I pull at the tight t-shirt. "Make it three days." I turn to John, his mouth slack. "Or should I go elsewhere?"

He closes his gaping mouth. "Three days, your suits will be here."

He pulls on his own suit jacket. "I'll leave the two suits you requested I bring today downstairs before I go."

"Thank you, John."

"It's Francis." He mumbles as he leaves.

I make a note of his name. "Thank you, Francis," I call over my shoulder and catch his eye in the mirror.

The generic suit fits me surprisingly well. I previously sent a few photos to Francis so he could gauge my size and bring me a few suits while he was measuring me. It would keep me tied over until he made me my new ones. Three days isn't much time, but it surprises me how quickly people can really do things when you push them.

I remove the tie and open the top button of my shirt. My black hair has grown longer than I would normally keep it, and I push it back; my fingers touch the puckered skin along the left side of my skull. Seventy-two stitches made up the scar that would forever haunt me.

Meeting my gaze in the mirror, I don't recognize the man who stares back at me. It's not just my physical appearance that's altered over the years. It's the hate I see in my eyes. I turn away from the mirror, putting on my watch before making my way downstairs.

Davy is waiting for me at the bottom of the grand staircase. "Eamon and Marcus are on duty. Mario is making the food."

"You should have him make you a meal."

Davy's lips drag up into a snarl. "I won't eat food from him; besides, I'm a mean chef."

I slap Davy on the back as I pass him. "You'd burn water." Taking a set of keys off a hook, I take one final look in the mirror. Nothing has changed in the last fifteen seconds. The same hard look in my gaze is still there.

"Don't wait up." I grin at Davy. It's a grin that tells him I've gotten lucky.

"I won't."

I leave through the kitchen and enter the garage. Three cars fill the space. I move to the one positioned at the end. I open the door, my nose assaulted by the smell of leather. I bought it a few days before my father tricked me and locked me up in the asylum.

The engine hums under the hood of the BMW.

The doors rise behind me as I reverse out of the garage and leave the house. I don't expect this little outing to take long, but Davy doesn't need to know that. A family gathering was called to welcome me home. My father expects me to show up with tales of my travels and business in Czech Republic. Where there is obviously no fucking phone reception because they bought into the idea that I could only text. I didn't believe the bullshit for a second. They just didn't care enough to find out what really happened to me. I could have been rotting away in a ditch.

Growing up, my father promised me the mafia world. The sad part is I believed him. I am addicted to his lies, the way he creatively folds truths with bullshit until all you see is what he wants you to see. I wanted to be just like him until my world went up in flames. I have no idea what I want anymore. My path has already been carved for me, so I just know what is expected of me. This anger and desire to smash and destroy all who have wronged me is all-consuming. One day I will allow it to consume me, but today isn't that day.

Slowing down the car as the hedge that lines my parent's property comes into view, I try to push aside all the hate that has taken up residency in my heart. It's not a fruitful exercise. The closer I get, the more my anger has my fingers tightening around the steering wheel. If my anger could manifest itself, I'd be fucking suffocating. I come to a complete stop at the entrance. The gatekeeper dips his head at me before the gates start to open. I'm tempted to rev the engine to make them go faster. Once they open enough for me to pass, I drive up the winding driveway until the house rises up in front of me.

A few members of my family have gathered at the front door smoking. I'm not surprised to see Shay, but like me, he's changed over the years. His demeanor seems more relaxed as he speaks to Jack, who looks the same as he did the last time I saw him. Both of them turn to my car as I park away from the door.

I angle the rear-view mirror and meet my eyes one more time. *You can do this.* I swallow saliva and all the pain of the last few years and get out of the car. I've been told my whole life I'm the mirror image of my father, so I give them the show they expect. Shay says something to Jack when he sees me. I don't expect a hug, but I also don't expect the hard jaw of Jack as I approach him and Shay.

"The prodigal son arrives home." Bitterness coats his words.

"Nice to see you too, brother," I respond in a monotone before turning to Shay, who is watching my every move, of course. I hold out my hand. "Congratulations on becoming a King."

He blows smoke out of the corner of his mouth before gripping my hand and shaking it. "You too, Richard."

If uncertainty had a smell, I'd be getting it in gales right now, and that's how I liked to keep things. Don't ever let them know where they stand.

"Is Mother inside?" I release Shay's hand and turn to Jack.

His jaw twitches, and I know he's waiting for me to congratulate him, too. I won't. He will never hold his place as King. He is just too stupid to know that.

"Yes." He grinds out the word.

"I'll speak to you both later." I step into the house, and thankfully no one is in the hall as I close the door behind me. Memories spring hard and fast, and I eliminate them one by one until I reach the kitchen.

She's my Achilles heel. I think she is for all of us mere mortals. I inhale the scent of her food, and when my mother turns from the stove and looks at me, I allow her to see her son.

A squeal of pure delight leaves her mouth, and she rushes across the space, wiping her hands on her apron.

"Richard!" She's so tiny as I pull her into a hug. "You're really here." She's gripping onto me, and I allow us to have a few more seconds before I start to mentally retreat.

It's like she notices and steps back. "Look at you; you're all filled out."

"Plenty of food in the Czech Republic," I say with a smile that's reserved just for her. It's still filled with pain and hate, but right now, it's the best I can offer.

"I missed you." She whispers, and the pain that reflects in her eyes tells me she just might know more than I think.

I stiffen as she pulls me into her for another hug, and she releases me, quickly cutting the hug short. "Go out back. Your father and uncles are out there."

My mother's gaze darts away from me, and she quickly returns to the stove. I know from the set of her shoulders that she's crying. I want to comfort her, but Jack and Shay arrive in the kitchen. Shay glances from me to my mother before heading out back.

"Mam, what's wrong?" Jack rubs her shoulders, and I watch like a stranger as she reaches back and grips Jack's hand. She leans into him, and he glances at me, giving me a death glare.

I leave before I snap. Outside, everyone is seated. If you look in from the outside, it almost seems like everyone is happy.

A big, happy, fucking, family.

Darragh cheers when he sees me and raises a glass. He gets up and half dances over towards me. He's wasted and sloppy, and I meet my father's gaze. Maybe Darragh should be the one we put down and not Finn, who I've spied in the corner, looking the part of the victim.

What a sorry-looking bunch.

Shane's darkness leaps from his body in waves. I dodge Darragh's attempt to hug me and make my way to Shane. He makes sense to me.

He greets me without words, using a sharp jerk of his head and raising his bottle of Budweiser before taking a drink.

"Nice to see you too, Shane," I say as I sink into the chair.

"Are you going to leave me hanging?" Darragh says, making his way back to the table.

"Darragh," I mumble in greeting.

His laughter is harsh. Time hasn't been kind to him. "You're just like your father." He drinks from his bottle as my mother arrives with food. She made a chicken curry, a favorite of mine. It's her way of telling me she cares. It also tells me there is a good chance she knew where I was and is feeling very guilty.

She fills a plate and, with a smile, reaches out to me. I want to take the food. She's looking at me with pride in her eyes.

"I ate before I came." I decline, and her face falls. "But thank you." I can't keep looking at her, so I focus on Shay, who watches me. The moment our gazes clash, he turns away and lights up a cigarette. Darragh takes one off him. My mother continues to dish out the curry but with little to no enthusiasm. She's rattled. I can see it.

I use the moment to look at my sad uncle. "Nice to see you, Finn." I move my chair, so I'm facing him.

He's holding an empty glass in his hand.

"Would you like another?" I don't attempt to move.

"No, I think I need to be the sober one. Darragh's drinking enough for everyone."

"Are you the designated driver?" I ask.

His jaw tightens, and he pushes his wheelchair closer to me. "You think that's fucking funny?"

His question has me laughing. I haven't laughed in a long time, but here is Finn, the pussy of the family, getting rowdy. "It took you getting shot to grow a pair of balls," I state when my laughter dies down. I keep my voice low, but Shane hears me.

"Leave him." Shane growls.

He can fucking eat that command. But I remember my place and sit back in my seat. Jack gets up, throwing his weight around.

I have an overwhelming need to take him down a peg or two. "A drink would be nice, Jack."

His glare swings to me, and I know he'd love to take a punch. I'm waiting for him to fire something back, but he just nods. "What's your poison?"

"A brandy."

He half snorts and goes back into the house. My eyes fall on a woman I don't recognize. She's watching me with a hooded gaze. She must be the killer.

"Maeve, is it?" I ask.

She sits up straighter like she's surprised at being called out. "Yes, and you are Richard, I assume."

I get up like the gentleman I am and approach Maeve, who sinks deeper into her chair. I reach out my hand, and she takes it. "I don't bite," I say and raise her hand to my lips just as Jack walks out. I turn her hand palm up and press a soft kiss there before releasing her hand, which she drags back quickly to her side.

"Your brandy." Jack looks like he wants to drown me with the drink. A part of me wants him to. I take my brandy from my brother. And turn to my uncles, mother, and Maeve. I raise the glass and stare at my father.

"To family, to loyalty, to belonging." I raise the glass higher. "An Chlann," I say our family motto. Darragh stands and salutes me while the rest repeat *An Chlann* like they wouldn't stab each other in the back at any second.

I look at the people who don't care about me. These aren't family or friends.

MAFIA GAMES

These people are the enemy

CHAPTER SIX

O'REAGAN
AN CHLANN

CLAIRE

I'm possessed.

Or that's how it feels. It's like each move I make, an echo of my action, is lagging behind me. I keep spinning, expecting to see something behind me, but each time I catch my reflection in the unbreakable glass. He said the glass was unbreakable.

Another sob tears from me. Trying to pull back my panic and fear is like trying to hold onto water. All it does is cover me in a wet layer of darkness that keeps growing.

He knows your name. The voice in my head whispers, and I swipe at my ear like I can make the noise stop.

I lose track of time as I search for a way out. I smash another chair against the glass to no avail, and my hope dwindles too fast.

"This isn't real."

Brown boots appear on the stairs; the legs come into view before a face I've never seen before has my heart jumping.

A man with sandy-colored hair walks towards me, holding a tray of food.

My Captor said he would get me food.

The man pauses at the doorway.

"Move back." His command has the air halting briefly in my chest.

He is going to enter.

"Move back **now!**" His bark has me moving back. My movement is a quick shuffle, and he raises a brow. "Five seconds or there will be no food."

I have no choice but to move back. My foot hits something, and I glance down. It's a piece of the broken chair. The man isn't watching me as he swipes a card at the door panel. The click is deafening, and the air changes as the door opens.

The signs are there in his gaze. Not to try anything, but I ignore the warning and scoop up the broken piece of chair. Violence isn't an option for me. I've grown up seeing too much of it. I've always sworn I'd never hurt another human being.

But these men aren't human.

He places the tray on the table and side-eyes me.

"Thank you," I whisper and move closer to inspect the content of the tray. To him, I am no threat. I see it clearly in his green eyes that don't smile at me, but they don't hate me either.

His gaze drags across my bare arms, and I don't want them to reach my hands, not before I get a chance to use my weapon. I keep the piece of wood pinned at my side.

"May I have a chair, please?"

Sweat makes a pathway down my spine. My shoulder blades drag closer, trying to ward off the sweat and fear.

"No." He steps away from the table and moves to leave. He turns away from me, and something else takes over.

It's not even that I've thrown caution to the wind. It's like all the fear turns feral, and it's not about escape; it's about elimination, so this ends.

Raising the broken leg of the chair high, the wood sails down into his shoulder. I'm expecting a sickening crunch, but the sharp piece of wood sinks into his flesh and stops. The force rattles up against my arms, and I'm nearly flung sideways as he spins, dragging me with him as he screams. My stomach churns as he tries to reach for the foreign object in his shoulder.

I don't wait but race for the door. My panicked feet slip on some of the broken wood, and the floor races upward. I hit the ground hard and start to crawl toward freedom. My hands cross the threshold of the doorway before I'm dragged back. My stomach is burning as pieces of broken wood poke and cut my flesh.

I spin in his hands as he flips me over. My feet kick out, missing their mark completely.

He reaches down with large, angry hands and drags me off the ground. I'm waiting for him to hit me. He wants to hit me, but instead, he releases me and pushes me aside. The back of my legs hit the table. I'm reacting without thought, and that's not always a bad thing. The tray of food flies towards his receding back. The plate shatters, and food is flung across the floor, but it's enough to stun him as he stumbles and falls to the ground. I run again, only this time I'm more careful of my footing as I make it out of the glass box. I turn and start tapping the panel to close the door, but it's not closing, and he's standing up, rubbing the back of his head. His hand comes away coated in blood, and I freeze at the sight of red.

"What is going on?" A voice behind me has me scrambling away from the door of the box. A man wearing a pair of glasses raises his hands. His bald head reflects the light of the room. The man who I just hurt walks out of the box and takes a threatening step toward me.

I move back.

"Go upstairs." The bald man doesn't look away from me, and he keeps his hands raised in a gesture that I assume is to make me believe he isn't a threat. He is here, so that makes him a threat.

"But..." The other man starts.

"Now!"

The warning I hear causes me to take another step backward.

The bald man doesn't speak again until we are alone. "Upstairs is filled with trained men, whom you won't get past."

My legs tremble with adrenaline. I rub the back of my shaking hand across my face. "I just got past him." My voice is small, and I don't recognize it.

The bald man smiles as he nods. He takes a small step towards me, like I might not notice, but I see the movement. "Yes, you did. Now, it's time to go back in the box."

I half glance over my shoulder; there has to be a door down here.

"There is no way out, only those stairs." The bald man slowly drops his hands, and I wonder if his patience has run out. "You're also bleeding, and someone needs to look at that."

I don't look down. I can feel the warm liquid along my stomach and legs. "Someone? You mean you?" I take another step back.

He exhales loudly. "You don't want to do this with me. Trust me, I'll win."

I turn, and he curses as I sprint around the outside perimeter of the box, I turn the corner, and he's nearly on my heels. I run until I hit another corner. There is enough space here in the basement for a car but I don't see any doors. Turning back toward the box, the only way out is the stairs.

Hands grip my arms, and I try to pull away, but the bald man's grip is surprisingly strong.

"Don't put me back in there." I'm screaming as he drags me back. "Nooo!" I kick my legs, but all I end up doing is hitting the ground. My arms are still in his tight grasp, which stops me from protecting myself against the concrete floor. My head takes the brunt before he drags me to my feet. The door to the glass box is right in front of me, and I'm pushed across the threshold.

Spinning, I watch the door close as the bald man glares at me.

It's not a calmness that settles around my shoulders. It's the hands of the grim reaper that keep me still on the floor as I wait for him to return. The lighting down here doesn't alter, so I don't know whether it's night or day. I'm on the floor with my knees dragged up to my chest. I have moments of clarity like I can make this add up like I can see a way out and know I just need to wait for another opportunity to escape. Then terror takes over, screaming that I'm going to die.

Tears fall hard and fast from my eyes, and I swallow one sob after another. There are worse things than death. I know this. Death sometimes almost seems kind.

I don't hear him come down the stairs. I can't say how I know he's coming; I just do. He's standing a foot away from the box in a suit that is made just for him; dark eyes that remove any light from the space are pinned on me.

My stomach tightens painfully. I should stand. I should be in a position where I can protect myself, but my limbs aren't taking directions from the signals my brain is sending them. Instead, there are only pools of darkness.

"You're hurt." His deep voice has my eyes fluttering closed.

"I want to go home." My voice isn't strong, and I look back up at him.

He juts out his chin sharply. "I've already told you, Claire. You aren't going anywhere."

My limbs push up, and I'm standing. "You can't do this." I can't accept this. "What do you want?" I'm half afraid of the answer, but my bones, along with my skin, are so tight, I'm ready to snap.

"When I tell you, you aren't leaving, it means. You. Aren't. Leaving." His hands move behind his back. With his head held high, his height really takes root with me. He must be well over six foot tall, and with wide shoulders, I had no chance of escaping him or fighting off someone his size.

"Trying to escape was foolish." His lip twitches before resettling. His hands leave his back as he takes out his phone from his trousers pocket. He raises the device, and I think he's taking photos of me, so I turn away quickly until I hear his deep voice.

"Bring down Eamon."

I spin around. Eamon? Who's Eamon, and what is he going to do to me? I'm moving backward deeper into the glass box, but there is nowhere to hide, just like the creator had intended.

The man I attacked, along with the bald man, step into the basement.

"Eamon." My captor's deep voice doesn't just rattle me, I see nothing but fear in Eamon's eyes that dart in my direction.

"Sir, I'm sorry." Eamon starts.

My captor cuts him off with a raised finger and a cutting smile that has me looking at the bald man.

The bald man's face is alight with excitement, and my fear triples.

"Sorry. You should never be sorry. You own what you did."

Eamon opens his mouth to speak, but my captor once again holds up a finger, silencing him. "What you did was to royally fuck up, Eamon."

"I'll do anything." Eamon's voice isn't strong.

"You can go." My captor directs towards the bald man, who doesn't look happy at his new order, but leaves.

Dark eyes swing back to me, and I step away from the dark abyss, only to hit the wall. The coldness seeps further into my bones, and I don't know what to do.

Eamon's body is jittery, and he shifts in his stance, the broken part of me is thinking, 'Don't run. If he chases you, I don't think you will survive.' I shouldn't care, but I've lived with cruelty and know the sight of it. It's standing in a black suit before me.

My captor steps up to Eamon, and it's like a shoe lined up against a dollar note. You can truly see the full size of the object. The object in question grabs Eamon by the neck and drags him to the glass wall. Eamon's face hits it hard, and my jaw tightens as green eyes widen.

"I'll do anything, Boss." His face is shoved up harder against the glass.

"Yes, you will." The words are spoken, but he's looking at me, and there is a lull, like that moment after the flash of lightning, as you wait for the rattle of thunder. The glint of a knife catches my eye, but it disappears seconds later. Red liquid sprays in an arc across the glass as life seeps out of Eamon's eyes. Fear chokes me, and my limbs give out as Eamon gasps and chokes as he makes a pathway down the glass before hitting the floor. The air thins, and I try to breathe in the sparse oxygen that doesn't fuel my body—spots dance in front of me. A movement to my left has my attention. He's moving toward the door.

CHAPTER SEVEN

O'REAGAN
AN CHLANN

RICHARD

"Stand up." I take a step away from Eamon's dead body, which lies at my feet. I move away from the blood-smeared glass so I can see Claire.

Her head snaps up, and she's crawling away from me.

A laugh bubbles up my throat, but it dies quickly as she curls herself into a ball.

"Stand up, Claire. Don't make me come in there because if I do, I can promise you, it won't be nice."

Her spine is rod straight as she stands swiftly. Like the clear waters of some foreign holiday resort advertised on television, blue eyes stare at me.

"Take off your clothes." My command has my cock hardening. I take another step around the box to get a better view of her for when she removes the dress; so far, she hasn't. Maybe she wants me to come in.

Threatening her twice isn't wise. The first time should be enough. I move to the door panel, and she sheds her dress, the white material pools around her ankles.

"It's off." Her voice is high-pitched.

I take my time starting from the tip of her toes all the way up her long legs; a few cuts still bleed. My fingers twitch with a need to clean her small wounds. Going into the box isn't an option. An old scar on her knee has a story that I want to hear. Her thighs are tightly pressed closed, a few more cuts mar the flesh, but they aren't bleeding.

White panties have my cock pushing against my zipper. My gaze drags across her flat stomach that has a few cuts all the way up to her perfect breasts that fill her white bra. I let my lip drag up as I reach her eyes. The ocean blue is a light behind her lashes.

"You've made a mess, Claire."

She shivers at my voice, and I step away from the door and move so I'm closer to her.

"I want you to run yourself a bath."

She drags her bottom lip in between her teeth. The action isn't meant to be sexual, but it draws me to her mouth. When she releases her lip, a droplet of blood is visible from how hard she must have bitten the plush flesh. The urge to lick the blood off has me exhaling.

She takes my heavy breaths as a warning and walks promptly to the tub that she fills. I'm also glad to see that the feet of the tub are no longer gold.

She keeps glancing at me over her shoulder like she's hoping I'm gone.

No such luck.

She fills up the tub and turns off the taps.

"Get in."

She doesn't turn to me; I'm faced with her back. My mind is stuck on her bleeding lip. She's ready to step in when I stop her. "Take off your panties and bra."

She lowers her foot to the ground. Her shoulders are taut with anger, no doubt. I hadn't expected her to try to escape. I hadn't expected her to fight so hard. I hadn't expected to want her so badly.

The bra falls to the floor before she brushes her long blonde hair across her back. It brushes the small of her back, and my gaze drops lower as she gets out of her panties and steps into the tub, but not before I get to see her perfectly round ass.

She hisses, and I move around the glass so I can see her face. I know she tracks me. Her head slightly moves as I move around the box so I can see her properly. She draws her legs up to her chest, covering herself. I could demand her to lower her legs.

"I will have the doctor come to check your cuts later."

She's ready to object but doesn't. Instead, she says nothing at all. I observe her as she stays huddled in the water. Annoyance grips me, and I feel the rush in my veins. I want to react. The thought flitters through my mind, and it's a split second, but it's enough to make me pause, and I don't react to my emotions.

My fingers relax, my hands uncurl from the fists they had tightened themselves into. This is what my father can do. This is what he wants me to do. Control my emotions, my impulses. The first reaction isn't always the right one.

The phone in my pocket buzzes. I didn't want to be disturbed, but Davy's name flashes on the screen. He's upstairs. I don't believe he's worried about Eamon; something else must be wrong.

I take the phone out of my pocket and notice how Claire's head moves, but she's not looking directly at me. Yet, she's listening.

With a flick of a button, I could cut off all sound to her, but I don't. I answer the phone.

"Jack is here." Davy's voice is stiff. He doesn't get wound up easily; Jack is on his shit list, along with most people.

"I'll be up." My cock is hard, and standing here watching Claire bathe this long is punishment enough. I hang up the phone.

Claire's gaze finally reaches mine, and she flinches before dipping her head.

I leave Claire and go upstairs to see what Jack wants.

The moment I step out of the basement, he's there pacing in front of the door.

"You've blood on you." Jack's words drag my attention to my shirt sleeve.

"You're right. I do." I let my lip move slightly like I might smile, but I don't. I remove my suit jacket and hand it to Davy, who doesn't look overly impressed to be my coat rack, but he wisely doesn't complain.

Jack doesn't ask any more questions about the blood.

"What did you say to Mam?"

I remove my cufflinks and place them in my pocket. I glare at Jack while I pass him and make my way upstairs. His footsteps click behind me.

"She was crying, Richard."

"And why do you think it's my fault?" My voice is emotionless. Once I reach the wide landing, I start to unbutton my shirt and enter the master bedroom.

"Three years, Richard."

I turn to Jack as I pull off my shirt. "I was busy doing business in the Czech Republic." The lie slips so easily off my tongue.

"Rough times in the Czech Republic?" Jack's voice doesn't hold the same amount of anger it had a few seconds ago.

I've turned my back to him. "I did it myself." I know his dissolving anger is because of all the scars on my chest and stomach. Stepping into the closet, I select a fresh t-shirt. Covering up my past in the snug material, I leave the room. "What do you want me to do?"

He's my big brother, but right now, he's a fucking stranger. One I want out of my home.

"You're a dickhead." He shakes his head. "You didn't have to leave."

He is referring to my homecoming. After my toast to the family, things had gone downhill. My mother wouldn't stop trying to force food down my throat, and Darragh grew drunker as the time passed. I had enough and left with my mother on my heels, asking me to wait for Dana, my sister, to arrive. If my sister had thought anything of me, she would have been there.

"You already have everyone half afraid to breathe around you."

I fold my arms across my chest. "What the fuck is your point, Jack?"

His temper flares like I knew it would. I drop my arms, wanting him to hit me.

"I don't know what's going on with you, but it's not adding up."

He's waiting for an answer. An answer I won't give him. Not a truthful one, anyway.

"I'm back here to rule with you and father."

Jack grinds his teeth. "You, rule?"

His tone is pissing me off. "Yes, Jack. Isn't that what Kings do?"

Jack runs a hand across his face. "Look. A lot of shit happened since you've been gone."

"Tell me," I say. Removing my phone and cufflinks from my pocket, I place them on the glass table top of my dresser. I see my reflection and relax my jaw.

"Finn, first of all."

I grin. It's a grin I can't stop. "Yeah, father told me."

"Did he tell you I was there?"

I look at Jack now and let my grin turn into a full smile. "Did it damage you seeing your uncle getting shot? Are you damaged from it? Do you need therapy?"

Jack snorts. "Still the same, Richard. I thought three years would have helped you shake off some of that cockiness and anger."

My anger has only grown.

"Again, Jack, I'm wondering what you are doing here."

"It's about Shay."

I laugh. This keeps getting better. "Not about mother anymore?" I ask as I leave my room. Jack follows.

"It's about both of them. I just want you to be a bit kinder to Mother."

I grit my teeth. I didn't want to argue about this. It would end up being a fucking pointless venture. "I'll do my best." I enter the living room and move towards the bar. Lifting the panel, I step behind the counter and lower the panel back down into place.

"Did she do something wrong?" Jack sounds exasperated.

"Do you want a drink?" I ask, removing two glasses from the shelf above my head.

"Yeah, whatever. Richard, I'm trying to fix things here."

I take down a bottle of brandy and fill both our glasses. I place them on the bar. "No, she did nothing wrong."

She did nothing.

Jack joins me at the bar and picks up the brandy. I don't pick up mine. I don't want to numb the turmoil in me. I watch Jack drink half his down, and when he sees I haven't drunk mine, he quickly spits the content back into his glass. His face pales. "Did you poison it?"

"You think so little of me." I pick up my glass of brandy and take a large swallow.

I want to see shame fill Jack's eyes, but we O' Reagans don't seem to own that one particular emotion.

Jack pushes the glass back toward me and faces away from the bar. "Shay's brother died a few years back, cage fighting. Do you remember it?" Jack turns to me.

I take another swallow of the brandy before answering. "Yes. I do."

He nods his head like it's great that we are on the same page. He steps up to the fireplace. "It wasn't a fight; it was a setup. The cage master had been paid to take out Shay's brother."

I knew all this. I remain silent.

"Shay tracked down the cage master and got a photo of a guy who had paid her to set this all up."

Jack touches a mahogany clock that ticks away on the mantel. "It was a ploy to stop Connor and Shay from fighting there. They were costing the establishment money by winning all the fights."

Connor, our half-uncle, who my father hated, was a savage with his fists. I grew up wanting personal lessons with him. I wanted to be as brutal with my fists as he was, but my father wouldn't hear of it. I spent most of my childhood admiring Connor from a distance and feeling jealous of Shay for having a father who could kill with his fists.

"Frankie was his name," I say after a moment.

Surprise lights up Jack's eyes because I remembered Shay's brother's name.

I don't think I will ever forget his name.

"Well, Shay found out that the uncharted territory that the fight club is on was sold."

I wait.

"The buyer is this guy. He's the one who paid to have Frankie killed." Jack takes something out of his jacket pocket and walks across to me. A photo slides across the bar and stops at my drink. A picture of a man with shoulder-length hair and a very distinctive tattoo walks away from a building. The teardrop tattoo on his cheek and the ink along his neck should make finding him easy.

"Did you find him?" I ask and pick up my glass and take a drink.

Disappointment has Jack taking the photo back and tucking it into his pocket. "No. I was hoping you might recognize him."

I did.

"I'm afraid I can't help you." There is enough truth in that sentence to make Jack believe me. "So now we are helping the North solve old crimes?" I ask and grin at Jack, who runs his hand across his face again.

I take my brandy with me and leave the bar. Moving across the room, I sit down on the couch. Jack returns to the unlit fireplace.

"It's not about the North anymore, Richard. It's about us Kings. Shay is a King and needs our help."

I wish we were all that loyal and willing to help each other.

"Did you ask Father?"

Jack's gaze darts away from me. I take a drink. Of course, he didn't. He is afraid of dear old Father. I don't blame him. Father has been hard on both of us. Jack got it a bit softer than I did.

When I look at Jack, all I see is our mother, and I'm like our father. Maybe that's what makes Jack soft, our mother's genes.

"You should ask him, Jack. I'm sure he won't bite."

Jack tilts his head from left to right in irritation. "I'm not afraid of him, Richard. I just can't tell if he's lying. So I won't really know."

Jack has me paying more attention. He has grown over the last three years. I take a drink. "I can't tell either." I'm honest for the first time in a long time. "But if you ask, and he knows something, Father will react. So look out for his reaction to your question."

Jack walks away from the fireplace and sits on the edge of the seat across from me. His gaze is intense as he leans in towards me like we are sharing a secret. "Explain that to me."

I pause. "When Father doesn't like us getting close to the truth, he normally does something to turn us off that path. So keep note of his movements over the next few days after you question him. Your answer is normally in there somewhere."

Jack sits back in the seat, and I finish my drink.

"You sound like you are speaking from experience."

"I am." I roll the glass in between my hands.

"What did you find out?"

"Be careful, Jack."

My warning registers with Jack. He answers with a nod of his head. The silence stretches out. The quiet is a place I'm comfortable in.

Jack isn't and sees the need to fill the silence with senseless babble. "So, how was the Czech Republic?"

I want someone to see past all my fucking lies. I stare at my brother, wanting to tell him the truth that for three years, I was locked away from the world.

A knock on the living room door has me holding all my words back. I get up from the couch as Davy half opens the door.

"Doc is here."

A nod of my head has him leaving. "Thanks for coming by." I compose myself as I turn to Jack.

He's still sitting, watching me. "I'm dismissed?" He smirks, but it's filled with annoyance.

Did he really want me to answer that? He still hasn't moved, so apparently, he does. "I have other things that require my attention."

He stands up. "You sound just like him." His nostrils flare, and he walks past me. He's speaking of Father.

I might look like him, sound like him, but I am not my father.

I am not a monster, and they would soon see that.

CHAPTER EIGHT

O'REAGAN
AN CHLANN

CLAIRE

I don't move long after he leaves. My body soaks up all the warmth from the water, leaving it cold. I try to focus on the only color I can find in this box; gold and blue reflect on the water from the overhead lighting. My fingers touch the colors, and like an illusion, the color disappears. Burying my head into my shoulder, my mind wanders towards the darkness that seems to be growing with each passing moment I spend here. I'm not sure which is worse... having my captor watch me strip and bathe or knowing there is a dead man lying a few feet away from me.

My heartbeat ricochets around my chest as I come to two realizations. One is that I am not getting out of here, and two is that there is a high probability that I'm going to end up like Eamon. Shivers assault my skin. I need to get out of the water.

I survey the glass box for cameras and don't see any. Did it really matter since he had seen me already? I get out of the tub, and the cold water runs off my body as I step out on the white floor. I take the towel from the free-standing rack, and wrap it around my body and keep my head tucked into my chest. Maybe, just maybe, I can pretend that I'm at home if I don't see too far ahead of me. I nod, telling myself that is possible. I shift my stance, and the color red catches my eye. The red is so stark against the glass. I shouldn't look, but I can't stop myself as I turn fully toward Eamon.

He's so still. There's so much blood. I take a step towards his body. What if he's alive? I keep walking, leaving wet footprints behind until I reach the glass wall. I lower myself slowly to the floor. His sandy hair is matted with blood. Through the blood streaks painted across the glass, I can make out the rest of his body.

My hand trembles as I reach up and knock on the glass. The knock is loud, or maybe it seems that way in the large space. I'm waiting for something to happen. Nothing does. I knock again—still nothing. My knuckles hurt as I start to knock rapidly on the glass, my heart beating as fast as my fists. "Eamon!" I call his name like he might rise up off the ground.

My body is hijacked as I reel away from the dead body. He's dead. He's gone, just like my parents. Only they weren't recognizable. They had to be identified from their dental records. But I already knew it was them. I had heard them die. I had heard their screams, their pleas, their frantic cries.

I drag my legs up to my chest and rest my head on my knees. Flames dance behind my lids as I close my eyes. Tears stream down my face. "I'm sorry," I whisper for the thousandth time.

I have a great belief in Karma. Sometimes the punishment that God hands out isn't always clear, but with time, when bad things happen, you start to understand that you did something wrong in life, and this is God's friend, Karma, who is getting you back.

This box is my punishment. Do I deserve to die in a box? It's where we all end up in the end. I raise my head and glance around my glass coffin. My fingers rub the scar on my knee; the puckered skin a comforting reminder that everything has a beginning. The day I got the scar was the first time I saw the cruelty in my brother. It was the first time I saw him relish in others' pain. It was also the beginning of my pain.

My head shoots to the left, and I stand abruptly.

He's back and with him is a man with a black bag. It reminds me of a Doctor's bag. My mind skips and jumps to a small hand saw, a knife, any weapon that could fit in the bag and cause the deadliest amount of pain. My attention is drawn away from the bag as my captor takes out his phone, taps it a few times before turning to the man with the bag of tricks. I can't hear them, and I'm tempted to touch my ears and wiggle my finger inside them to unclog any trapped water.

"Hello," I speak quietly, and neither of the men turn to me. They continue to speak. They can't hear me, and I can't hear them.

I'm ready to speak again when my captor turns to me. Dread infiltrates my system, and I step back as both men move to the door.

The click of the door is loud, and the man with the bag steps in.

"I'm Doctor Hanlan, I'm going to take a look at your cuts."

I don't look at Doctor Hanlan; I'm watching my captor, who stays at the threshold. He doesn't step across it, and that both terrifies me and also gives me some hope. He stays put as the door closes, and it's just the Doctor and me.

"Help me," I whisper, barely moving my lips.

"That's what I'm here for." He places his black bag on the table. He doesn't remark about the smashed furniture, the smeared blood on the glass wall, the dead body, or the fact I'm in a glass box. Has he seen this all before? Is he here to finish me off? It didn't make sense to bring me here just to let some man kill me.

My heart thrashes against my chest, and the blood roars in my ears. I'm staring at the Doctor, looking for some glimmer of hope.

His long black hair is tied at the nape of his neck. The more I study Doctor Hanlan, the more he doesn't exactly look like a doctor. His thick black mustache makes me question his age. His hair coloring isn't natural.

"If you want to lie on the bed, I can take a look."

I tighten my hold on the towel. "I've been kidnapped," I whisper and take a peek at my captor, who watches us. I'm hoping the doctor isn't a killer. There has to be some good left in this world.

He turns to me with a handful of bandages and small white packages. *No handsaw.* "Claire, I'm here to clean your wounds." His gray eyes are surprisingly soft.

"Am I the first?"

"The first what?" He appears a little more unsettled the longer we stand here. I want to tell him that his boss can't hear us, that if he wanted to help me, he could answer me.

"The first person you fixed up who was kept here against their will?" My nails ache from the death grip I have on the towel.

"Claire, do as the doctor says."

I jump at his voice, and a sensation like a million spiders races across my back that has me moving to the bed. I lie down, keeping the towel around me, and close my eyes. He was listening the whole time.

"I'm going to examine your legs first." The bed dips as Doctor Hanlan sits down. I try to control my breathing and remind myself that he isn't going to kill me. Not today, anyway. I race through my arsenal of memories, and like some movie, I hit play.

I focus on red lips, red lips that widen and smile at me. "Claire, that's too much maple syrup."

"No such thing, mother." I tease and squirt a little more, forcing her to remove the bottle from my hand.

"Did you finish your math last night?" My mother turns with a stack of pancakes that she places in the middle of the table. My dad reaches over his newspaper, takes one, and rolls it up before diving back into reading while eating.

"Yes, I did," I answer, but my mother is still focused on my dad.

"George, no paper at the breakfast table."

My dad folds up the paper and finishes the pancake.

"Good girl, Claire. Leonard!" my mother calls as my dad places two more pancakes on his empty plate. He squirts plenty of maple syrup and looks up at my mother, who is pouring out a glass of orange juice. With her back turned, my dad splashes loads of maple syrup onto my plate. He winks and sets the bottle down just as my mother turns around and walks to the table. She puts down two glasses of juice and shakes her head, looking at the door that leads out into the hallway. "Leonard!" She calls again, but I'm staring at my dad. His secret smile just for me is still there on his face.

"It's only minor cuts. I've cleaned them with disinfectant wipes, but otherwise, there isn't much I can do. Let's take a look at your stomach."

I'm pulled out of my memory. The smell of maple syrup fades. A tear runs down the side of my face, and I don't wipe the tears away. I unfold my towel and allow the doctor to examine my stomach. My eyes are closed, but

I feel like I'm in a room with a million people scrutinizing me. My eyelids flutter open, and I see my captor has moved along the side of the box. His dark gaze roams across my flesh, and every wound stings and burns like he physically touched me. My gut twists, and a new kind of fear has my breath growing shallow. Dark eyes snap up to mine, robbing me of everything.

"Only minor cuts. There is no need for bandages; they will heal fine on their own."

I can't look away from my captor.

"Your job is done, Doctor." His deep voice rolls across my skin and releases me from the depths of his black gaze. I'm quick to drag the towel back over my naked body.

I don't move as the doctor packs his bag. I don't move as he leaves the glass box. I don't move as both men leave the basement completely.

My early realization is confirmed again. I am not getting out of this box. Anyone who comes down here works for him.

Panic overrides my body, and I don't fight; fear is choking me, and when my panic overflows, I grow numb.

Time passes in a blur before I get up and mechanically go to the wardrobe. The same white dress stares at me. I let the towel fall to the floor and rip one off the hangers before pulling the material on. I slam the door, the loud bang making me jump. My heart hammers as I glance around, expecting him to be there. But it's just me and Eamon who hasn't moved.

He's dead.

I close the other door gently before walking back to the bed and sitting down. I can't look away from the body. He's really dead. Will they leave him here to rot? Will the stench fill the box until all I can smell is his rotting corpse?

My stomach lurches. The image of my parents assaults my mind. They had been burnt to a crisp. The phrase never really made sense to me until I saw both of them laid out. Their skin was completely gone. Muscle and tissue incinerated, their bones black.

"How did you get out of the house?" The Gardai had asked me. Leonard held me tight against his chest. "I carried her out." His voice was calm, with a touch of happiness.

The Gardai looked back at our burnt down home. Fire engines still roared into the night sky, and the smoke was still in my mouth. I wanted to reach up and grip the Gardai's coat. Maybe I had moved because Leonard tucked me against his chest, smothering my words smothering me.

"You are a lucky girl." The Gardai placed his hat back on his head and faced us. Paramedics raced to Leonard and me, and for the first time, I could breathe. It had nothing to do with the oxygen mask that was placed on my face or the fact that I'm moving away from the house and placed on a stretcher. No, it's the separation from Leonard.

He watched me while a paramedic assessed him.

His smile crept across his face, and there wasn't enough oxygen in the mask. I'm pointing to him like I'm seeing him for the first time. The paramedic who was taking care of me pushes my hand down. "Take a deep breath."

I wanted to scream at her, but she thought something was wrong with the mask she pulled from my face.

Darkness consumed me hard and fast, and I'm lifted into the back of the ambulance. Even in my state, I'm glad I got away. One door slammed, the other took longer, but I'm being lulled into sleep until a hand takes mine.

"It's okay, Claire. I'm here."

A whimper left my lips at Leonard's words. The second door slammed, locking me in with this monster. The sirens roared as the ambulance drove us away from our home.

I return to the here and now and get off the bed. I let all the water out of the tub and use the towel to dry the inside. Once it's dry, I drag the blanket off the bed and climb into the tub, covering myself with the soft material. It's a small victory finding a place to hide, but one I cling to and allow my body to finally give out.

CHAPTER NINE

O'REAGAN
AN CHLANN

RICHARD

Any other time I would demand her to get out of the tub. This time it suits me. I make sure the sound is off in the box as Davy and Marcus remove Eamon's body. He's made quite the mess on my floor. Both men get to work without a word or objection of cleaning up their comrade's spilled blood. They know how this works. The life span of any member of the Mafia isn't long. We all resign ourselves to that. Each day we open our eyes and put on our suits could be our last day.

I keep an eye trained on Claire, who has created a little hiding spot in the tub where I can't see her. All my planning and I hadn't thought of her using the tub as a place to hide from me.

A war rages inside me, threatening to defeat my resolve to not step into the box. If I do, I'll take her, and I wasn't about forcing myself on women. I never had to. As the doctor cleaned her wounds, I took the time to really look her over. Each cut on her flesh screamed for attention, and I would gladly spend my time on each tiny graze.

Marcus and Davy leave with Eamon's body. It doesn't take long for Marcus to arrive back with a bucket and scrubbing brush and start cleaning up the blood. Davy re-appears at my side. He doesn't speak, and that makes his next words very loud.

"Is she an enemy's daughter?"

I don't answer and fold my arms over my chest—his first warning not to proceed.

Davy is brave today. "We spent a year building this box, Richard. Just tell me that you didn't lose your mind, and I gave in to the madness with you."

A laugh catches in my throat, and I cough. The half-laugh leaves like a puff of old air. "I did lose my mind. There really was no other way in there." I turn to Davy.

He doesn't appear disappointed with my truths. I walk to the box and touch the glass. I know if I focus, I'll see my reflection. "It's a real mind fuck." I half-laugh before looking back at Davy. "You can see through it, but you can also see yourself, just not clearly. It's a mind fuck," I say again.

I step back from the glass and re-cross my arms. Davy grows silent beside me.

Marcus finishes cleaning the blood up and removes a pair of large green gloves from his hands before hanging them over the side of the bucket.

"I want the broken chairs cleared and replaced."

Marcus nods while gathering up the bucket that sloshes as he moves.

"Not you." Marcus is too loud on his feet.

"You." I point at Davy.

Davy doesn't pause but goes to the door and opens it. He moves quietly as he gathers the largest pieces of wood and places them outside the box. Marcus leaves and returns with chairs that Davy takes and puts inside the box. Once all is done, as I said, they leave the basement.

I stay for a while staring at the tub, remembering how she looked lying on the bed. I get up and walk around the box, stopping directly across from the bed. Small dots of blood are still visible on the sheets, blood that bled from her body. My cock hardens at the thought of running my tongue across her damaged flesh.

I pause and turn to the tub. I had sworn the quilt shifted. I stare long and hard, and when nothing happens, I leave her. My father had called another meeting with Shay and Jack. The four mighty kings are to meet and discuss the future of the Irish Mafia.

What a crock of shit. He would be the master handing out our job roles like we were lackeys with no brains.

We meet at one of my father's hotels. Cabra Castle rises up in front of me. The castles original foundation sank deep into the ground as the rest of the castle was re-created to its former glory. I never really looked at the castle when I was a kid. All I saw with this place was restrictions that my father laid down. I could never drink or act like other teenagers. When I was here, I was working. But now, after being locked up for so long, I see the potential for the first time. The potential to have Cabra Castle as my home. My father won't just hand it to me. I will have to take it from him.

I park up in one of the designated parking bays. I meet my gaze in the rear-view mirror.

Showtime.

I get out and lock the car as I make my way to the side door of the castle. Five steps rise up to a set of smaller double doors that the front doors would dwarf.

Shay stands at the entrance, smoking a cigarette. He's wearing casual clothing, a green sweater, and slacks. His gaze darts across my full navy suit. "Didn't know this was formal." He takes a final drag of his cigarette before flicking it onto the ground.

"Meeting with my father is always formal." I sound like a prick.

"Me and your da have gotten close." His grin is one that's telling me to go fuck myself.

"I'm glad to hear it, Shay. I really am."

Shay's gaze narrows slightly before he grins again. "I hope we can, too."

"I'm sure we will get as close as you and my father have." I pull down the sleeves of my white shirt unnecessarily and smile a real fuck you smile before climbing the steps to the door.

Shay doesn't speak again, but he isn't one to be brushed under a carpet. Shay is one person I've always liked. He's smart and, most of the time, does whatever the fuck he wants. We pass a set of medieval knights that were kitted out with swords. I'm sure they cost my Father a decent penny. He had not just had the castle restored to its former glory on the outside but inside as well. He spared no expense. Every little detail, even down to the hallways, are picture-perfect.

We leave the main hallway and move down a smaller one that leads to a passageway for the staff. I glance at Shay over my shoulder. "You've been this way before?"

"Never. Castles aren't my thing." Shay's voice always holds an accusation, or maybe it's laughter. It's hard to tell with him.

"What is your thing?"

"I'm more of a country boy."

I snort at that lie. We reach a set of large arched doors, and I push the left one in. We enter the room that my father uses for entertaining corrupt politicians and members of the public sector that will turn a blind eye to our underhanded dealings.

Jack is here sitting at the table while my father stands looking out one of the large arched windows. Both of them are wearing suits. Shay looks shabby in the room with the three of us.

Jack's gaze dances from me to Shay. He settles on a nod as a greeting.

"All the Kings are here," I say while unbuttoning my suit jacket and sliding into the nearest chair. I want this to end as quickly as it has started.

"Can I smoke in here?" Shay asks, but he's already got a cigarette in his mouth and the lighter in his hand.

My father turns away from the window and faces us like he is the mother-fucking King of all Kings, and we are truly his pawns.

"Secrets are deadly. They create speculation and fester."

My father's words hold all our attention, and Shay doesn't light his cigarette. Instead, he slides into the chair beside me, like a student late for class, trying not to draw the headmaster's attention.

"So we need to clear the air," Father says.

I quickly look at Jack. His gaze is focused on Father.

"Would anyone like to go first?" My father doesn't look at any of us in particular.

"Since you started, why don't you?" I speak, and I see a flicker of irritation in his gaze. If we were all spilling secrets, no better man than he.

My father widens his arms like he has nothing to hide before joining them together. "I have no secrets from you. All you have to do is ask me a question, and I will answer it."

He might answer the question, but it won't be truthful. I'm tempted to get up. I don't want to listen to his twisted words that are being spilled for some fucked up reason.

No one speaks, and the noise of Shay lighting his cigarette has me fighting a grin. He blows smoke into the air. I think he's secretly telling my father to fuck off. That action raises Shay in my estimations again.

"Fine." My father makes it sound like he gave us a chance, and now the time is over. When his gaze swings to me, I hold still. *What the fuck is he doing?*

"Richard wasn't in the Czech Republic. He was in Mullingar Asylum."
Son of a bitch.

"What?" Jack sounds stunned and spins fully in his chair, so he's staring at me. His eyes normally remind me of Mother's, clear, crystal blue but not now; they darken as they dance from me to father.

"Makes sense." Shay's voice is low, but I hear the fucking insult that makes my earlier estimation of his worth drop. I glare at him before I face Jack.

"For how long? And why?" His hands are tightly gripped together on the table.

"He killed a man." My father is all for talking for me today.

"I killed a nurse while there." I correct him. If we are spilling secrets, then I am all for that too. "Father put me in there to teach me a lesson about emotions."

My father has the nerve to shrug like putting his son in a madhouse is no big deal.

"You did what?" Jack's brows draw down with anger that's directed at my father. "He's your son." He's pointing at me now, and I have a moment of shock. Jack's anger towards my father surprises me more than anything right now. No matter what our father does, we don't react like this. Maybe we are growing up, stepping out from the shadow that he has cast over all of us.

"I'm well aware he's my son. That's why I placed him there. It was for a few days. Minor. He killed a member of the staff, and he's lucky his incarceration was only three years. His time locked up would have been a lot more in prison if I hadn't stepped in."

Jack drags his hand across his face. "That's such bullshit. You told us he was in the Czech Republic."

I sit back and try to appear like I'm enjoying the show. I hide the truth of this moment. I'm proud of my brother, but as he continues to call our father out on his bullshit and in front of Shay, I start to fear what will happen to him if he doesn't stop.

"It was a holiday, like Disneyland, really." I grin as I sit forward, and Jack's hands fall to the table. He's looking at me like I'm mad, and I play up to it. "Don't look so serious, brother. I enjoyed the break. Now let's hear Shay's secret."

I turn to the man in question. His gaze is steady as he looks at me. "I've lots of secrets. Just none that would interest you boys."

"Try me," I say quickly.

Shay sits forward in his seat. "I jerk off to Wonder Woman. She's hot in her tight clothes." Shay gets up and searches for an ashtray. He's deflecting, but it doesn't matter.

I turn to my father, who watches me, and I want to know why he spilled my secret. Everything he does, he does for a reason.

"What happened to you in there?" Jack still hasn't let it go.

"Before or after I killed the nurse?" I ask. My voice has grown deadly serious.

"I don't know." Jack confesses. He's thrown by this. Is that my father's purpose for this meeting? The King himself sits down, and Shay returns to the table.

"Now that we have cleared the air let's begin." My father speaks for the next thirty minutes about our positions as Kings, what he expects us to do.

Jack is to oversee the drug trade that we built our wealth on. Shay is to oversee arms as most of them came through the North, and I am to work on my father's other ventures that include the hotels and brothels.

"Jack, you'll work with Darragh. He's very wise with the streets and how they operate." That is a nice way of saying he can mix with the riff-raff and rub shoulders with politicians and the corrupt people my father paid off.

"What about Finn? He could help us out." Jack's question has me really watching my father. This should be interesting.

"I'm going to have Finn help Richard."

I'm ready to laugh. Of course, he is placing Finn in my killer hands. Jack doesn't look convinced, and I want to tell him I'll take good care of the cripple, but saying that would be one big fucking lie.

"I'll work with Connor and Shay." Another surprise leaves my father's mouth.

"And Shane will help Richard and Finn." The cripple and the dark one. Great, we would make some team.

Shay taps his box of cigarettes on the table. "I'm not sure my da will be up to working." The tapping of the box is something I file away to see if he does the action again before speaking of his da. It might be a tic that could come in useful. I'm sure my father is doing the same. Jack is too busy staring at me like he's trying to figure out if I'm fucked up from my stay in the asylum.

"When he's ready." My father says. Connor, who's Shay's father, was shot in the leg by some moron seeking revenge. They found the man and dealt with him. I don't think for one second my father is okay with Connor resting up. I'm surprised I haven't been asked to clip him, too, since my father is such a noble and caring brother.

"So everyone knows what they are doing?"

"Crystal clear," I say.

My father nods at me. "Good."

"Does Mother know about Richard?" Jack points at me again, and he's looking more lost as the time slips away.

"Not quite."

My heart hammers. I don't want her to know. I want my mother to believe that I have been in the Czech Republic. That way, I don't have to hate her for not coming for me, for not at least trying to get me out of there.

"She believes he was in the asylum instead of prison."

I laugh, and I can't stop it. "Half-truths," I bark.

"You should have told me." Jack's voice lowers as he quickly looks at Shay like he's only noticing him now.

"What would you have done, Jack?" My father's question has me really paying attention.

"Visit him."

My father's laughter is quick and sharp. "Do you really think a man who has lost his freedom wants to see a brother, a friend, a mother, even his priest come and chat nonsense, then get up and leave him behind in his cage?" My father is a man of few words, and the room expands with his words. They grow and wrap around us all, and for a moment, it's like he's speaking from experience.

The lull in the room is uncomfortable and allows too many questions to expand.

"It's better than my brother thinking he was forgotten."

I've underestimated Jack. I've thought about this so many times since I got home. He is different.

"I can step outside if you want to have a family pow-wow." Shay stands up, and I want to reach across and drag his smart ass back into the seat.

"You are fine to go, Shay. We will be in touch." My father, ever the diplomat, stays calm. His earlier show of emotion is buried, and I wonder if I imagined it.

The moment Shay leaves the room, I want to ask my father what the fuck he did that for. Why spill something like that about not just me, but us as a family. I don't get a moment to ask because his phone rings, and with a wave of his hand and the turn of his back, he dismisses us.

"Talk to me, Richard." Jack follows me out the doors, and I want to open the top button of my shirt but resist doing it.

"The scars on your stomach, did that happen in the asylum?"

I turn to him. I want to confide in someone. Looking back up at the castle, I wonder if our father is watching us, thinking how weak we are.

"I'm fine, Jack. It was a break from father. I rather enjoyed it." I grin and turn, making my way to my car.

"I'm not him, Richard. You can talk to me."

My gut tightens, and I want to so badly. "Great chat." I wave two fingers in the air and climb into my car. I reverse around Jack as he hasn't moved. Our gazes clash, and I'm tempted to stop and roll down the window, but that is an invitation to talk, and talking isn't what I want to do now. The only way I can control the anger that is growing hard and fast is with the blade and the spilling of blood.

I push my foot to the floor and tear out of the gates of Cabra Castle to find my release.

CHAPTER TEN

O'REAGAN
AN CHLANN

CLAIRE

My back and head complain intensely as I sit up in the tub. It's like a bad dream roaring to life as I glance around my cage. Gripping the side of the tub, I climb out. My heart jumps for too many reasons, but the number one is him. He's standing like some avenging God outside the box. The navy suit fits his large frame flawlessly.

It's another reminder of how insignificant I am compared to him. My palms grow clammy, and I don't blink. He moves forward, and my heart leaps.

"I can't imagine you slept well."

It's only now I notice the tray in his hands that holds my breakfast: a bowl, a mug, and a plate with toast laid out on it.

"Go to the back of the box." His command has my stomach quivering. I don't hesitate but turn quickly, wanting nothing more than to look over my shoulder. At the sound of the click that I associate with the door opening, my shoulders draw together as I walk faster. I reach the end and spin. He has placed the tray on the table and is leaving.

My body settles when the door closes, that is until his dark gaze pins me to the spot. If Lucifer was to take human form and wear an Armani suit, I'm sure this man would fit the profile perfectly. He's harshly beautiful.

"Claire, I want all your food eaten."

His voice drags across my flesh. I don't move from the back of the box. The distance makes me slightly braver. "What do you want with me?" My voice is weak, but it still carries to him.

His gaze zeros in, and I don't need his words; it's in his eyes. It's true that the eyes are the windows to the soul, and from meeting his gaze, I know he doesn't have one.

Blood roars in my ears, and my core tightens. I straighten at the sensation, not expecting to feel this way at all. Confusion at my body's reaction to him overwhelms me.

"I'll be back later." The devil turns on his expensive heels and leaves me reeling for air. What is wrong with me? I can't find him attractive. I do. I shouldn't, but I do.

My feet feel as though they are cemented to the ground, and it takes me some time to move. I pass where Eamon's lifeless body lay. None of this feels real. It's like a bad dream, one I'm yet to wake up from. I pause and step closer to the wall of glass, looking down at the concrete ground. The area is free of any blood. It's like Eamon never existed.

The chairs I smashed have been replaced. I drag one out and sit down, staring at my breakfast. My stomach rumbles loudly, but I don't eat. I examine the tray. The silverware holds my attention. I swallow saliva as I pick up the knife. Running my finger along the blade, I pull away and hiss, not expecting the tip to be so sharp. A metallic taste fills my mouth as I suck my damaged finger between my lips. The bleeding stops after a moment, and I get up with the knife and walk back to my bed. Lifting up a pillow, I place the knife there for safekeeping.

I walk back quickly to the table. My heart pitter-patters in my chest. The sensation grows and accelerates as I think of him discovering the knife. What would he do?

I'm ready to race back and remove the knife from under my pillow, but I manage to stop myself. Having a weapon gives me a better chance at getting out of here. I had to take it.

I eat the dry toast quickly, not bothering with the selection of jams or the butter. I wash the food down with hot coffee. I barely taste the cereal as I eat in record time. My stomach appreciates the food, and I'm still alive, so he hadn't poisoned the breakfast.

Once I have everything eaten, I mess up the tray a bit more. Opening two of the small pots of jam, I scoop out some of the contents. I do the same with the butter. I'm hoping he won't check the tray, just hand it to his housekeeper. A man who dresses like he does is bound to have a housekeeper or two.

When I feel as satisfied as I think I will be, I leave the table and make my way back to the bed. I bring the blankets back from the tub and remake the bed. I keep checking to make sure the knife is still there. It is.

Relieving myself is another thing I have to do, but each time I step closer to the toilet, I step away until my bladder demands to be emptied. I finally use the toilet and quickly wash my hands and face after. Sitting back on the bed, I wring my hands. I have no idea what I'm meant to do.

I check the entire box again for something to use to get out of here. But there are no weapons. Only the sharp butter knife that I stole. My mind sings. A sob presses against my throat, pushing my palm against my chest doesn't stop the onslaught of panic that tries to devour me.

It's the click that has me swinging towards the door. He's here again. He doesn't have to say a word. I instinctively dart to the back of the box. I need to appear obedient, so he can relax and hopefully give me an opportunity to use the knife. I want to look at the pillow where the knife lies but keep my focus trained on him as he enters the box. He's carrying something that he places on the table before picking up the tray. Without a word, he leaves. The door closes. He climbs the steps and disappears out of sight.

I count to one hundred waiting for him to reappear and demand the knife back, or worse, use it on me. My throat grows dry as I wait, but he doesn't come. My steps are slower as I approach the table where a box sits. It's the size of a shoebox. I keep checking the stairway, but each time it's empty. Picking up the box, I flip open the lid, and small puzzle pieces fall out onto the floor. Quickly I kneel down and scoop them up, placing them back in the box.

A puzzle?

Most of the small pieces are gray. The material in the image looks like stone. As I shift the pieces, I see the greenery of fields and trees and the blue of a river. I glance at the stairway again, making sure he isn't there, and when I'm satisfied, I look back to the puzzle. My fingers itch to make it up. Why give me a puzzle? Is this some weird way of telling me why I am here?

With that thought, I spill the puzzle out across the table. Flashes of my family doing this have me stumbling from the table. Emotions surface hard and fast, and I cover my face like I can keep them down.

Would my family be searching for me if they were alive? I know they would. My parents would have been distraught. I wonder what life I could have led if they had lived. Would they have noticed how cruel Leonard was? Would they have gotten him help before it went too far? Before, it cost us everything.

I bite my lip until the pain has me refocusing. *Make up the puzzle, Claire.*

This is what I spent weekends off doing. With that thought, I tell myself it's just a normal weekend as I sit down and get lost doing the puzzle. It's something that has always numbed me, and all that matters is completing the puzzle. The image takes shape as I fill in the edges and continue this pattern, watching the landscape develop. A river is running alongside fields. With each piece I add, I see more of the picture, and my heart races. Why give me this? The castle starts to take form, and my stomach squirms as recognition takes shape. I know the castle. I know where this is.

Cabra Castle.

Not far from where I live. Why show me this? Is this puzzle one he had upstairs and just gave to me to pass the time? Or could he know doing puzzles is how I spent dwindling away my spare time. My hands start to shake as questions assault me.

Three questions dominate all the rest, and I'm looking at the stairway again. Why am I here? Why me? And what would he finally do with me?

I'm not getting out of this place. The chair hits the ground hard as I stand abruptly. My fists smash down on the stupid puzzle, and I tear into the image like it's a living thing that I can pour all my anger out on. Flinging the contents across the floor, I join the puzzle pieces on the ground. Tears burn my eyes, and I let them flow as I scream out my fear and frustration towards the glass ceiling. I stay on the floor for a while until my body is all out of tears and hope.

I crawl across the floor, picking up the gray box, and start putting the pieces back in. It's like my life, really. When I fall apart and spiral into the darkness, I often wait for someone to pull me out, someone to hold me and tell me it will be okay. That never happens. I resurface even for a small amount of time and have to pick myself up off the ground. I have to convince myself it will be okay. That life will get better.

The lies, I tell myself. My fingers wrap around the small pieces, and I anchor myself to gathering up the pieces and placing them in the box. Once I've gathered them all up, I put the box back on the table and pick up the fallen chair.

The silence is driving me mad. At home in my apartment, I kept a radio going or the TV on. I never allowed the silence to fill the space; with silence came my pain.

I hum off-key as I move to the back of the box and sit down on the ground. I have a clear path to the door, but I'm the furthest away if he comes back.

He does. He's changed out of his suit and has swapped it for a t-shirt and jeans. He looks more deadly, and my heart thump thumps in my chest as he places a tray on the table. No warning is given, and once he leaves, I muster the strength up and go to the table. A steak dinner steams from the tray. Silverware and a napkin are placed to the left. A tall glass of liquid is what I pick up first and drink it down in one go.

The food doesn't go down so easily. My stomach rebels through the large meal. I hold up the steak knife, tempted to take it, but I got away with one; a second knife going unnoticed isn't likely. The steak parts like butter under the steak knife. Once all the content is cut up, I take the plate to the toilet and scrape all the food into the bowl. I have to flush several times, and sweat starts to gather on the back of my neck. Flushing the toilet seems so noisy in the surrounding space. I hum to try to calm myself, and it works as I walk back to the table and return the plate to the tray. I reluctantly leave the steak knife behind. Grabbing the puzzle box, I take it with me to the back of the room, where I sit down and start to make the puzzle again while continuing to hum. I've made up the puzzle five times when he arrives again. He removes the tray and, just like the last time, leaves something on the table for me. He pauses this time and doesn't leave immediately. I hold my breath, not moving a muscle until he finally leaves.

I hate the small swell of excitement that pushes my feet faster across the flooring. I reach the table, and it's another box—this one black. Opening the box, the pieces are smaller and the quantity larger. Taking one final peek at the stairway, I take my puzzle with me and hug the box to my chest as I return to the back of the space. Sitting down on the ground, I finish off the first puzzle before starting the second one. These are just random fields with cows and some far-off mountains in the background. Once again, I recognize the landscape, or maybe it's like all the back roads in our area that are overlooked by the Loch Leigh mountains.

The pattern happens again. He brings me tea. This time the tray holds a sandwich and a mug of coffee. I eat the food this time, and when he collects the tray, another package is left. I nearly smile as I race across the cube and pick up the package; it's not a puzzle but a brown bag. Opening it, I take out several adult coloring books and a set of coloring pencils. Fear tightens its hands around my throat. This is another thing I do to pass the time. Has he been watching me? How did he know these things about me?

The coloring book makes me feel unsettled. I leave the book and the pencils on the table, not wanting to give him any more of myself. I do keep remaking my puzzles until I can nearly do them with my eyes closed.

Days grow repetitive. The one thing that changes is that he stops bringing my food. The bald man named Davy brings the trays instead. No one has to tell me to stay at the back of the box. I spent most of my day there, biding my time to use my knife. Food comes and goes, and more puzzles and coloring books are left behind.

My fingers itch to color, and I give in to another thing I did with my mother. Coloring calms me, and I give in to the call and start to fill the pages with vibrant colors. I want to fill the washout space with colors too, not just the pages. Everywhere in the box is white. Why white? Everything is white, even the clothes on my back.

The violet coloring pencil I slide across the white flooring and smile at the line it creates. My smile wobbles and my hand tightens around the pencil. It snaps. The sound of the cracking wood causes me to startle. Closing my eyes, I take a calming breath and start to hum. It settles me again, and I pick up a blue coloring pencil and start to paint my freedom on the floor.

CHAPTER ELEVEN

O'REAGAN
AN CHLANN

RICHARD

"You want me to push you?" I ask Finn as we make our way to the hotel in Kells. It's our first check-in of the day.

"No." His word is barked.

Shoving him out in front of oncoming traffic has crossed my mind. My father has been on my case. So this would be the perfect opportunity to remove another thing from my to-do list.

"I still can use my arms." His remark is spoken through gritted teeth.

"Make them work faster. We are losing daylight hours," I say without looking down at him.

He stops spinning his wheels, so he's facing me and also blocking me from going any further. "You will show me some respect." There is no force behind his words, and I'm ready to tell him he hasn't got my respect, but my attention is snagged by Shane, who jogs across the road.

He is accompanying us today. My father must think we are delinquents as he sends three of us to check in on the running of the hotels.

"I got caught up," Shane grumbles to me. "Did you hear from Darragh?" He directs his question to Finn, who's all red in the face from having a go at me.

"No, why? What has he done now?"

Shane exhales loudly while rubbing his jaw. "He's not answering his phone. He was meant to initiate new members."

Shane takes out his phone. "I'll try him again." While Shane rings Darragh, I'm here standing on a footpath in the middle of Kells. These brothers are such fuck-ups.

Shane shakes his head, glaring down at the screen on his phone before cutting the call.

"I'll initiate the members. Just tell me where," I say.

Shane's smirk is brief as he raises both brows. "You think Liam would want his son doing groundwork?"

"If it's good enough for Darragh, it's good enough for me."

Shane's smirk returns, and he glances at Finn, who also finds this fucking amusing.

"Are you sure?" Shane tilts his head like he's giving me a way out, and I should take it.

But standing here with these two clowns isn't doing it for me.

"I'm positive, Shane." I don't flinch.

All humor flees Shane's face as he directs his attention to his phone. Mine vibrates in my pocket, and I remove the device.

"That's the address."

"Have a good day," I tell them and leave. I'll have to kill Finn some other time.

The new members are runners for the drug trade, and all vary in age. The only common thing they share is that they are all male, and all are here for the money. Two men I've never met before make their way across the warehouse toward me.

The first wears a leather vest with nothing underneath. His dark black hair is slicked back. Muscles bulge as he holds out his hand eagerly for me to take. I take his hand but want nothing more than to wash my hands immediately after.

"Shane told us you were coming. Great to meet you, Richard."

I stare at him as I release his hand. "Your name?"

He stands a little taller as the second man steps up beside him. His attire is cleaner, with slacks and a royal blue shirt.

"Mike, and this is Eddie."

Eddie holds out his hand, and I take it quickly.

The noise in the warehouse is growing quieter as the men start to notice my arrival.

"So the boys have been primed and are raring to go," Mike says proudly, and I step around him toward the men who would do the actual donkey work. These men might be the lowest paid, but without them, this ship would sink. I just needed to make sure that if the ship did sink, the captain would remain on dry land.

"Who has spent time in prison?" My question has the men mumbling. I focus on a young boy, maybe eighteen, the pristine white tracksuit and shoes that haven't seen a day's work. That would change. He's at the age that if he throws his weight around like that, it makes him more of a man.

I single him out. "What about you?"

He turns to the other men, half laughing before facing me. "Nah, I'm too quick to get caught." He lifts the baseball cap off his head before sliding it back on. Laughter bubbles up behind him.

I grin, not fucking amused.

I look at an older man.

"You?" I ask.

"No, Sir." His gut hangs out over his trousers, and I move along the line of men.

"Anyone?"

A lanky man, whose face is covered in acne scars, steps forward. "Two years in Mount Joy."

I place my hands in my trousers pockets as I make my way down to him. I don't ask him about his crime. That is irrelevant.

"In those two years, how many times were you beaten?"

"Too many times." He laughs, but the pain and anger reflect in his eyes.

"How about getting raped?"

The next question has his face growing red, and he's ready to step away from me and back into formation with the other men.

"You will answer my question."

He looks to Mike and Eddie, who are approaching me fast like they are sweeping in to do damage control.

I know it's Mike who will take charge before he opens his stupid mouth.

"This isn't what Darragh does, Richard. We don't interrogate the men."

I nod, and the man who hadn't answered my question tries to sink back into the line. "Stay where you are." I warn him, and he pauses.

Turning to Mike, I grip his shoulder. "It's Mr. O'Reagan to you."

His jaw hardens, but he keeps his big mouth shut.

"I'll do this my way." I turn back to the lanky man. "Were you raped in prison?"

"Yes." He admits through gritted teeth. Men snort laughter around him, and I take a step towards them.

They shut the fuck up.

"Working with us may seem like quick money. Easy earnings." I walk the line, making sure each man hears my words. "But if you get caught, prison is how you pay for your quick money, and in prison, you will be beaten." I stop and point at the lanky man who admitted to being raped. "What's your name?"

"Jared." He grumbles reluctantly.

"Just like Jared was beaten and raped, so will you."

The men aren't laughing now.

"But let me tell you something, if you get caught and breathe the O'Reagan name, rape and a beating would be a blessing compared to what I would do to you." I stop, and the young boy who had never been to prison has paled as he looks up at me. The baseball cap dragged a little closer to his eyes.

"I enjoy hurting people," I speak to him before stepping back. "I'm very good at it." I allow a slow grin to grace my face. "I can't give you references because no one survives."

I clap my hands, and they startle. "So let this be your warning. It's money on the table, but the consequences are deadly."

I turn to Mike and Eddie. "How did I do?"

Eddie looks to Mike, who tightens his jaw. "Very well, Mr. O Reagan."

I step up to Mike and slap him gently on the cheek. "That's a good boy." He needs to remember he is in the presence of a king.

No one laughs or speaks. The room is deadly quiet as I look back at the men.

"That is your initiation. Mike and Eddie will give you further instructions." I take my leave from the group of silent men.

I think it went well.

I have no intention of returning to Shane and Wheels. My mind has been fixated on Claire whenever I gave my mind a break from thinking about work. She fascinates me. So much so that I had Davy take over bringing her food because the pull I felt toward her kept growing. She is the perfect image of damaged, and instead of mending her, I want to completely open her up until she is unfixable.

"That wasn't wise."

A thrill shoots through my body and I turn to Mike, the knight who races across the asphalt toward me.

"The men are pissed, and I had to ring Darragh."

I fold my arms across my chest and let this fool continue to divulge.

"He's Mr. O Reagan to us, and I mean no disrespect, but what you did to Jared in there wasn't right."

I nod my head like what he is saying is fascinating.

I could lash out easily and take this fool's life. I remember my lessons. Take something else from him. It would be his power in this case.

"You're right, Mike." I unfold my arms.

Mike smiles. "Look, I get it, man, I know what you were doing, but that doesn't work on my guys."

"Your guys." I grin.

This stupid motherfucker grins back. "I'm the boss when Darragh isn't here."

"Let me apologize to the men."

Mike's brain kicks into gear. "Really?" It's his first time looking skeptical.

I walk back to the warehouse. "Yeah, Mike, really."

He jogs until his steps match mine. "I mean, they would appreciate that. Especially coming from you."

I pull open the door to the warehouse, and like the gentlemen I am, I allow Mike to enter first.

The hush falls around the space quickly, but I want to make my point.

I clap my hands several times. "Gentlemen." I garner their attention. "Mike here thinks I've treated you badly."

Mike steps up beside me, his shoulders held back with pride, like he just tamed a lion.

"Anyone else agree with Mike?" I ask.

I take a slow, drawn-out look at the men. Not one of them moves, not even poor Eddie who looks gray. The royal blue shirt he's wearing sports sweat patches.

"Looks like you're on your own, Mike."

"These are my men." His growl pisses me off.

I keep my temper in check. I'm proud that I don't extract my gun and make him eat bullets.

I step away from Mike. "Ten G's to whoever shoots this clown."

Mike's face grows white, and he spins, ready to run. Three rounds are fired in quick succession. One drills a hole into the back of his head. It's all over in a second as he hits the floor, blood pooling around his head like a halo. I turn and note the three men who had withdrawn their guns. The young boy with the baseball cap and white runners lowers his gun. "Never liked him." He's a cocky little fucker, but he's like a starving dog. Throw him a bone, and he will become loyal.

"The three of you will get your blood money," I announce to the group before approaching the boy.

"You will apprentice under Eddie."

He puts his gun away, and his eyes sparkle as his ego grows.

"What's your name?"

"George." He nods several times as he speaks.

"Well, George, here is your chance to shine."

"I won't let you down, boss." George bites his bottom lip like he's trying to contain his excitement. Like he can't wait to tell all his little friends that he's a boss.

"No, you won't, George. Because if you do...." I don't finish that sentence, and he swallows, looking unsure for the first time.

I've had my fun with these donkeys.

"All yours, Eddie."

Eddie's shirt is worse for wear with his growing sweat marks. Where did Darragh get these men?

"Change your shirt." I bark, and he starts peeling it off as I leave them to squabble.

Taking off my suit jacket, I get into my car and drive away from the warehouse. I don't get far before my phone starts to ring, it's Shane. "Yes, Shane."

"Killing the staff isn't wise." His growl vibrates down the phone.

I unbutton the top of my shirt. "I didn't raise a finger. My gun is cold."

"Your father won't be happy, Richard."

I grit my teeth as I join the traffic on the roundabout before veering off for Monalty. I want to say I don't give a fuck what my father thinks. "I'll take it up with him, then."

"Jack would never behave like this. You need to follow your brother's example."

I laugh as I merge onto the road. Jack is responsible for his son's death. I wonder if he knew the truth, would he still sing his fucking praises.

"I'm going to give you some advice." Traffic zooms behind Shane's words. He must be walking outside.

My laughter dies down as I wait for his words of wisdom.

"I didn't survive this long in this game by being foolish."

"I was making a point." I state.

"No, you were showing your power."

Same difference.

"Let me give **you** some advice, Shane." I'm getting sick of tip-toeing around my uncles like they are gods. They are old and worn out. "The reason you survive this game isn't because you are careful. It's because my father wants you alive. Otherwise, you would be dead." There it is, the truth of all this.

We don't die from some street gang or jobs gone wrong. We die because of my father. Either he wants you to die, or you get caught in his crossfire of dirty deeds, but ultimately it all comes back to him.

Shane is silent, and I listen to the zoom of traffic down the phone as I approach my home.

"You are right. Your father favors me. He always has. That is something you should remember." With his final words, he hangs up like it's some threat.

The only threat here is my father. And what do you do with threats? You eliminate them.

CHAPTER TWELVE

O'REAGAN
AN CHLANN

CLAIRE

Time no longer exists. The thoughts of witnessing the day fade into night or the rebirth of a new day seems unimaginable. Days morph into weeks. I think it's weeks. Maybe it's longer, and maybe it's shorter. The lighting never alters, so differentiating from night and day is impossible. I can only rely on my body clock. My mind buzzes, and I have that frayed feeling I had when my parents died. Any small thing would set me off. I'm teetering on that line; waltzing with madness is how I've always pictured it. I bite hard on my cracked lip, and the skin splits easily. It contorts the smile that I don't want painted on my face. It's not a happy smile or a sad smile. It's one that shows how broken I am.

The black colored pencil is down to a stub as I run it across the white wooden flooring. An image manifests in front of me. I've been drawing without paying attention. My stomach twists as I'm dragged into the vortex of his dark eyes. Why did I draw him? My mind, even when I'm not focused, is fixated on my captor.

My palm turns black as I try to rub away the image with a ferocity that burns my skin. Everything inside me twists painfully, and I'm afraid. Afraid that I have been locked up in this box for so long that it has turned me inside out, and I'm losing my mind again.

And again.

And again.

"Shut up," I mumble under my breath as the picture on the floor blurs. I blink back the tears. I sit back slightly, and I'm stuck on the figure.

He materializes at the end of the box. I haven't seen him since those first few days. He's here, and he's observing me. My heart jumps into my throat. It's his eyes, no, his height; no, his build; it's all of him that terrifies me. I drop my head.

The picture of his eyes glares at me with judgment. He's moving in my peripheral vision along the side of the box. I don't want him to see what I have drawn. Gripping the bottom of my white dress, I use the material as a scrubbing brush until the image is distorted enough to resemble a black blob. Yet, as I stare down, I swear he's staring back.

I'm breathing heavily and stay kneeling with hunched shoulders. If the glass didn't separate us, it would only take a few steps, and I would be able to touch him.

"You've stopped eating." His words have my shoulders drawing closer together. My fingernails bend under the pressure as I dig them into the flooring, into the picture of his distorted eyes.

"Why am I here?" I turn my head and watch him through a curtain of disheveled blonde hair. When I slowly lift my head, my strength buckles under the weight of his stare.

A red stain on his white shirt draws my attention. The blood is fresh along the side.

"What have I done so wrong?" My words grow louder, and I wonder if he can even hear me. Is this Karma, Is this God, or is this just a man's wrath?

He bends his large frame until he's sitting on the ground. The position looks odd on such a powerful man. He drags his legs half up and rests his arms on them, his hands dangling across his knees. He has blood on his hands.

"I used to go to this priest, Father Flynn. He was a giant of a man. Seven-foot tall. I often questioned how he fit into the confessional box as a kid."

My captor stares at his bloody hands, and all I can think is he killed the priest. A man of God. "You killed him." The words tumble fast and hard out of my mouth.

"Some might say my confession didn't fare well on him." His lip twitches like he's fighting a smile. But it falls flat, and all I see is anger. "No, he died of cancer."

I'm sorry for your loss is on the tip of my tongue.

My captor returns to staring at his bloody hands, and I return to trying to stay calm and breathe. He's too close to me. I know he can't get through the glass, but my skin tightens across my bones. I feel like I'm up close to a lion, or an ocean of water is leaning against the glass. One small crack, and I'd be dead.

"He listened to me every Saturday night. I would tell him my week and everything I did during that time."

I somehow doubted that what he did included cooking Sunday dinners or drinks with friends.

"Three Hail Marys, one Our Father, and all my sins were forgiven." He looks up at me. "Do you believe in God, Claire?"

I could easily answer yes or no. "What do you think? I'm stuck in a glass box." I rise as the unfairness of this situation roars to life inside me. "I'm stuck in here listening to you."

He stays on the floor, and I dare to take one step closer. My temperature soars. "Talking about your priest, and your life, while you took mine. Why am I here? What did I do?" My body trembles as my voice hits a peak of hysteria. I need to shut up, but I need to know more.

"What do you want?!" My roar has him rising, and I stumble back.

"The same as you, Claire. I want what was taken from me. I can't get time back. But I can take time."

My feet falter and trip as I race to the glass, terrified that he might leave now that he has started to talk. "That's what you are doing. Taking my time?" I'm confused, and he moves and hisses. The red stain bleeds deeper into the fabric of his shirt. He won't answer. My fists hit the glass. "Tell me." My words end in a whimper.

"You will eat your food." His dark gaze grows darker, and he starts to walk away from me.

"I won't. I'll starve." I'm following him, clinging to the glass screaming. I can't be left in here again. I can't accept this. "I'll die my way!"

He pauses, and when he turns, his lip rises slightly. "The only person who is taking your life, Claire, is me." Once again, his smirk doesn't form completely before it dies.

"No!" I'm walking away.

"No?" he repeats, his question follows me.

"No!" I'm giddy as I race to my bed.

"Claire!" The warning in his voice pushes me quickly to the bed that I leap upon. My hand frantically feels around under the pillow. The cold steel has me half laughing as I pull the knife out. I spin on the bed and face my captor. "I said no."

"Put the knife down." His warning is low, and he's rooted to the spot.

"No." My voice is calm. I've spent so much time sharpening it along the inside of the plughole of the tub. It has whittled down the steel, and I have tested the blade on a few dresses.

I raise the knife to my wrist, and when I look at my captor, his eyes look panicked.

"How does it feel to have all the power taken from you?" I ask and press the knife to my wrist. Blood pools fast along the small nick. My blood roars in my veins, and I don't know if I have the guts to continue. I don't want to die, but I don't want to wait until he kills me. Is this the lesser of two evils?

"I'll tell you." His words are quiet. His hands curled into fists. "Put the knife down, and I'll tell you why you are here."

He's lying. He has to be.

"Claire." His voice rises, his gaze is pinned to my wrist that's bleeding heavier. Without thought, I had pushed the knife deeper.

With shaky hands, I drop the knife on the bedspread and watch the blood flow from my wrist.

My vision wavers, and I blink. He's gone. Now I wonder if he ever was truly there. I've officially lost my mind.

It's the click.

The click of the door has me scrambling to stay alert. I raise my head, and he's in the box. He's walking toward me. His large steps eliminate the space between us. I turn as terror rips through me. My weakened body isn't strong enough to get off the bed in time. I remember his smell. It's here again. Strong hands touch me, and I'm screaming with the last ounce of strength I have. It's useless as he spins me around, forcing me onto my back and pressing me into the mattress. I lash out at him, and blood drips from my wound back down on top of my chest.

"You're making it worse." His angry words have no effect on me. Not while his hands are on me.

"No! Get away from me!" I'm screaming and feeling for the knife. I can't let my life end like this. My fingers touch the steel metal, and for a moment, my vision clears. He's above me, and all the air is sucked from my lungs. Dark hair falls into his eyes as he glares down at me.

Darkness dances along my vision; it's a warning that I heed. I wrap my fingers around the knife's handle, and my scream propels the blade towards him. He swats the knife away like it's an annoying fly. The knife bounces off the floor, and it's the sound of doom.

"That wasn't very smart, Claire." I can't look at him. A fresh wave of fear devours me. I buck and scream under his weight that grows heavier, and I cry as my lungs refuse to work and my sight fails me. I roll my head to the side, squeezing my eyes closed, darkness envelopes me, and the last word I hear is his curse.

CHAPTER THIRTEEN

O'REAGAN
AN CHLANN

CLAIRE

The pillows behind my head are soft. I move my head to the left. My eyelids feel heavy, and I don't open them straight away. My mind is muddled, and I'm waiting for it to clear. It's the smell that has me cracking my eyes open. My body sinks further into the pillows like I might get away from him.

"You lost a lot of blood." His tongue flicks out, and he licks his bottom lip like he's tasting something.

My heart trips, slows down before going into a full gallop at his closeness.

"I knew you had the knife. I thought you would try to use it on me when I decided to give you the opportunity, that is." His lip quivers, or maybe I imagine it.

I hear his words, but I can't focus. He has changed his clothing. His black shirt sharpens his dark features. Features that when he's angry become more defined, more ferocious. I can't imagine what could possibly soften the sharp edges.

"Using it on yourself...." He trails off and steps even closer to the bed. "I didn't see that coming. You caught me off guard." He sounds almost proud of me.

He's sick.

He's twisted.

And he's standing at the end of my bed. He's way too close.

My heart thrashes painfully against my chest, and I want to reach up to keep it in my body, but I don't dare move.

"It won't happen again, Claire. A lapse in judgment on my part." He turns away from me and glances around the space. "It's not nice being on this side of the glass. Three years I spent behind a wall of glass." He pivots back to me. "I didn't have this kind of room. A single bed, a locker, and a toilet."

Did he want me to think I was in luxury? No matter what size the box is, I am like a caged animal.

The silence drags out, and his sharp laughter twists my stomach. "I thought you would have lots of questions now that you have my attention. That is why you hurt yourself, isn't it? To get my attention." His words are more of an accusation.

"I don't want your attention."

He raises a dark brow, and I swear I see amusement in the depths of his eyes. "Don't you, Claire?" His voice drops a few octaves.

A shiver races along my neck and brushes my arms. "Are you going to tell me why I'm here?"

"It depends." He spins on his heel and walks over to the drawing on the floor that I had smudged out. "What were you drawing here that you tried so hard to cover up?"

"I don't know. Scribbles."

His smile is all teeth and no humor. He waggles his finger at me like I'm telling lies and really shouldn't.

"You," I say quickly.

The light catches his gaze, and his eyes dance brightly, and for a moment, it lightens his eyes, and they appear brown. He blinks, and I see the soulless creature who has taken me.

He stares back at the ground and tilts his head, trying to make the distorted image out.

"I've never had anyone draw me before. Maybe you will do it again so I can see." He doesn't look at me as he speaks. His gaze transfixed on the floor.

He rolls his shoulders before glancing back at me. My wrist becomes his focus. It's only now that I notice it's been bandaged.

I reach across and touch the bandage lightly. My fingers dance across the white material.

"It's going to leave a scar." His words confuse me. He sounds like he cares. But that can't be true.

"It won't be the first." I find myself saying.

He turns fully, and my senses rise too quickly, making me dizzy. The feeling settles when he doesn't advance any closer.

"The scar on your knee. I'd like you to tell me the story behind it."

"I will," I swallow a pool of saliva that keeps refilling in my mouth, "If you tell me why I'm here."

He's watching. He's thinking. He's moving towards me again, and I'm pushing myself up to try to increase the separation. No amount of distance from him would settle my racing heart.

He doesn't speak. So I try again. "Are the puzzles a clue?"

"No." His jaw clenches, the muscle working quickly like I've angered him. His gaze fixates on my wrist again.

"Now tell me about your scar." He repeats.

I want to say no, that he has told me nothing, but under his heavy stare, I find myself giving in. "barbed wire when I was twelve."

Silence. He's waiting.

"My brother made a swing on one of the old oak trees that grew close to our house." The memory rushes back, and I touch the bandage on my wrist and push a finger down. The pain burns my arm but forces the memory away so I can just speak without emotion. "He insisted I went first, so I did. When I was swinging, he hit me with barbed wire. It caught in my knee and held me in the air. It felt like an eternity." I press down heavier on the bandage. "Until the skin snapped, and I was released."

A flash of anger across his face has dread making me curl into the pillow.

"You're bleeding." The words are barely audible as he speaks through clenched teeth. He's moving towards me again, and all I want to do is get away from him. He's quick and takes my forearm; my skin reacts to his touch like flames on my flesh. I try to drag my arm back, but his grip is iron.

"Stay still." His large fingers circle my arm as they move down, leaving a burning path behind them until the tip of his fingers touches the bandage that's leaking blood. It must have started when I pressed down on it. He releases me, and I'm ready to pull my arm back, but he unravels the bandage at a speed that's almost panicked. The stained bandage floats to the floor, and he touches my arm with a gentleness that runs as deep as the cut. His touch takes over my senses, and it's all I feel.

"Who hurt you?" I ask.

His hand tightens briefly before his touch loosens, but he doesn't let my arm go. He won't look at me. His gaze is on my arm. I don't care about my wrist, I care about getting out of this box, and he is the only way I'm getting out. "I'm sorry if someone hurt you."

Dark eyes finally focus on me, and I hold still, even against my body's instincts to sink away.

"You think someone hurt me?" His tone is mocking.

"Yes," I answer honestly because no sane person would do this. He had spoken of time stolen. He had said he spent three years in a box like this. I have to use the small snippets of information I receive. I just hope I am going in the right direction with this.

He returns to my arm. "I need to re-bandage your wrist." He releases my arm and gets up. I think he's leaving, and I should feel relieved, but I don't. A coldness seeps into my bones.

Running water has me looking at him as he dips a cloth under the stream. He returns to the bed, and I hold myself still and try not to flinch when he sits down and takes my arm with the same care he had moments ago.

"Please, let me go."

"Stay still." He dabs the cut, and I feel the burn along my wrist for the first time. My adrenaline is slowly receding, leaving a coldness in its wake. I face away from him as he continues to clean my wound and re-bandage my wrist. The bed dips as he gets up. "I can't let you go."

Regret.

I hear regret in his voice. "Can't or won't?"

I don't know who senses the bald man first, my captor or me, but we both look toward the door at the same time.

No words are exchanged. My captor tightens his fists and storms off. I don't look away as he meets up with the bald man. The door closes, and I'm alone again.

His words should drive fear into my heart. *"I can't let you go."* They don't. They pump hope into my system, and I get out of the bed. I grip the edge of the mattress and wait for the dizziness to pass before picking up my discarded black colored pencil. I move to the center of the room and sit down and start to draw.

No matter how afraid I am, I had to try to win him over. He had said he couldn't let me out. I had to give him a reason to free me. With that thought, I draw his face on the floor of my glass cage.

CHAPTER FOURTEEN

O'REAGAN
AN CHLANN

RICHARD

Davy doesn't speak until we leave the basement.

"Shay is at the front gates."

"That's what you dragged me up here for?" I ask. My feet are itching to turn around and return to Claire.

Davy shakes his head. "You need to see this for yourself."

I follow Davy into the security room. Marcus gets up from his seat to let me lean in on the desk, so I can get a clear view of what exactly the problem is. Five screens show different perimeters of the house. I focus on the screen positioned to my left, which displays the front gates. Shay is standing outside my gates; a cigarette hanging out of his mouth, the wrath of a King twists his face as he holds up...

"Is that a head?" I look closer. *It's a fucking head.* "Jesus Christ. Let him in before someone sees the stupid fucker."

I march out of the room and to the front door. I'm halfway down the driveway when Shay's car tears up towards me. Our gazes meet, and like a deranged man, he roars past and jams on the brakes at the front door. I jog back to the house. My gun is tucked in the band of the back of my trousers; I yank my shirt out to cover it.

"You want to tell me what is going on?" I demand.

Shay jumps out of the car, and blood flecks his face and clothes. He's made the kill recently. He doesn't speak but reaches back into the car and extracts the head. He grips it by the hair, and all I see is the back of the head. It spins, and I internally curse.

This isn't good.

"Is this like a welcome home gift? Someone who pissed me off that I forgot about?"

Blood drips all over my driveway. Davy appears at the front door with Marcus on his heels. I hold up my hand, and they don't advance any further.

Shay lifts the head until I'm staring Carlos in the eyes. "This piece of shit had my brother killed."

The teardrop on Carlos's face, along with the distinctive ones on his neck, which Jack had asked me about days ago, is what would have gotten Carlos caught.

"Your point?"

Shay takes a step toward me, and once again, I have to hold up a finger to Davy not to intercede. Shay might be one hell of a fighter, but I am a good shot.

"Carlos here talked a lot before I killed him."

"Once again, Shay, what is your point?" I take a step towards him until our chests almost brush.

"Your father ..." Shay stops talking, his brows drawing together. "Your father did this." He blinks like a man who can't accept the betrayal he's speaking of. "Your father is the owner of the uncharted territory up in the North. That's why I couldn't buy it."

I know all this. I've always known who was behind Frankie's death. My father. Lucian Sheahan wasn't a fan of Shay after he betrayed the IRA over a bombing that killed women and children. Shay had disagreed with them over the bombing, and that went against the IRA's beliefs, placing Shay on their shit list. So when my father asked to buy the uncharted territory, Lucian agreed, with one condition that my father arranged for either Shay or Frankie to die. Connor was their best fighter and took too much of the profits. If he fought, he won, and Shay walked in his footsteps.

No matter how tall you are in this world, there is always someone taller ready to knock you on your ass.

Shay's gaze fills with pent-up anger, and he's on the verge of crying. "He cost me my brother." He roars the words in my face.

I lunge forward. My hand tightens around his neck. "I'm not him."

"You're a bigger cunt than he is," Shay says. His lips are a little too loose for my liking. Loose lips are a very dangerous thing. Shay grips my neck when I don't release him.

"Take your hands off him now." Davy comes forward and cocks the gun that's pointed at Shay's temple, but Shay squeezes tighter like his life isn't on the line.

"You're all a bunch of cunts," Shay sneers.

"We are," I admit. Releasing Shay first. "Davy, put the gun away."

Davy reluctantly removes the gun from Shay's temple, and Shay releases me.

"Why?" Anger forces his question out.

"Money, Shay. It's always about money and power. You know that. You killed Amanda, I believe, but she would have told you that your dad was eating into their profits."

"You mean your fucking father's profits."

"Give us a minute," I say to Davy, who hesitates. I flash him a warning look, and he goes back inside with Marcus.

"My father bought the territory. But he didn't run the cage fights. They just paid him a cut for allowing the fighting to continue."

Shay moves to the steps of my front door and sits down, plonking the dismembered head beside him. He pats his chest pockets before taking out his cigarettes and lighter, leaving more blood on his shirt. He lights one up, and I give him a moment to compose himself.

"I'm going to kill your father," he says while calmly blowing smoke into the air.

I laugh at his boldness. I admire it, but I won't tell him that.

"He'll kill you first," I say the truth. "He will know Carlos is dead. He won't leave a loose end dangling."

Shay's gaze swings to me, and he inhales a sharp pull of his cigarette before blowing smoke out in my direction. His smirk is vicious as he rises. "Let him fucking try."

"Does Jack know?" Shay asks.

Everyone loved fucking, Jack. No one wanted him to be the bad one. I'm tempted to say yes, but the truth is he didn't.

"No."

Shay nods and reaches down, and picks up the head.

"Why did you come here, Shay?" I ask. If he is so hell-bent on killing my father, he came to the wrong place.

"I needed to make sure Carlos wasn't lying. You confirmed it for me."

"I might be lying." I grin.

"You hate your old man as much as I do. I saw the hostility at the meeting. You don't want to protect him. Just like he won't protect you." Shay tilts his head and steps closer, his pain raw on his face. "He took my brother. Frankie…" He turns away and gains his composure before turning back to me. "Frankie never hurt anyone." Shay shakes his head. "He's a fucking monster, Richard."

"Isn't that what I am too?" I ask. Everyone sees me as his shadow.

Shay steps back up to me. "No. He wants us to see that. He wants us to fear you. We did."

"What changed?"

"The woman who died. They said you tortured her in front of her kids, and that's why you were sent away to the Czech Republic. That's the story that your father fed us. Like a bunch of cunts we ate his lies right up."

I don't confirm or deny what he's saying.

"You didn't do it. You tried to stop it."

"And how do you know that?"

Shay seems to know a whole lot about me.

"I have my sources."

I shake my head. "That won't work with me, Shay. You want mutual respect? Tell me how you know that."

"A man my father drinks with was there. We haven't seen him in years. He popped back up and had one too many and told us the story."

It takes me a moment to let that all sink in. I didn't think he was lying. There were several Northern men there that night.

The gates open down the road, reminding me of my actual appointment I had this evening. The Range Rover drives slowly up the drive, the windows are tinted, and it passes us, driving out back.

Shay walks back to his car and throws the head in.

"I'd maybe put that in the trunk. You don't want to have to try and explain why you have a head in your car if you get stopped."

Shay glances at me over his shoulder. "No one is going to stop me."

His anger will get him killed. He climbs into the car, and I walk over to the window that he rolls down. I lean in, placing my hands on the door frame.

"Don't do anything stupid."

His grin is back, but it's like someone carved it out with a knife. "What, like kill your father?"

I release the door frame and stand up, moving back as he starts the car. "Yeah, something like that."

He reverses quickly, and I watch him as he leaves my home. I could ring my father and warn him, but I won't. Shay won't kill him tonight, and I won't warn my father. That way, I will gain Shay's trust.

Davy lingers in the hallway. "He's unstable." Davy starts.

I'm not amused. "We are all unstable. Every last O'Reagan. It's in our blood."

Davy doesn't answer as I walk to the back of the house. The second garage is out here, and that's where the Range Rover is parked.

"Bob," I say his name as the back window rolls down. A pair of wild green eyes widen, and recognition slowly drips into his foggy brain. They've beaten him badly. I had said rough him up, but not enough that I couldn't enjoy this moment.

"Richie?"

Fuck me. I hated that name.

"What's going on?" He looks to Andrew, who sits beside him. I nod my head at Andrew and move away from the Range Rover as Andrew drags Bob out. Bob starts shouting and cursing immediately. I walk around to them.

"What is this?" Bob tries to pull away from Andrew, but the action does nothing but burn away his energy reserves.

"Let me show you something, Bob."

Andrew drags Bob behind me as I follow through on the plan I had all along. Only now I hesitate at the top of stairs that lead into the basement. I don't want Claire to see this. I hadn't cared before.

"Look, Richie, you got to tell me what's wrong. Come on, bud."

Anger escalates until all I see is red, red blood that poured out of me that day as they left me to die in a pool of my own blood. Each step I take reminds me that what I am doing is right. The moment we step into the basement, I look to Claire, who's too absorbed in what she's drawing on the floor.

Bob stops, and his face contorts with fear and confusion. "What is that?" He squints at the glass box. I nod at Andrew, and he pushes Bob, who keeps looking back at the glass box. "Is that Claire?" He tilts his head, and I didn't think anything could ever make me angry apart from what they had done to me, but him looking at her has me spinning on my heels.

The satisfying crunch of his nose under my fist makes the blood splatter on my shirt worthwhile. Bob reels and falls back, squealing like a pig being slaughtered.

Claire moves, drawing my attention. I focus on her long enough to watch her stand before returning my attention to Bob.

I won't give in.

We keep walking until we reach the glass coffin. Bob tries to run, but Andrew grabs him and twists his arm to the breaking point, forcing him back toward me.

"Richie, don't do this." His whimpers are music to my ears.

I help Andrew put him in the coffin before sliding the top closed. He's screaming, trying to get out. I open the small window, and he gasps for air.

"I'm sorry about what we did to you. It was Patrick's Idea."

I close the panel, and his face grows red as panic sets in. More banging on the glass, only this time it's not coming from Bob. I look up when I know I shouldn't. Claire's eyes are wide with horror as she watches me.

"Get me the hose," I speak to Andrew but never take my eyes off Claire. She's screaming, but I've turned off the sound. Yet, it's clear she's begging me to stop. Does she recognize him, too?

I open the window and let Bob gasp for air. "I'll do anything."

I really look at him. "Anything?" I ask.

Hope grows fast and hard, and he sobs. "Anything."

Andrew hands me the hose, and Bob stares at it. "What is that?"

I soak up his fear. "It's a hose."

His cries grow more frantic. "Please, man. Let me out."

I turn the nozzle on before pushing the hose into the coffin and letting the water trickle in.

Bob screams as he tries to move in the tight coffin; it's as immobilizing as I thought it would be.

All the hairs rise on my body as he thrashes and screams in the tight space. I push the hose deeper into the coffin.

His thrashing slows as he looks up at me. "Please. Don't do this. It was Patrick. He threatened Lenny and me." His ramblings mean nothing.

The water continues to rise. "You have no family."

My statement is met with fragmented focus as he watches the water rising like if he looks away, it will fill quicker. "No." He admits.

"If you had, I would have found them and caged them, too. Just like I've done to Claire." My stomach twists with guilt.

They brought this upon themselves. Each one of them deserved this.

My gaze darts to Claire, who's crying. Her fists keep pounding the glass, and I want to tell her to stop before she hurts herself. The bandage on her wrist is bleeding again, and I grit my teeth at the sight.

"Please!" Hysterical words I should be relishing, but Claire is taking all the enjoyment of this moment away from me.

Water pours over my hand, and I look down to see Bob submerged. His eyes wide as he kicks and punches the glass. It's useless, but it's human nature to fight to the last breath. I want my face to be the last one he sees as he loses the battle that he's fighting with his deprived lungs. It's that moment when he opens his mouth when he has no choice but to let the water pour in and fill his lungs. The drowning slows his thrashing; his eyes close as his body gives out, and I know he's dead; one down four to go.

CHAPTER FIFTEEN

O'REAGAN
AN CHLANN

CLAIRE

My fingers move faster than my eyes can track. I want to slow down, but the burning need to complete the drawing has me pushing the pencil across the floor over and over again until the image starts to take shape in front of me. I'm almost smiling at how realistic this one has turned out. His eyes, they hold too much all at once—a bottomless pit.

My stomach squirms as I stare down at the drawing. Hunching over, I continue from memory of his sharp brows, long thick lashes, moving down to his sharp jaw; I pause once again as the rest of his face takes form. His face is for the front of magazines or movie stars. I shiver as I think of what lurks behind his face that's designed to lure people in—a man who has locked me in a glass cage.

My fingers tighten around the small colored pencil that I've worn down to a nub. I sense his presence in the basement, but I don't look up. I'm waiting for him to enter. I'm waiting for the click of the door. I'm waiting, and nothing happens. I finally risk a glance in his direction. He's not alone. A man who's been very badly beaten is dragged by another man who doesn't look fazed at all. I can assume the unfazed one is one of my captor's men. My gaze darts to my captor, who keeps walking deeper into the basement, the lights flickering on, lighting the way. My captor stops, and it takes me a moment to make out the coffin. My stomach heaves as I get off the ground and move to the wall of glass. The man whose face is swollen and coated in bruises looks at me, and I swear he says my name. His green eyes bounce around the space, and I can see he's looking for an exit. I should tell him it's pointless, that I tried. He rushes forward out of the security man's grasp. He might have gotten five steps away before he's restrained and dragged back kicking and screaming. My heart races as they take him over to the glass coffin.

No.

They both grab him, and the beaten man has no chance as they stuff him into the glass coffin and seal the lid shut.

"Stop!" My voice is low, but the word rumbles to life in my chest and makes its entrance on stage to no crowd.

Curling my hands into fists, I bang on the glass. "Stop." My fists hit the glass again. *What are they doing?*

My captor looks up at me, and I already know it's a losing battle, just as sure as I know the glass won't shatter no matter how many times my fists collide with it.

His security man leaves briefly. A reel that I hadn't noticed before is where he walks to. He turns a handle and takes the hose off the reel, dragging it back to the coffin.

"No!" My knuckles ache as I repeatedly bang the glass. I don't stop; my voice is hoarse as they fill the coffin with water. The man fights. My vision blurs with tears as my captor glances up at me before he watches the man die. I know when he's dead. He stops fighting, and my captor stands up, running his hands through his hair. I stumble away from the glass. The wound on my wrist has reopened, and fresh blood soaks into the bandage. He's staring at me, and when he takes a step toward the box, I move away, not wanting him to enter.

Trepidation moves my feet faster as I seek refuge at the back of the box. I know I can't realistically hide from him, but my fragile mind needs this right now. He moves to the front of the box, and a whimper lodges itself in my throat. I don't want to die. It's horrible, but all I can think of is not like that, not drowning in a coffin.

He walks past the glass box with the security man beside him. A sob pours from me as they leave the basement, and I'm left with another dead body. When will it become me who's dead? My cries die down. I don't think I have any more liquid left in my body.

Sinking to the floor, exhaustion tugs at me. I don't think I can sleep, but my mind leaves the glass box and relives simple moments with my family. Moments that would be insignificant if they were still alive. If they were still alive, the small memories would fade over time. They are all I have, so I cling to them and paint each tiny detail in high definition.

I miss the smell of the newspaper. I miss the smell of oil that constantly stained his clothes and hands. I miss the smell of the porch on a hot summer's day.

I miss my parents.

I don't think I've thought about them this much in years. It's this box. This place makes me think of them so much. Rose, my therapist, would be so proud that I'm finally allowing them back into my heart, but with each memory, my heart breaks a little bit more. The truth fills me up, and the exhaustion leaves me with no fight, even as the door clicks open, and he enters with fury fuelling his steps.

I think this is it. This is when I die. He doesn't speak even as he reaches me. He reaches down, and I'm waiting to be pulled up roughly from the floor, but his fingers wrap gently around my forearm as he guides me to my feet. His fingers are hot on my cold flesh, and he doesn't release me. I refuse to look up at him. I refuse to look death in the face. Maybe I'm a coward, or maybe I'm exhausted. But no matter what, standing this close to him is terrifying. He towers over me, and I'm insignificant beside him. He doesn't release me even as he walks me through the box.

We stop, and he isn't looking at me; he's staring down at the floor. He's staring at the picture I drew of him. His fingers release me quickly as he kneels down in front of the drawing. I'm looking at him over my shoulder, and I don't want him to look at my drawing. I have a sense of embarrassment. I look away and notice the door is open. My heart lurches. I could run. I could try to escape. My gaze darts over to the man who is still in the coffin.

"You have a gift."

I shiver at my captors compliment. His voice is gravely against my flesh. I fold my arms across my chest.

He rises and takes the two steps towards me. When he reaches for me, I unfold my arms, and he gently takes my arm again. He walks me to the door, and I pause. A soft tug has me stepping across the threshold.

"Is this the part where I die?"

"Not today." He looks at me over his shoulder, his fingers trailing down until he circles my uninjured wrist.

There are worse things than death.

The stairs feel strange to my limbs as I climb the steps. How long has it been? Days, weeks, months? It feels like a lifetime. We leave the basement; my bare feet touch dark oak flooring as I'm led through a hallway. I feel dazed by all the lighting and wonder if this is a dream or maybe I had been in the coffin. My gaze jumps to my captor, who still holds my wrist. If this is a dream, then what is he doing in it? As if sensing my thoughts are on him, he glances at me over his shoulder again. His dark gaze has me dropping my eyes to the floor. I keep my head down as we move through the hallway until we reach a set of double doors that he pushes open.

I blink up at the blue sky. The sun looks glorious. It looks larger than I remember. I have to shield my eyes as we step outside and into a warm breeze. From the way the sun sits, I'd say it's early afternoon. The patio stones are warm under my feet. My captor doesn't stop there. He leads me out onto grass that cushions my feet. After we walk through the lush grass and past an apple tree, he releases me.

I want to ask why I've been granted this freedom, but I don't. Thoughts of going back to the box creep in, and panic squeezes my stomach painfully. I need to separate myself from that and try to just live in this moment with the sun on my face and the breeze in my hair.

"Have you always drawn?" The question smashes into my illusion.

He's walking close to me, but I'm afraid if I move away, it will anger him, and he will put me back in the box.

"No. I've only been drawing the last few years," I answer honestly.

"Well, it's exceptional."

His compliment makes my heart swell. He doesn't seem like a man who handed out many compliments. "Thank you."

He stops walking, and so do I. "You're welcome, Claire." He says my name with such familiarity, and for the millionth time, I'm wondering why I'm here.

"Why am I here?" I blurt.

"I thought some fresh air would be a nice reward for the drawing."

Bullshit. He hadn't known I had drawn it when he had arrived. I don't call him out on his lie. I wouldn't dare. His gaze drops to my wrist, and his jaw tightens.

"You need to stop hurting yourself."

You need to stop killing people.

"I'm sorry."

He exhales loudly and runs his hands through his hair. My stomach dips, and shame at even admiring him for one second raises my body temperature to an all-time high.

Movement in my peripheral vision has me following the large dog that darts through the grass. The closer he gets, it's clear he's a greyhound. His zig-zag pattern is bizarre but seeing a dog has me forgetting everything and ready to call to him.

I hear the cock of the gun and spin towards my captor. It takes my brain a second to realize what he intends to do.

"Don't." I reach for the gun that he pulls away from me.

The dog races closer. I see another flash of black. "Please don't." I move away from him and towards the dog, who slows down enough for me to really see him. His mouth is white, and it matches the large white patch of fur along his stomach.

"Claire." The warning in my captor's voice has me stopping but so has the dog who half hunches in the grass. I see the damage. He's been beaten badly. I hold out my hand. "It's okay, boy." I swallow a lump at the cruelty before me.

"Claire, come away now."

I ignore the second warning. "It's okay." I stretch my hand out, and the dog raises its head slightly. It's weary, and I don't blame him as my captor pulls me upright. "Fuck's sake, it could have rabies." His words are barked into my ear.

I don't look away from the greyhound. "He's been beaten. He's served his purpose on the track, and no one wants him."

My heart hammers in my chest.

"How can you know that?" My captor sounds irritated.

I take a peek at him; he's still holding the gun. The dog hasn't run away, and that's encouraging.

"My father was a betting man; he took me to the dog races sometimes. Just let me check him." I plead.

I don't expect the answer I get. He curses and puts his gun away. "You stay back. I will check him."

He takes a step towards the dog, who whimpers and cowers.

"You're frightening him." I fold my arms across my chest, my fingers itching to reach for the dog.

My captor ignores me and bends his large frame. The dog doesn't run but lies on his belly while whimpering. People can be so cruel. This world can be so cruel. As my captor reaches the dog who growls, I watch a moment of redemption, a moment of a beast transforming into a man. His hand touches the dog, and he rubs his bowed head. "Easy, boy."

The dog's whimpering ceases. I take a step closer.

"Claire!" The warning has me stopping in my tracks but also causes a low growl to rumble from the dog.

"Easy, boy." He touches the dog again, and the growling stops, much to my amazement. "He's been beaten badly."

I take another step closer and try to look over my captor's wide shoulders. He's separating the dog's hair, gently looking for wounds. His long fingers are gentle; he's a conundrum. I just watched him kill someone in such a cruel way. A shiver races across my bare arms at the memory.

"Why did you kill that man?" My thoughts evolve into words.

I don't know what I expect him to do. Spin around and hurt me, kill me? I don't know. But he doesn't stop assessing the dog for damage. Through some whimpers and growls, he continues.

"He deserved it. He beat me nearly to death."

I'm sorry is on the tip of my tongue, but I don't say it. Yet I'm looking at his back and remind myself that he never laid as much as a finger on me. He took me from my home, but he hasn't hurt me. I kneel down beside him. He shifts but doesn't say anything.

The poor dog has several cuts. I reach out and gently touch his side. The dog's head whips to me, and he bares his teeth. Leaning away, he stops.

My captor turns to me, ready to say something, but his gaze trails down to my bandage. "We need to change your bandage."

Dark eyes travel up to my face, and my heart grows frantic in my chest. No matter what happens, his gaze will always haunt me.

"Help the dog first," I whisper. We are too close, and I have the odd sensation again that I don't want to put my finger on because my thoughts toward him are inappropriate when I'm not half terrified. My face heats, and I refocus on the dog. My captor is still watching me. His gaze burns a path down the side of my face. It seeps into my skin and fills my stomach, making it queasy.

"Fine, I'll help the dog, then I will change your bandage."

I can't look at him, so I give a sharp nod of my head.

He exhales loudly. "Easy, boy." He speaks to the dog as he rises slowly. I get up and watch in astonishment as the dog gets up and starts to follow us back to the house. It's like my captor has cast a spell on the dog. Maybe that's how he gets his victims here, that or drugs them.

I take a peek at him, and he's watching me again. We reach a door that he opens. "You first, Claire."

I hesitate. I didn't want to go back inside. As if he reads my thoughts, he pushes the door open further.

"If you don't, I'll shoot the dog."

His unfair threat has me moving past him. His smell encircles me as I enter an empty garage space. My captor encourages the dog in, and once the dog has entered the garage, he closes the door.

I focus on the dog that's sniffing around with his tail dragging on the ground. The dog's ears are pressed to the side of his head. To hurt an animal is like hurting a child. It is wrong.

I kneel down as my captor makes his way to an intercom on the wall.

"I need some water, cloths, and bandages."

"He needs a vet," I say.

My captor's sharp gaze swings to me. His jaw is tight, and I want to hide. I've overstepped. He turns his back on me.

"And a vet." He lets the intercom go.

Clicking my tongue, I gain the dog's attention. He's still half afraid of coming over to me, but when I reach out, he lets me pet him. I want to tell him I'm afraid, too.

"He's hungry." The dog's bones prod into my hand.

"One thing at a time, Claire."

The dog relaxes slightly as I rub around any wounds. My captor is leaning against the wall with his arms folded, watching me. I try to ignore him, but that's a hard thing to do. He's there. You can't not notice him.

The door opens, and it's the bald man who enters carrying the items my captor asked for. He doesn't look surprised to see a dog here or me.

"Thanks."

He hands everything to my captor and, without a word, leaves. My captor stuffs the bandages into his black trousers' pocket.

"Let me do it." I rise and hope he will allow me to clean the dog.

The set of his jaw and the tightness of his shoulder gives me my answer before he speaks it.

"No. He's an injured dog, and he isn't going to like anyone handling him."

I stand up but don't move away. My captor brings the bucket and cloth with him. Kneeling down, he takes my place and calls the dog to him. The greyhound comes but whimpers again.

I can't look away as he cleans the dog with a tenderness that doesn't make sense. The image of the man thrashing in the coffin of water pummels my mind, causing me to momentarily lose my breath.

"Why a coffin?"

"Why not a coffin?" He answers back. The dog is standing, but he doesn't stop my captor from gently cleaning him.

"I think that will have to do until the vet gets here." He stands up with his bucket.

"What will happen to the dog?" Did it really matter?

"I'll find him a good home."

His words make me want to laugh. It's not the kind of laughter that's belly deep or high pitched; it's one that is drowning in tears.

"Just don't kill him." I frown as I say the words.

He watches me again before stepping closer. My heart beats harshly against my chest. He's too close.

"Now, let me look at your wrist."

CHAPTER SIXTEEN

O'REAGAN
AN CHLANN

RICHARD

She was hesitant about leaving the dog. I repeated my earlier words that I would find him a good home, but she still looks doubtful. I can't blame her, but it still annoys me that she won't take my word for it.

I happen to like animals. Just not ones who have been beaten because it makes them volatile. Claire follows me down the stairs as each step takes the light out of her crystal blue eyes. Now she's the one looking like a beaten-down dog. My gut tightens. The sensation is new to me and one I associate with Claire and Claire alone.

Guilt.

I press the card against the scanner, and the door into the box opens. She's staring at the empty coffin off to our left. That's why I took her for a walk. I didn't want her to see us remove the body. I regret her seeing me kill him—regret, another emotion that felt wrong to me.

She still hasn't moved. "Come on, Claire." I keep my back to her, giving her time to come into the box herself. I really don't want to force her, but if it comes to it, I will.

She passes me in a flash of white. She's disheveled looking and tired, but it doesn't take away from her beauty. She folds her arms across her chest, and I step in behind her. The space is filled with her scent. Her smell is something sweet and earthy. I stop at the drawing on the floor again. It's remarkable.

"Maybe I could get you an easel and some paints," I say.

Her head jolts up to me. Her cheeks tinged pink. "Charcoal."

I nod my head. I hadn't seen an easel or charcoal in her apartment. I had found stacks of filled-in coloring books and an endless supply of puzzles. Giving her these, I am hoping to ease her homesickness.

I take the bandage out of my pocket and walk to the small sink. Running the tap until the water is warm, I take a towel and hold it under the spray. "Sit on the bed." I command, without looking at her.

I squeeze out the towel and turn off the tap before looking at her. She's sitting on the bed, picking at the edge of the bandage. The moment I step towards her, her bowed head rises, and crystal blue eyes track my steps.

I like how she looks at me. She's half afraid, but behind all that terror are questions, intrigue.

I don't think her intrigue is as deep as my fascination is with her. I don't think anything has cut me quite this deep.

I want to sit down beside her, but the slight tremor in her hands has me kneeling at her bare feet. I should have gotten her shoes. Another oversight I will fix.

"Give me your arm." I hold out my hands, and she does as I say. I love the feel of her skin under my fingertips, and the urge to caress her flesh has me unwrapping the bandage to give my hands something else to do. The bandage floats to the floor. Fresh blood still pools from the wound. I hold her arm, so her palm is upright. I don't clean the cut straight away. I'm transfixed on the red liquid. My cock grows hard in my trousers. My thumb inches closer, I stop over her racing pulse. Her heartbeat is erratic, and when I glance up at her, she's watching me with wide, frightened eyes. I let my thumb trail to her wound. She inhales sharply before pulling her bottom lip in between her teeth. I want to taste her. I want to taste all her pain.

So I do.

Bending my head, I bring her arm up to my lips and press a kiss to the open flesh. She tries to pull her arm back; it's a weak attempt that I easily fend off and tighten my grip on her. My tongue flicks out, and I taste her blood before looking back up at her.

Her blue eyes fill with panic. They shoot up to my lips. Horror reflects in her voice as she speaks. "You have blood on your lips."

My tongue flicks out, and I lick the blood off.

"My blood." She speaks again while staring at my lips, and I want to kiss her. I want her to taste what I taste.

I don't have to rise to meet her lips. All I have to do is lean in. My fingers are still wrapped around her wrist. Her pulse pounds ferociously.

I want to capture her face in my hands, I want to touch her hair, I want her trust.

I want her.

Claire's lips part as I inch closer. With her blood in my mouth, I pause; her chest rises and falls rapidly. She hasn't pulled away from me even through her clouded fear.

I smile at that internally.

I move back, like the spell that her beauty casts over me is broken. Her lips tug down, and I wonder if she is about to cry. I'm almost tempted to wait until she sheds more pain. I just might taste her tears too. It's the fear that tightens her jaw and gives her a wild look that has me knowing I need to hold off. I don't release her wrist but loosen my grip and break eye contact. I pick up the damp towel and clean her wrist softly, trying not to put pressure on it. I don't want to be tempted by more blood. Once I have her wound clean, I re-bandage her wrist. My cock doesn't ease down, it painfully throbs in my trousers, and I rush through the rest of the job as the want for her increases. Once I'm done, I march from the box, lock the door and make my way upstairs. I need space. The distance does nothing to help my raging hard on.

Marcus stands in the hallway and opens his mouth to speak. I hold up a finger in warning, and his mouth snaps shut as I go upstairs to my bedroom.

The door bangs as I slam it. Anger at how she makes me feel has me marching to the bathroom and turning the shower on cold. That should cool down all the hot blood that pulses through me. I loosen the belt on my trousers and shove them down along with my boxers. My cock is almost painful to touch as I stroke it, picturing her, imagining her mouth around it. A groan is ripped from me as I pump harder. Licking my lips, I taste her blood again. I want so much more of her. I let my cock go as I take off my clothes and step into the shower, turning the temperature up. I don't step under the stream but lean against the tiles and resume pumping my shaft. I picture her in her white panties, on her knees, sucking my cock. Her small tongue flicking out and licking my balls.

"Fuck." I pump faster with the image of her in my head. Three final jerks, and it's all over as my seed flows across my hand. Opening my eyes, I step into the spray and wash it all off. I'm only coming down from such a high, but I still keep an eye out. I'm still wary in a shower. That's where they nearly beat me to death; where they took too much blood from me. My hands run down my torso that's coated in scars.

I will have my blood debt paid back in full. With a renewed determination, I wash and get ready to make another one of them pay.

CHAPTER SEVENTEEN

O'REAGAN
AN CHLANN

RICHARD

I've built this moment up too high, and I can't seem to reach for the door handle and open the fucking car door. The building looms over me, and the fear of being trapped inside the asylum again has my feet stuck to the floorboard.

To the world, I'm my father, unbreakable, indestructible, a King. My father placing me in the asylum made me realize I'm just a man.

A man he broke and destroyed.

A man who can't wear a crown.

My fists smash into the steering wheel repeatedly, the pain radiates up my arms, and I drink agony in like it's the fucking cure to the madness in my head. I don't stop until blood drips down the steering column and the air decreases in my lungs. I raise my head and glare at the building that holds all my demons and Lenny.

He deserves to die. I glance at the brown envelope on the passenger seat. I will torture him first with these images. Grabbing the envelope, my blood starts to soak into the paper, but I do nothing to clean my wounds. Climbing out of my car, I lock it and walk with my head held high like a man who isn't weighed down with his own thoughts. Instead of the memory of what they did to me, I focus on what I'm going to inflict on them.

Lenny will meet his maker soon, just like Bob had. They will suffer by my hand. I jog up the steps and push the front door to the madhouse open.

I'm weary. I hide it well, but I'm weary as I enter. It's like reliving what happened the first time. How naïve I was when my father brought me in here. I hadn't expected to be attacked from behind. Now all my senses are on high alert.

The red-headed receptionist picks up a phone when she sees me, her gaze bouncing to my bleeding hands. She speaks quickly into the phone as I reach the glass shield that protects her. I rap the shield with a bloody knuckle, leaving smears of blood behind.

"I am here to see Leonard O'Reilly."

"Mr. O'Reagan. Leonard won't be having visitors today." Her voice shakes.

I don't remember her. I hadn't exactly had time to take in the front desk before I was attacked.

A silent red light comes on, and seconds later, a door to my left opens. Two security men step out into the reception area.

"Is there a problem?"

Cam is the name I read on his name tag. What kind of fucking name is that? He chews gum, and the smell of his cologne is overbearing. This is his life. He's one of those types of people who thinks they own the place.

"Yes, there is. I want to see Leonard O'Reilly now."

"You're bleeding on the floor." Cam stares at the drops of blood before smiling at me and then resumes chewing. I take a step towards him. He drags up his trousers by the belt that holds a baton. That's what I will do. Beat him with his own baton. These people need to learn who they fucked with.

"That's enough. Let him through." The voice sounds over the speakers, and I know who it is—the director. I spot the cameras parked in all four corners.

Cam shrugs his shoulders like being told to stand down is no big deal. It's clear that it is, as he chews his gum a little harder and slower. I don't step away from him, forcing him to back away from me. Cam opens the door for me, and I pause before entering.

"That's a good boy," I say as I pass him.

"Is that really necessary?" I ask, not giving two fucks that Leonard is chained to a table. He's an animal, and that's all he deserves. For now, I will keep playing the friend for the next twenty seconds.

"Leonard isn't up to visitors. Honestly, I'm surprised they let you in." The nurse speaks under his breath.

"What, is Leonard unstable?" I ask loudly and grin.

The nurse's thin jaw tightens. "You have fifteen minutes."

He leaves, and I turn to Leonard. "I tried to get the cuffs off." I hold up my hands as I speak.

"They're a bunch of fucking muppets..." He's still ranting, and I pick up the chair and let the legs drag along the floor, making his words grow silent. I sit down and tap the desk with the envelope.

"How are you doing, Lenny?" I ask.

"Can you get me out of here?" His serious question, I ignore.

Opening the envelope, I stare at the image of Claire inside the glass box. Each one is her doing something different, sitting on the edge of the bed, eating her dinner, sleeping. As I continue to flick the images, they get more personal. Claire bathing; she looks petrified. Another picture of her crying and they go on to the final image of her cutting herself. My gut tightens, but I know this one will have a huge impact on Lenny.

"Did you hear me, Richie, can you get me out of here?"

I look up at him. "Can I get you out of here?" I repeat his questions.

His brows drag down like he thinks I'm thick.

"I'm going to be really honest with you, Lenny." I lean in, and so does he. His eyes lit up. "I could call the nurse into the room, get him to remove your cuffs, and we could walk out the door together."

His smile splits his face. "Let's go, brother." He tugs at the chains, and I don't move back.

"No."

"What the fuck is with you, man? Did all the fresh air go to your head?" He finally looks down at the photos in my hand. "What are they?" His leg starts to shake under the table. I feel the vibration along the table.

I slide the pictures across to him, and I drink it all in as he flicks from one photo to the next.

"What the fuck is this? Someone has my sister?"

"Yes," I answer.

He returns to flicking through the images again. He tilts the pictures. "Is she in a box?" His confusion and upset continue to grow.

"Yes," I answer again.

Leonard releases the photos and tugs on his chains. The force lifts the table before it slams back down. "What do they want?" His roar bellows from him.

"You," I say.

He tugs his chains again, coming out of his seat, but they are keeping him restricted. His gaze darts to the photos. "I'm here. Tell the fucking cowards I'm here if they want me."

I stand abruptly and lean in, gripping the back of his neck pulling his face close to mine. "I know you are here, and you're going to die in this place. I think your sister likes me. It's such a pity I'll have to kill her. I might fuck her first. Real hard."

Lenny's chains rattle as he tries to reach for me, but I scoop up the images and stand back. His roar has him launching himself towards me, dragging the table with him. I take another step away and put the photos into the envelope.

"You're going to die here, Lenny." I remind him as the buzz of the door has me stepping towards the exit. He's roaring and dragging the table towards the door to get at me. Three nurses step around me, and I turn and grin at Leonard.

He is still screaming as they take him to the ground and drag down his trousers. A syringe is emptied into his ass, and I leave the building, knowing what I did will kill him. His sister was his highlight each week as he waited for her to visit. He had a twisted obsession with Claire, and I knew taking her from him would be the ultimate revenge for what he had done to me.

His roars follow me all the way down the hall long after he has stopped. I re-enter the reception area. No one is here. I glance up at the cameras. The director might be still watching. I grin as I push open the front door. Each step to my car has me breathing a bit easier. I would make sure Leonard died there, and if he didn't soon, I would finish the job myself.

Killing Claire was my plan all along. As I climb into my car, I allow myself to fully accept that won't be happening. Killing her isn't an option anymore.

"Patrick." I stand outside his door.

He's not very fucking welcoming. He sticks his head out past me and looks left and right. He's paranoid as fuck.

"Richie." That name will die with them all.

"I was in the area and wanted to see how you were doing."

He focuses on me now. "Yeah, fine."

"Can I come in?" If he didn't allow me in, I would force my way in.

He steps back and wears a look that suggests he wants nothing more than for me to leave.

"Nice place," I say as I step into the small hall. It's a shit hole; the walls stained yellow from cigarette smoke. A line of hooks holds too many coats that reek of the offending substance.

Patrick closes the door behind me. He's thinner than I remember, easier to break. He steps around and enters a small living space. Everything is old and frumpy. An elderly man in a gray vest sits in a recliner. He's drinking a can of beer. His attention rests on me for a second before he returns to watching the TV.

"Another debt collector?" He asks.

"No, a friend," I respond.

"From the asylum." Patrick fills in and sits on the couch that has seen better days. He tugs a cushion to his chest.

The elderly man half laughs. "You look like you are going to a funeral."

"I just wanted to drop in on Patrick first." I sit down beside Patrick, who shuffles away.

The elderly man takes a long drink from his can before belching loudly.

"What do you want, Richie?" Patrick speaks up, his voice weak, and now I wonder if he knows why I'm here.

"Richard. You can call me Richard. I always hated that name."

"Fine, Richard. What is it you want?"

The elderly man laughs again. "You're a pig in knickers, Patrick. Make the man a cup of tea."

Patrick's face darkens. "He's my uncle." Patrick rumbles as he gets off the couch to make me a cup of tea. I wait until he's up before moving to the edge of the couch.

"Patrick here wasn't always so quiet." I speak to his uncle.

He grunts like he doesn't give a shit. His finger moves to the remote to turn up the volume.

"He beat me nearly to death," I say.

That gets the uncle's attention.

"It wasn't just Patrick. There were two others."

I glance at Patrick, who appears paler than he had seconds ago. I grin. "Well, there are only two now. Bob drowned in a coffin," I say.

The uncle laughs again. "You need to go back to the asylum. Drowning in a coffin? Now I've heard it all." He's still laughing.

"I'm sorry." Patrick's words are quiet, but I hear them.

"It's too late for that. Bob said it was your idea before I killed him."

"I ... I ... I'm sorry."

"I'm struggling to believe my lad would do that." The uncle mutes the TV, takes a drink from his can before placing it on the ground beside him. "So I think it's time you got on your way. Don't want to be late for your funeral."

I stand up.

"Richie..." Patrick starts before correcting himself. "Richard, don't hurt him."

I remove my suit jacket and fold it before placing the jacket on the couch.

"I've waited three years for this. So..." I grin at Patrick as I roll up my sleeves. "It's going to be slow."

The uncle tries to stand. I move fast. My foot connects with his gut driving him back into the seat. "And painful," I state as he gasps for air. I glance at Patrick, who doesn't move an inch.

"I'm sorry."

His words roll off my back. "So you keep saying, Patrick."

He wasn't sorry when he drove his foot into my face repeatedly. At the end, I think all three danced on my head.

"I don't have to ask why," I say as the uncle gasps for air and tries to get out of the chair. I walk away, not stopping him from his feeble attempts to protect his nephew.

Patrick seems frozen to the spot like his feet are cement blocks. His head moves as I walk past him and open his kitchen drawer. The knives rattle. "You all wanted to prove that you were men." I hold up a knife that's blunt and drop it back into the drawer.

I look at Patrick. "No, I think it was boredom. After they locked you up like animals, you just wanted to release all that rage." I grin as I take out two knives. The uncle has managed to get to his feet.

"This is how it's going to work. First, I kill your uncle and then you." I pass the cooker that has a pot on it with yesterday's spuds caked to the bottom. Picking it up, I reach the uncle and smash the pot into his face. He falls back into the seat sideways.

I twist his limp body around, so he's sitting correctly in the seat. Moving around, so I'm facing him, I take a look at Patrick. "Sit down on the couch."

He shakes his head.

I drive a knife into his uncle's leg. He's awake now. His screams are high-pitched. Patrick moves quickly and sits on the couch.

"Enjoy the show," I say as I slowly start to kill his uncle.

I make him watch each stab, hear each scream, and also let the knowledge sink in that he is next.

Patrick doesn't scream as loudly, but he cries a lot. I make his death last longer, and when he draws his final breath, I drop the knives on top of his dead body. The room has blood splattered on every surface. Even the TV that still flickers with life has a stream of blood across it. The uncle's sliced throat trickles blood. I had to cut off his screams at the end.

My shirt is covered in blood, along with my hands.

I make my way to the small sink that's tucked away in the corner. The sound of the water seems loud after the silence that followed their deaths. I wash my hands. There is no soap. Opening the cabinet under the sink, I find a bottle of dish soap. Filling my hands with the liquid, I wash them and turn off the tap. I shake my hands out. The towel looks like it would leave my hands dirtier. I pick up my jacket and put it on before taking my phone out of my pocket. I dial Davy's number.

"I need a clean-up."

"How many?" Davy asks.

"Two. I'll send you the address." I hang up.

I leave the apartment, telling myself I have two more people to kill. But really, it's only one. Killing Claire isn't an option.

I've decided I'm going to keep her.

CHAPTER EIGHTEEN

O'REAGAN
AN CHLANN

CLAIRE

The memory of him licking my wrist, licking my blood, seems more unrealistic as time passes. Had I imagined it? Yet, his lips had been stained with my blood. The image drilled into my mind. The sick part of me had felt divine. The idea of him tasting my blood is so wrong, but somehow it felt right. I'm disturbed by my own thoughts. It's been days, I tell myself, and I need to move past this.

I refocus on the drawing at my feet, I just started to draw, not thinking, and it's the oddest thing that's formed under the pencil. My kitchen table and chairs from my childhood are sketched on the floor.

I pause, my hand hovers above the floor, and I tilt my head, aware of his presence. My heart starts hammering. How does he do that? He's standing along the side of the box, watching me. I hadn't even heard him enter the basement. Maybe the sound is off again.

I don't get off the floor but stay seated. I want to touch my bandage but keep still, not wanting to draw attention to my wrist, yet he's brought back the memory of what happened last time.

"How is your wrist?" He asks, his voice clear.

His hands are folded behind his back. The blue shirt stretched across wide shoulders. He takes a step to the left, and I turn so I keep him in my view.

His dark eyes look lighter like he's smiling, but it's a contradiction to the stern look on his face.

"Better," I answer.

His dark gaze flickers down to the bandage, and my stomach clenches. His eyes sing the truth that he has tasted my blood. It had shocked me, but something else has taken root that I don't want to face.

He doesn't walk any further; his hands leave his back. I notice his knuckles appear damaged like he had a fight with a wall.

I think back to him saying he had been beaten. Maybe he was a fighter; like the ones on TV. The thoughts of him walking around a ring in shorts have me dropping my gaze to hide the growing color in my cheeks.

"Were you in a fight?" I ask.

"With a steering wheel."

My head snaps up, and I crack a smile without even thinking. His answer is bizarre to me.

His lips twitch. "You find that amusing?" He asks.

My smile melts off my face like ice cream on a hot day. "No." I sink my hands into the floor to ground myself and try to slow my heart rate down. "Yes." I take a peek at him. I'm not sure what sets him off, so I want to be careful. "Maybe."

His face hardens, and his gaze pivots towards my new drawing. "A table and chairs?" He steps closer to the glass, and I want to move back but force myself to stay still.

"From my home."

"I didn't see that in your home."

His answer shouldn't shock me or make me feel more violated, but it does. He had taken me from my apartment. I just didn't like the reminder.

"My childhood home." I correct him.

"Did you have a good childhood?" His question has me staring down at the table and chairs.

"I had great parents." I answer. "Did you have a good childhood?" I fire back and cringe, wondering if I have overstepped. I don't think he did. I'm picturing a lot of dissected frogs and headless Barbie dolls if he had a sister. My standards are coming from a documentary on a serial killer.

"My mother did her best."

My stomach twists. "Your father?" Is he the weakness here? Maybe he isn't around. Most psychopath's had mommy issues.

"He did his best, too."

Did his best? What did that mean? So far, I'm still looking for the broken childhood that turned him into a raging lunatic.

Silence follows. I do have lots of questions. The number one question is: why am I here? But I don't speak.

He is the one who breaks the silence with a half-smile that startles me. "I had a small victory recently."

I'm holding myself steady as he continues to smile. I want to smile at him. My stomach quivers. "I wanted to share it with someone, and I thought of you."

Surprise has me widening my eyes.

His smile grows. "I was surprised too."

This time I don't fight with my own smile. My heart races as he continues to smile at me. The longer his smile lasts, the more unsettled I become. I can't explain it. Smiling at each other feels too normal under the circumstances. That thought kills my smile. Yet, I don't want him to leave. I don't want to be alone again.

"What was your victory?" I ask.

He observes me as I stand. I wipe my hands together like it might remove the lead marks from the side of my fingers.

"I gave a man who hurt me a visit." His own smile dwindles away, it's a slower pace than mine, but I'm waiting for the blow that he no doubt will deliver.

"He was in his home with his uncle. I could tell from the look in his eyes that he knew why I was there."

I swallow. I didn't want his confessions. "I don't want to know." The words tumble and rush from my lips. I'm waiting for the backlash, but all he does is nod his head.

He starts to walk around the box, and I regret stopping him from talking, but I didn't think my mind could take much more. He had killed them. It is there in his eyes. I just don't want to hear it. I pivot as he moves until I'm facing the door that he stands outside. He doesn't take his eyes off me as he reaches up and presses a card against a scanner. The door clicks, and I'm sure the color drains from my face.

He steps in.

"My mother made pancakes most mornings. I spent every night with a ruler scratching my back from all the sugar." I swallow the saliva that pools in my mouth as the door closes behind him, and he walks towards me.

"The sugar made me itchy, but it was worth it." I'm rambling. I'm trying to reach for something that will make him stop.

I'm afraid.

"Maple syrup..." words fail me as he reaches out and touches my chin, lifting my face, so I'm looking into dark eyes. "I loved maple syrup." My words are low. His gaze darts to my lips. His large frame shadows mine. His hand could encase my face if he wanted to. "I loved sunny days." Something in my chest tightens and clicks. "I loved to watch movies on a Sunday." I try to hold on to some of the fear that's leaving me, and all I'm filled with is loss and sadness. I want the heartache to fade, but it's flourishing.

"I loved the smell of the newspaper." My captor still holds my chin gently, his face so close to mine. "I loved the way my dad said wee. It was a wee road. In a wee while we would be going for ice cream." I smile through my pain. "I miss them," I admit. "I miss my parents."

Surprise filters across his face, and he releases my chin. "They died?" He takes a step back, and I want to reel in all my words that I've shared with him.

I wrap my arms around my waist, feeling cold. "Yes."

I want to walk away, but I don't move.

"Let's take a walk."

It's my turn to be surprised as he leads me out of my cage. Once we reach the first floor of the house, he picks up a box that sits on a chair. He opens it and takes out a pair of red slip-on sneakers and socks. He holds them out to me.

"These will be more comfortable."

The socks reach my ankles and disappear once I slip my feet into the sneakers. He waits patiently until I'm ready before leading me outside again. It's a sunny day and my confession about loving sunny days has me wondering if that is why he brought me outside.

"So you have a sweet tooth." The way he says it makes me fight a smile. I feel silly sharing such small details about myself with him.

"I like sweet things myself." He continues to talk.

I can't stop the laugh. It's abrupt, and I glance at him. "Like what?" I can't picture him eating anything sweet. His body didn't look like he fed it anything wrong.

"Frosties. I had a sick obsession with Frosties when I was young."

"Frosties?" I ask.

"The cereal."

"I know what Frosties are." I kick my sneaker into the grass, trying not to laugh again. It felt unnatural.

"I had three bowls in one sitting."

I want to tease and tell him he's so bad. But he is. He's worse than bad. My smile disappears again. He's a murderer and a kidnapper.

"What happened to your parents?" He asks.

I stop walking. "Why am I here?"

"You said you loved sunny days." He takes a step towards me, and I hate when he's too close, he clouds my judgment.

"Here's another one for you. I love my home. I love my freedom. I want to go home." My voice rises, and I'm waiting for him to grab me and stop me from shouting, but he just takes a patient step towards me.

"In time, you may earn your freedom."

My heart lurches. "How?" Is he messing with me? Could I really go home? My vision blurs, and I swallow the emotion.

"You can earn your freedom by talking to me." He reaches out and cups my face just like he had done earlier in the basement.

"Talk about what?"

He tilts my head back. "About you, Claire."

Irritation claws at me. None of this made sense. "So if I talk about myself, you will let me go?"

He doesn't answer. "I'll give you freedom."

He is playing with words as he releases me, and I inhale a wobbly breath. Being outside is better than being stuck in a box.

"Can I ask you questions?"

He nods his head. "Yes."

"Am I going to die?" I hold my head up high like I can take the truth. My knees weaken, and I lock them, so they don't buckle.

"Everyone dies, Claire." His lip twitches.

I want to scream at him and tell him to stop playing with me.

It's like he knows I'm close to cracking.

"Not by me." His admission surprises me more than it should. He takes a step back towards me. "Not for a long time. I can imagine you will be old and grey. Still beautiful. Still angelic."

Angelic?

No one has ever described me as angelic before, and I hate how much I like it. He looks at me like he really sees something different from what I know is there.

"The dog." I sputter, anything to refocus my mind. "Did he go to a good home?"

He takes a step back and places his hands behind his back. "Connor is still with me."

"Connor? You named him."

"You want to see him again?"

I nod and follow my captor to the garage that he had brought Connor and me into only the other day. The dog leaps out the moment he opens the door and races past us. I think he's escaping, and I'm ready to go after him, maybe leave with the dog.

"Wait." My captor's hand touches my arm. The heat of his fingers keeps me still. I try to keep my attention straight ahead as I wait.

Connor disappears completely before reappearing and races back towards us. He stops at his new owner's feet.

My captor removes his hand from my arm and kneels down, rubbing Connor's belly. I just observe while being taken by the laughter that bubbles from my captor's mouth as he plays with Connor.

I stand long enough for him to look up at me. "I thought you would be happy to see him."

The stupid part of me is wondering if that's why he kept the dog.

I kneel down close to Connor and reach out my hand. His head bows, and he lets me rub him.

"I am happy to see him." I smile at the dog and not at my captor.

"His wounds are healing." I'm surprised all over again at the care he has given the dog.

When I turn my head, we are very close. The dog becomes forgotten under my fingertips.

"If I tell you about myself, I win my freedom?" I ask again.

His lips twitch. "Yes."

"I can do that," I answer.

His laugh is soft, but it slams into me hard and fast. Black eyes turn brown. Angles that are hard on his face soften, and he turns from a monster into a very attractive man.

A man who had the capabilities to ruin me in more ways than one.

I can only hope I get my freedom before he captures another part of me that I might not recover.

CHAPTER NINETEEN

O'REAGAN
AN CHLANN

RICHARD

It's her smile; a clear reminder of why I took her. For revenge was one reason, but capturing an angel, for a guy like me, was just irresistible.

She's still smiling. It's not directed at me any longer; she's focused on Connor. I had been tempted to shoot the dog, to put the animal out of its misery. Watching Claire, I knew I made the right decision to keep him. Slowly she would open up to me. Slowly, I would gain her trust. Slowly, each part of her would become mine.

Her head swings towards me again. A flash of fear has me reaching out and touching the bandage on her wrist. The air gets caught in her lungs, her mouth opens, and she looks stunned. She doesn't pull away from me. I seek out her pulse and find the beat of her heart thrashing under my fingertips. She releases a shaky breath, and I lean into her. I want her. I want her like I've never wanted anything in my life. This even feels stronger than the want for revenge. It's taken everything in me not to have my way with her. I move closer to her lips, and surprisingly, she doesn't pull away.

My thumb stays over her racing pulse that pumps faster. My cock grows hard in my trousers, and I clench my jaw. One taste. Just one.

My lips brush hers, and she inhales a sharp breath at the contact. I release her wrist and capture her face instead. I want to taste every part of her; I want to sink my tongue into her mouth, but I keep the kiss soft, coaxing. She doesn't respond, but I'm aware she hasn't tried to pull away. My tongue flicks out, and I lick her lips before pressing another kiss to her mouth that suddenly moves under mine. It's like a gun being fired, and I'm gripping her tighter, deepening the kiss—my control slips.

"I hope I'm not disturbing anything?"

I remove my lips from Claire but don't release her face. Fear that I can't fully explain has me clinging to her. If I let her go, my father will have a full view of her. He must have seen us kiss—a kiss of death.

I release her, and her gaze flickers across my face like she's searching for answers. I can't say anything, so I stand and try to block her from his view.

"I've been ringing." It's a statement from my father.

"I've been busy." I respond. Connor is barking beside my leg. I'm about to reach down and settle him when Claire's small hand runs along the dog's back. I glance down at her as she continues to soothe Connor. I thought she would be running and screaming for help. Maybe she senses the evilness from my father, who is looking right at her. The wheels in his head are working, no doubt.

The glass box had been her cage. Maybe now the prison I built would be for protection.

"I assigned you a job that you never completed." His gaze flickers to Connor and Claire. "Playing happy family, are we?"

I step away from Claire and Connor. I don't like leaving them, but I can't have my father around them any longer.

Behind my father is Davy, watching, waiting for instructions. I never thought I'd feel relief at seeing Davy. "Take Claire back to her room."

My father's head turns, and he dismisses Davy, who moves past us to Claire, who's watching the exchange.

I'm tense as Davy takes Claire by the arm and leads her towards us. She's within hearing distance when my father steps towards her.

"Claire, you look remarkably like Leonard."

"My... my brother." I know Claire is staring at me with the question in her mind.

If I could reach out and wrap my hand around my father's throat, I would.

"Yes, your brother. Richard is friends with him."

"Richard," Claire repeats my name.

I jut out my chin at Davy to move her now. He does, but she keeps looking at my father and me over her shoulder.

"You want to explain to me what she is doing here?"

"Actually, I fucking don't." I bark at him. "I'm not killing Finn," I add. That's what this is all about. Finn is still rolling around, alive and semi-functioning. Now I wish Shay had killed my father to save me from this grief.

"You seem tense, son."

"What happens under my roof is my business."

My father's jaw clenches. My words clearly get to him, so I continue.

"None of yours. I don't like you on my grounds. So what do you want?"

My father's half-baked smile has me reconsidering my words. I need to be clever around him, or I might end up on a hit list.

He turns away from me, stuffing his hands in his suit pockets. "I've called a meeting but can't seem to get a hold of Shay."

My father faces me again.

"I haven't seen him." I lie.

"He is no good to us if we can't reach him."

Connor arrives at my feet. I didn't care for the dog, but Claire did. "Let me lock him in, and I'll ring Shay."

"Yes, get your priorities straight first." Sarcasm isn't my father's forte.

"I finally am." I call Connor over and open the garage door. He's slow to come to me, and it takes me calling him several times before he finally arrives at my legs and enters the garage.

"I didn't know you liked animals."

"Love them." I respond, closing the door.

"Carlos was found with his head missing."

I'm glad my back is to my father. It gives me a moment to brace myself before I face him.

"His family would like his head returned."

"Are you asking me if I did it?"

"Yes." My father is direct for once.

"No, I did not kill Carlos."

My father removes his hands from his pockets. He's ready to say something else about Carlos but stops.

"One hour: the meeting will commence. If you could let Shay know, that would be great."

I watch him as he leaves my property. All I want to do is run downstairs and check on Claire, but I don't have time. Taking out my phone, I check to see she's back in the box. She is sitting on the edge of the bed, biting the tips of her fingers. I've seen her do this when she's nervous. I close down the image of her and bring up my contacts. I didn't expect Shay to answer me, but he does.

"My father is alive and kicking. He's been ringing you," I say.

I make my way upstairs as we speak.

"I overreacted. I have no intention of killing him."

Disappointment, that's what I feel about Shay's words. Disappointment and exhaustion from trying to keep up with everyone's games.

"There is a meeting in one hour. I can pick you up."

"I'll be there." Shay hangs up, and I move faster, getting dressed.

I need to get there before he does, so I can try to figure out what has changed since he arrived at my home with Carlos's severed head. I also wanted to warn Finn without warning him.

I change into a clean black suit.

I pause in front of the mirror. Since when did I care who died? I finish buttoning up the white shirt.

She's in my thoughts again, but I need to silence that part of my mind and focus on the meeting. My father had called a meeting for a reason. The reason we would soon find out.

I have no idea if I've arrived before Shay. I'm not sure what he drives. I park close to the front door of Cabra Castle. I stay in the car, not wanting to look too eager or worried, by standing on the steps.

Shay pulls up in a green Range Rover. He hops out with a cigarette in his mouth and tugs a black leather jacket closer to his neck before walking across the asphalt. I get out and look up at him.

"Shay."

He nods, but I feel the hate roll off him like heat.

He flicks the cigarette on the ground and grabs the door.

"A word?" I ask.

He pauses but doesn't turn around.

"Please."

His smirk is instant as he turns to me. "The magic word."

Behind his smirk, I see the shark's circle. He is out for blood.

"I never got to explain everything about my father and the fighting rings."

Shay takes a step closer. This topic is one that he can't seem to control from showing on his face. It's burning him alive, and he doesn't even seem to notice. He's blind to the pain I see on his face. "I know what happened." Shay starts, and I let him proceed. "You told your father I was coming for him, so you both built a story about what really happened because Uncle Liam is only doing right by us."

Not much makes me laugh these days, but his words take the prize. I laugh, and he grows angrier by the second. I know explaining myself would be wise before I lose him.

"Uncle Liam isn't fit to rule." I start.

Shay shakes his head like he's trying to push my words away. "Don't patronize me, Richard. I won't touch your father, so you don't have to try to convince me otherwise."

I'm curious why he is backing down. "Why? You were hell-bent on killing him."

"You wouldn't understand." Shay fires back. I glance to my left and see Jack's Range Rover parked across from us. Our time is almost up.

"Try me."

Shay spots Jack, too. "I have someone now. I can't risk her getting hurt." He pulls open the door and leaves me on the steps of the castle.

"Any ideas why he called another meeting?" Jack asks as he steps up beside me.

"No, but I'm sure it will be riveting", I answer, forgetting about my usual composure.

Jack pauses. "Are you okay?"

"Let's not get all soppy, brother." I open the door and enter the castle.

"You're clearly not okay. But if you want to act like a complete gobshit, then be my guest." Jack moves past me, and I take my time walking to the meeting room, wanting to be anywhere else but here.

I step into the room. Shay is seated where he sat the last time, he's already smoking. My father isn't standing but sitting at the head of the table. Jack to his right, a seat half pulled out to his left. I walk to the end of the table and sit as far away from him as I can.

"I have some bad news." My father starts. He doesn't continue, but he has everyone's attention. My eyes are drawn to Shay, who has his head bent as he continues to smoke. I'm waiting for him to snap and pull out a machine gun and kill us all. They think I'm unstable. I disagree. Shay is as unstable as a three-legged table.

"Our shipment up north was stopped."

My father is looking at me. These things happen in our line of business. We always give a percentage of wiggle room for losing money due to shipments being frozen.

"By Lucian Sheahan." My father finishes.

"I thought he was on our side," I say, directing this to Shay, who puts out his smoke.

"One of his men was killed recently, and he isn't very happy with us." My father answers.

All I can think is, here we go. The table is going to fall over.

"I didn't kill anyone," Jack speaks up and then half shrugs. "Anyone associated with the RA."

I grin at my brother, and he smirks back.

I know he's talking about Carlos, but I still speak up. "My four kills were personal."

"Four?" my father says and shakes his head.

"Three were planned. One was for bad management."

"I haven't killed anyone." Shay looks up at my father. "I have no dealings with Lucian Sheahan. So if you called me in here to be your fall guy, I can't help you."

He's pissing on my father's leg.

"No, Shay. I called you in here because you are a King."

Shay's out of his seat, and I have no idea what's happening until he's bent over my father. "I'm not a fucking King." He's barely containing the rage. Jack's standing and has a gun pointed at Shay's head.

"Jack," I warn, getting out of my chair slowly.

He doesn't react.

"Jack," I speak louder, and he cocks the gun like I didn't just warn him. "Put the gun down."

He glances at me before looking back at Shay. "Get away from my father, or I'll drop you where you stand."

Shay is stiff but finally straightens up, holding his hands in the air. He smirks at Jack and makes a gun motion with his thumb and forefinger. "Calm down, pretty boy." Shay takes a pack of cigarettes out of his pocket and lights one up.

"Jack, put away the weapon." My father commands, and Jack finally lowers the gun.

Shay blows smoke into the air before looking down at my father, who is the only one seated.

"Why don't you take my crown." Shay pretends to lift a crown from his head. "And shove it up your ass."

He smirks at us all. "You are all a bunch of cunts." He turns and leaves the room.

I don't need to see my father's face to know what's going to happen next.

I follow Shay.

"Where are you going?" Jack shouts after me, but I don't stop.

I catch up with Shay on the stairs. "You said you had someone you were protecting." I start.

He doesn't answer me.

"I'm sorry you can't smoke in here." The receptionist speaks to Shay, whom he ignores along with me.

"You just signed her death warrant."

He stops. I knew that would get his attention.

"I'll keep her safe."

I'm shaking my head. "Where? Up north? You think you're safer up there than here?" I fire.

Shay throws his cigarette in a large glass bowl that's for decoration purposes before slamming the front door open.

"You have more chances of surviving down here than up north."

"They are my people up there." He's ready to get into his jeep.

"Lucian Sheahan is the one who gets the money for the cage fights, not my father. You killed his man, Carlos."

Shay finally stops. "So, what? I stay here and wait for your father to kill me?"

"No." Shay wasn't making this easy, but I could see his frustration clearly. "You help me."

He's laughing and pulls the Range Rover door open. I reach around him and slam it shut. "I really need you to hear me out, Shay." I grit my teeth.

He's a loose cannon, and I can only hope he will hear my honesty.

"We can't become my father. I don't want to have no one to trust anymore where there is no loyalty, where there is no trust. I want a family. An Chlann."

Shay turns around. "You really buy into that lie?"

I step away from him. "No. But we could have it all. We can rule side by side. No more scheming. No more hurting each other. We are family. No matter what, we are Kings."

Shay's fighting with his demons, and I don't think I'm getting through to him.

"I want to rule with you and my brother. I want us to be loyal to each other. Trust each other. We can't become my father and his brothers. They destroy each other."

"You really believe we won't become them?"

I consider Shay's question. "I know I want to try to be better."

Shay appears calmer, but I don't get an answer as he climbs into his vehicle, and I'm left watching him drive away, hoping some of my words sink in. I meant each of them. I am tired of my father's games, and if we don't break free soon, none of us will survive this.

CHAPTER TWENTY

O'REAGAN
AN CHLANN

CLAIRE

Richard. His name keeps spinning around in my head. "Richard," I say his name under my breath, trying it out over and over again like saying his name might eventually start to feel normal. Saying his name makes him more human. Monsters don't have names.

Richard.

He knew my brother. They were friends. None of this made sense to me. The man who had spoken looked exactly like Richard; only he's older. At first, seeing another person out in the garden had my instincts wanting me to run to him and tell him that I have been kidnapped, but like the wheels of a watch spinning, the scene before me had me pausing as I took in the details of our new arrival. His dark eyes, dark hair, and the overall air around him made me think of my captor. Even the tailored suit that coated his frame-like armor reminded me of Richard. As I looked longer, I knew he wasn't one of Richards's men but his father. The most disturbing part I had become aware of was that Richard was afraid of his father. Someone who was crueler than Richard? That made me afraid of the man, too. The word fear had developed an entirely different meaning to me since I'd arrived here.

I lick my lips—that kiss.

I'm pacing the box. It feels smaller, and the air feels thinner. I want out of it. The small taste of freedom and fresh air had left my skin itchy being back in this box.

I bit my bottom lip as the kiss continues to resurface in my mind, demanding I give it the full attention it clearly thinks it deserves.

He had kissed me. I kissed him back. I shouldn't have, but with his lips gliding gently over mine, time had ceased to exist. Our history no longer came into play. All that mattered was the moment. The feel of his lips on mine, I had been lost in the kiss. That never happened to me before. I bit the inside of my cheek at the memory.

His name, the kiss, the fact he knew my brother continues to circle in my head until pain starts to grow like my thoughts are nurturing the ache.

I've been locked in here for hours with no idea what has happened on the outside. I'm wondering if Connor is okay. I'm wondering if Richard is okay. That's the part I'm trying to bury, the part that has any real feelings for him.

I walk across the table and chairs that I had drawn on the floor but stop at the image of him— the image of Richard with his dark eyes and dark soul.

My heart palpitates unnaturally in my chest.

This time I'm aware he's there, but I get my breathing under control before I look up at him. He's in a fresh suit, but his eyes look worn out like he's lived too many lives and just wants to lie up somewhere and rest.

I want to ask so many questions, but I don't.

"Are you okay?" He asks as he clears the last step of the stairs and joins me in the basement.

"No. I'm not." I answer.

His smile rocks my reality, and I'm unstable. "You don't like your shoes?" He points at the red sneakers on the table.

I had taken them off the moment I had been returned to the box. They felt almost unnatural on my feet.

"You know my brother?"

"Yes." His answer startles me.

I knew his father had said they were friends, but to hear him say it makes this whole situation a bit clearer.

"Did he tell you to do this to me?" I step closer to the glass. They must have been laughing at me all this time. Watching me slowly lose my mind.

I kissed him. I had kissed Richard back. My cheeks heat up at how foolish I must look right now.

Richard's lip twitches.

I march the rest of the way to the glass, and my fist smashes into the wall. "This isn't funny." Tears burn my eyes. "When will this stop? When will he be happy? When I've completely lost my mind?" The questions fall fast from my lips.

"I did this ***to*** him." Richard walks around the perimeter of the box until he comes to the door.

"Don't come in." I plead.

The door clicks as he disregards my request. He steps in but doesn't move toward me. "There are some things you don't know about me. Your brother didn't know much about me either. I think if he did, he wouldn't have beaten me nearly to death."

My mouth opens, but I close it quickly. I couldn't defend Leonard; it sounded like something he would do. He's always had such a vicious nature.

"I don't remember you." I finally say, knowing if I ever saw Richard, I would have never forgotten him.

"I was in the asylum with your brother."

I don't have to ask why he was in an asylum. Yet Leonard had been unbalanced. Richard didn't seem that way at all. I wouldn't have thought him unhinged. A killer, yes, but not unstable. There is an order to Richard that I've never seen in Leonard.

"My father placed me there as a form of punishment." His confession meets me head-on with disbelief.

"The man who arrived in the garden?" *Just as we kissed.*

Richard nods. "My father."

Each word is becoming too much, and I need to sit down. The table and chairs are right beside Richard, so I opt for the bed because that's the furthest point away from him.

"So I'm here to what, to hurt my brother?"

"Yes. I saw how happy you made him."

I laugh when all I want to do is cry. "I don't make him happy." A fist curls in my stomach.

"Does he make you happy?"

I look at Richard, the question not sitting right with me. "No."

Richard steps up to the table and chairs.

"So, how were you going to use me against my brother?" I ask the question I wanted to ask the moment he had mentioned my brother.

"Kill you."

All the hairs rise along my body, and I fall silent.

Each step he takes toward me has me closing my eyes. I smell him. The air stirs in front of me, and I know I should open my eyes. Alarm bells ring loudly in my head as his fingers touch my bandage.

My eyes snap open. He's kneeling in front of me; there is a softness in his gaze that I've never seen before.

"I told you already you won't die by my hand."

I nod my head.

He could order someone to kill me. The bald man whom he had called Davy springs to mind.

"My father..." He starts, but his words trail off.

Holding his stare becomes too much, and I look away.

"He will be the one who kills me?" I ask his feet.

Richards's fingers touch my chin. "I won't let that happen."

I'm staring into rich brown eyes, and I want to believe him, but he put me in this box. He had planned to kill me.

"I want to go home."

He hangs his head. "Claire, that's not possible."

I'm ready to get off the bed, but his fingers curl around my wrist, the touch sinking deep under my skin and keeping me seated on the bed.

"Please." It's a whisper.

Richard glances up at me, his fingers still wrapped around my wrist. His brows rise, and irritation widens his eyes. "I said that's not possible."

I bit my lip to stop from shouting. I am going to die in this god-forsaken box.

"Is my brother dead?" I find myself asking.

"Would that upset you?" Richard answers my question with a question.

If this were anyone else, I would question how serious they were. The sharp gaze that Richard holds me under tells me he's very serious.

"Of course." The moment the words leave my lips, I'm questioning them. I didn't care for Leonard, but him dying made me feel even more alone in this world. I would have no one left.

The sadness of that thought has a laugh dribble from my mouth. Richard loosens his hold on my wrist.

"You're going to kill him, aren't you?" I ask, but I don't want the answer.

Richard's gaze holds the answer that his lips don't form.

He would die, and I would be alone.

Tears fall from my eyes without my consent. They are silent tears like my emotions haven't caught up with them yet.

"I told them he wasn't right." I pull my hand out of Richard's touch. "I told them he hurt me." I'm mumbling. I focus on the glass over Richard's shoulder. He's silent as he remains kneeling in front of me.

I'm in a confession box, and I'm ready to spill my sins. "They didn't see it. Maybe I didn't convince them enough about how dangerous he was." I'm focused on Richard. "Maybe if I had tried harder." The image of Richard wavers, and I blink, allowing the tears to fall down my face. "Maybe they would be alive today."

I swipe at one eye and glance away from Richard again.

Another laugh rumbles my chest, and I slap my chest like the laughter had no right to make an appearance.

"But I'm sure you and my brother exchanged war stories." I wipe my other eye angrily.

"He hurt you?" His words are low.

I really look at Richard, taking in how dark his eyes have grown, a dot in an inkwell. His jaw twitches several times.

Is he angry?

"He never told you why he was in the asylum?" I tilt my head, trying to see Richard from a different angle.

"No." He growls. "But you will tell me."

The demand has me sitting up straight. "No."

Richard gets up and towers over me. His hands are curled into fists, and fear grips my shoulders and drags them back. I'm waiting for him to strike me. I'm waiting for this to end. I don't look up at him. I'm not that brave, but I know better than to run. Men like him would love that rush, and I refuse to give this man or any other more power over me.

He doesn't move but remains stoic in front of me. My heart gallops in my chest; the wait is often worse than the action.

My head snaps up. I stare at his back as he walks away from me, exits the box, and closes the door. He never looks back, even as he climbs the steps and returns to his life while I rot in this place.

CHAPTER TWENTY-ONE

O'REAGAN
AN CHLANN

CLAIRE

This time when tears come, I let them fall fast and hard. My stomach twists painfully. Richard said he would kill Leonard, and I didn't beg him not to. I am as big of a monster as they are. This place is making me lose my mind. I'm off the bed; I've never wanted to hurt someone, but I want to hurt Richard.

I'm pacing again, and the glass walls that rise too high are closing in on me until I stop walking. I'm back to staring down at the image of Richard on my floor. Even when he's not here, he's all I see.

I take quick steps to the sink and stuff a large towel in the basin. As I turn on the taps, I don't care about all the excess water that pours over the towel and out onto my dress.

I don't try to stop the onslaught of water.

Without turning off the taps, I drag the towel out. It's heavy with water as I hold it over the image of him. His dark gaze is warning me not to remove his face from the floor. I slap the towel down on the image and fall to my knees. The drawing slowly disappears under the towel that turns from white to gray very quickly. Once the image is removed, I sit up. The bottom of my dress is soaked, turning the fabric translucent. The taps still run, and the noise of rushing water is better than the silence. I continue my path of destruction, attacking the picture of the table and chairs I had drawn. I don't want to share these parts of myself.

Time continues to slip away as I turn everything upside down and inside out. Maybe I'm finally having that breakdown that I feel I should have had when my parents died. When Leonard purposely set that fire, only he knew he wouldn't let me burn. I would live with the knowledge that he burnt the house down and saved me because that's the kind of power he had. Another reminder of how little control I truly have over my own life.

"You have made a right mess." Richard's voice should startle me, but it doesn't.

I continue my destruction as I pull all the dresses out of the wardrobe. I ignore him as I throw the clothes into the tub and turn on both taps.

"What are you doing?" His voice carries over the rushing water, and I give him a quick look before walking back to my bed and dragging the quilts off it. Everything goes into the tub, and I get a feeling like I'm drunk and the world is dissolving around me as I build my own. This world is filled with water. All the towels join everything else in the tub.

"You want to tell me why you are destroying your room?" He's right behind me, and I pause in my path of destruction.

I think of my answer as my heart pounds in my stomach. I can feel my heartbeat in my teeth; the flicker should be a warning, but I am drowning, and I don't think I want to breathe.

"No." I bark and move to the table and chairs. I don't break them but knock them over. Richard stays standing in the middle of my destruction, and he doesn't stop me. He looks amused, and that really sets me off.

The puzzle boxes are stacked at the back of the room, and I gather them before walking up to Richard. I open up the first one and let the puzzle pieces rain down over him. Elation at doing it has the blood burning in my veins. My temperature soars as I open the next one, ready to do the same thing.

Richard's hands reach out quickly, and he drags me fast and hard against his chest. His touch is a splash of cold water on my face. I'm waking up from my meltdown, and I dare tilt my head back and look into his angry eyes. I swallow as fear grips my throat. His hands on my wrists are tight, but I don't chance to move a muscle. I'm already wondering what I was thinking, throwing the puzzle at him.

The water still rushes in the background, and along with it, I hear the racing of my frantic heart. I'm waiting for the blow, but it doesn't come.

He releases me and takes a step back. The space isn't enough. He's towering over me, and all I feel is wet and frazzled.

Richard walks past me, and I don't move as the sound of running water stops. I glance over my shoulder as he turns away from the basin.

"You've ruined all your clothes."

His words drag my attention to my dress, which is soaked. The white material is clinging to my skin.

I swallow as he steps towards me, his gaze drinking me in, making me feel like I don't have a scrap of fabric covering my flesh. He stops only inches away from me.

"I want to know what Leonard did to you?" It's a question, a demand, a death sentence for Leonard.

"No." I jut out my chin and hold my head high.

I think I see a smile in his eyes, but if I did, it's gone before I can conjure a second thought. I'm turning towards the door that never closed when Richard entered. I hadn't noticed the door open before. How had I not noticed? I take a step towards freedom.

Richard moves past me to the door. I'm waiting for him to leave, close the door, and disappear up the stairs.

"I have food prepared for us." He looks at me over his shoulder. "You will have to change first."

I don't state the obvious that all my clothes are soaked in the tub.

"Come upstairs." He steps out through the door.

It's a trick. Then stay here, Claire.

My mind taunts me.

I wrap my arms around my waist and follow Richard out of the box. His gaze snaps to my bare feet, and his jaw tightens.

He returns to the box and picks up my red sneakers off the floor where I had thrown them. He holds them carefully between his fingers as he climbs the stairs. I'm stalling again, wondering what really awaits me upstairs. But I've been up there twice, and each time no harm came to me. My feet are silent as I climb the steps.

We emerge into the hallway, and Richard places my shoes on a chair across from us. I don't expect the contact and jump as he wraps his fingers around my bandaged wrist. He guides me through the hall. Two men I've never seen before don't even blink as we pass them in a larger hallway; it's grander than the last. The heavy chandelier above our heads is lit, with a million lights that reflect and dance off the dark wooden flooring beneath my bare feet.

My heart plummets into my stomach as an open staircase appears before us, and the steps soon disappear under my feet as I climb numbly.

Some of the worst thoughts race through my mind as we reach a landing. I would admire all the marble flooring and high arched door frames, but all I feel is sick as he opens a set of double doors that lead into a bedroom. He releases my wrist once he steps in, and I'm at the foot of a huge bed. The gray sheets and cream covering give the room an almost pleasant feel. That is, except for Richard, who walks toward a door positioned to the left of the bed and disappears into it.

A torture room? Maybe he has more women in there. That thought has something tightening my chest and not because some poor soul is trapped. It's the idea of him kissing another woman.

The thought lodges itself painfully in my throat, and I want to cough, but I swallow the dryness as Richard reappears, holding a blue t-shirt in one hand and gray sweat pants in another. He's not looking at me; he's staring at the clothes in his hand. "These will have to do for now." He looks up at me, and I fear he can see the thoughts written on my face, that for one second, I was jealous that I wasn't his only captive.

I let the cough out to distract myself.

He reaches me, and I curl my fingers around the garments. "Thank you." I'm flustered, and when he doesn't release the clothes, I look up at him.

"You are welcome, Claire." His words are spoken clearly and hold a small amount of humor.

He finally releases the clothes and points to a door that sits to the right of the bed. "The bathroom is in there. You can change."

I move faster than is necessary, but I need to get away from him. I need to get away from my thoughts. Closing the bathroom door gives me little solace. My gaze zones in on the electric toothbrush that sits alone on a glass shelf below a round mirror. I walk over to a cabinet that sits under the sink and open the doors. Aftershave, toothpaste, all bottles of hair care products fill the space. It's his room—his bathroom. I take a peek at the enormous shower. I stare at it for too long when a rap at the door has me dropping *his* clothes.

"Everything okay?" His words are spoken at the door.

"Yes," I say.

He knocks again. "Claire?"

I clear my throat and speak louder. "Yes, I'm nearly done."

"Okay."

I wait a beat. His footsteps move away from the door, and I pull the wet dress over my head before dragging on the fresh clothes. The t-shirt falls to my knees, and all I smell is him. The jogging pants are huge, and I'd need to use both hands to hold them up. I remove them. I don't want to go out in just a t-shirt, no matter how long it is.

"The pants are too big."

His footsteps are back at the door. "That's all I have. You'll have to make do since you destroyed your clothes."

I'm ready to tell him I'm not coming out in a t-shirt.

"Open the door." His command is low, and something stirs in my stomach.

"No." I don't expect him to hear me, but he does.

"You want me to break down the door?"

I don't doubt he will. I unlock the door, holding the jogging pants in a death grip as Richard slowly takes me in. He starts from my bare feet, and it feels like an eternity before he reaches my eyes. I swallow from the look of hunger in his eyes. Hunger I can't ever imagine someone like me could satisfy.

It's a click of a finger, and the look is gone. "You will be fine as you are."

I'm ready to protest, but he flashes me a warning. I hand over the sweatpants and follow him out of the room in just a t-shirt. The material grazes my knees, but I still feel naked as we go downstairs. Once Richard is in the hallway, he pauses, waiting for me. I can't see his eyes. The cold wooden flooring under my feet does nothing to extract the heat that burns through my flesh.

I don't look at the security men stationed in every room of the house that we pass. But I'm aware of them. Now I'm staring at Richards's wide back, wondering exactly who he is. Someone extremely wealthy, judging by the grand rooms we move through until we end up in a dining room with a table long enough to seat over twenty people. I count the chairs all the way down to the end, where it has been set for the two of us.

Twenty-two seats, I count. I wonder why he needs so many. How many people live here? And why all the security? Too many questions swirl in my mind, but none make an appearance as Richard pulls out a high-back chair for me to sit down.

I do, and as he pushes the chair in, I keep my hands in my lap. Richard takes his seat at the head of the table with me to his right.

It's beyond awkward. I'm too close. The table is too big. The room is too silent. It's too wrong.

CHAPTER TWENTY-TWO

O'REAGAN
AN CHLANN

CLAIRE

The food that I place in my mouth is tasteless. My heart is refusing to slow down, and this is a new kind of torture: Sitting here with him while he watches me like I'm the most interesting thing he's seen in a long time. He hasn't touched his own plate.

"Stop," I whisper, glancing down at my lap.

"Stop what?" Richards's voice holds a pinch of humor.

I look up at him and my stomach twists.

"Tell me what Leonard did to you." The question flows like an average question, but I hear the depth of what he's asking.

Did it really matter? I place my knife and fork on the plate. My appetite never showed up anyway, so I could stop the pretense of enjoying the meal. "He burnt my parents alive while I listened to their screams." My voice doesn't sound like my own. No emotion is attached to the words; right now, I just can't allow myself to feel that depth of pain.

"I remember as a child he loved hurting animals, and soon it turned to people." I glance back up at Richard. "Soon, his love for inflicting pain turned to me."

I stumble over the next sentence. I hadn't even told Rose, my therapist, any of this. The words always lodged themselves in my throat with fear, fear that Leonard would find out I told someone and make my life worse. I think it's safe to say that my life has hit rock bottom. There is nothing more anyone can take from me.

"Two weeks before my parents died, there was this stupid cat stuck up in our old tree house that Dad had built for us." I place my hands in my lap and squeeze them tightly together like they might hold me together. My hands grow damp with the memory. Somehow I find the strength to continue. "Leonard loved hurting small creatures, and I knew when he told me the cat was up there, he was giving me time to save it, or he'd kill it. He liked playing games. I went up, and of course, there was no cat." My gut twists painfully. I reach across the table and pick up a glass of water. I don't drink the liquid. I'm not sure whether my throat is capable of any more functions beyond letting my story pour from me. I want to ask Richard to allow me to stop. That I don't want to talk about this, but I have no control as the words continue to flow. "He was there in the hut, grinning at me the moment I opened the trap door. I had no time to react. He kicked me in the face, and I was falling. I couldn't move, not even as he joined me on the ground, not even as he broke my leg. The fall had broken the other."

I look at Richard again. His face is impassive. He's stoic. The look on his face should be enough to make me stop, but there is no stopping the pain or my words. "I was bedridden. I never told my parents what he did to me."

"Why didn't you tell someone?" Richards's words are low, too low.

I should take my words back. "He said he'd hurt our mom." I blink, and tears fall. I wipe them away quickly. I don't want to feel right now. "They were screaming, and I couldn't save them. He made sure I couldn't." I'm up from the table, their screams propelling my steps. It's too much. I should have saved them. I should have dragged my body out of bed. I should have told them the first time I found a jar of wingless butterflies in his room. I should have told them when I found the countless dead cats or dogs hidden at the end of our garden. He always said he wouldn't do it again, or his reason changed as we got older, that he would hurt our mom and it would be my fault. I exhale a shaky breath as my mind leaves the pain, and I take in the surrounding space. I have no idea where I'm going, but I'm moving past doors— an endless stream of doors. A security man steps out towards me, but something has him stepping back.

I glance over my shoulder, knowing there would only be one person who would have that power. Richard is walking behind me, his eyes pinned on me. Knowing he's behind me doesn't slow me down. Nothing does. I have no idea where I'm going. Ahead I see a set of double frosted glass doors that I push open. The air changes as I enter a pool room. The water reflects off the wall tiles, giving the room an illusion as if it's all water. I stop running and move closer to the edge of the pool. My body shimmers with the water, and I'm staring at myself, standing alone, in his t-shirt, that is, until he appears behind me towering over me. When his hands touch my shoulders, I close my eyes at the contact, but his touch doesn't make me cower. It extracts more of my confession from my lips.

"I did nothing," I say. His fingers tighten on my upper arms, he still hasn't spoken, and that has me opening my eyes. I try to turn in his arms, but his hold is firm and keeps me in place. I'm drawn to the image of us that distorts in the water.

A kiss is pressed to the top of my head, and this time when I try to turn, he allows the movement by dropping his hands. He doesn't move away from me, making me crane my neck back to look up at him.

"I didn't know." His words confuse me.

"How would you?" I ask.

His jaw clenches. "I know now."

The tightness of his jaw has me wanting to reach up and touch his face. So I do. The muscle in his jaw twitches under my touch. "I used to pray for him to die," I admit, not looking Richard directly in the eyes. Richard is a dangerous man who does dangerous things. Maybe he will understand my dark thoughts. "After the fire...." I let my hand slip from Richard's face. He catches my un-bandaged wrist and turns it palm up. Shock races through me as he presses a kiss to the inside of my wrist. "...I stopped praying." I finish my sentence.

Our eyes lock, and something I see has me touching his face again. He's looking at me with understanding, and I'm wondering once again what made him into the man he is today. What made him so cruel one moment but so gentle the next?

Richard bends his head, and I do nothing to stop the kiss; instead, I fall into him. I open my mouth and let his tongue gain entry. His large hands grip my sides and squeeze. It's a reminder of his sheer size, and I break the kiss. A shiver assaults me as our gazes clash. His hunger turns his eyes almost black, and I know I'm not getting away from him. He drags me back and claims my mouth. My hands automatically wrap around his neck, and he uses the moment to grab my thighs and lift me up off the ground. The moment my feet leave the ground, I wrap them around his waist. He moves us to the wall. The cool tiles push against my back as his large erection presses into my stomach.

His lips slip from mine, and he presses one kiss after another along my jaw. I cling to him as each kiss chips some of the hardened pain away from me, revealing the rawness underneath. How long has it been since I shared more than a kiss with a man? I never allowed myself to go too far. I never wanted to feel.

My head feels light like I'm drunk, and my hands glide from his neck to his face. Richard's kisses stop, but he doesn't release me. He's waiting, watching me and our breaths mingle heavily together.

My core throbs. I want him. He wants me. His head dips closer, and I eradicate the distance and kiss him first. His body presses heavily against mine, and I push my core toward his shaft, wanting to satisfy the yearning that makes me wet.

He releases my legs and slowly lets my feet slip to the floor. He doesn't break the kiss, and the air catches in my lungs as his hand touches the bare skin of my thigh. His long fingers move the fabric of my panties aside, and his finger circles my clitoris. His other hand races down my arm and touches the bandage. He leaves my clitoris, and his finger dips inside me while his thumb presses down on my wrist. His lips leave mine, giving me a moment to breathe harsh and deep breaths that roar through my body. I'm light-headed as he plunges two fingers inside me. His lips crash down on mine again as the force behind them sends me back into the wall. Pain erupts in my back at the impact, but his fingers send waves of pure pleasure through me. His teeth graze my lips, sending a jolt of electricity through me, but I'm distracted as he moves his fingers faster and harder inside me.

It's like someone turning up the volume on a stereo. A soft bite to my lip pulls me away from the bliss, but Richard's thumb works my clit, moving in fast circles, which reignites my pleasure.

The nips to my lip get deeper until I'm a mix of pain and pleasure. Each time he bites me, he spends longer on my core, giving it exactly what it needs and sending me into a spin. I sense the skin splitting on my lip but once again, I don't fully register it as Richard's expert fingers move, bringing me close to my climax. I taste the blood in my mouth as another finger enters me, and I grip his shoulders as I moan loudly. I cry out my release. Each time he enters me slowly, it sets off small sparks behind my eyes and shocks throughout my system. He removes his fingers, and I dare to open my eyes. His gaze makes me swallow the saliva and blood. My tongue automatically flicks out, and I lick fresh blood from the cut on my lip. Richard is staring at my lips, and he bends his head and presses a kiss to the cut. The suction sensation frightens me but also stirs something deep in my belly as he sucks my blood. When Richard leans out, his lips have my blood on them.

He moves closer and presses another kiss to my lips. With his arms pressed against the wall, I'm boxed in. I'm trapped under his large frame. His breath fans across my neck, and I'm wondering if he's going to bite me. I'm waiting when his large hands leave the wall, and they touch my hips, but there is no pressure under his fingertips.

"He'll never hurt you again." It's a promise. It's everything I wish I had heard a long time ago. It's a death sentence.

"Don't kill him." My voice is devoid of emotion. I have to say those words, but the truth behind it is I'd be happy if he died. That thought has me wanting Richard away from me. My thoughts are wrong. I shouldn't wish anyone dead. What would my parents think of me? My father would be disappointed.

A kiss to my neck has shivers racing across my body, and when Richard steps away, I want him back immediately so he can fend off the cold.

"You think he has a right to live?" Richard's question has me folding my arms across my chest, causing the t-shirt to rise. All the flesh draws Richards's attention, and I drop my arms to my side, not forgetting for one second how hard he was against me.

I try to focus on his words. "I have no right to say who lives or dies."

"That's not what I asked." Richard steps away from me, putting more distance between us. I don't move from the wall.

"No, he has no right to live. But that doesn't mean he should die. He's locked up where he can't hurt anyone else."

Laughter echoes in the pool room. It's not kind laughter, it's cruel and angry.

"He continues to hurt people," Richard says when his laughter stops. I see it in his gaze. My brother hurt him too.

"I'm not playing God. We have no right to take a life." It's stupid to say these words to a man who took the life of two people in front of me.

"There is no God, Claire."

I'm ready to tell him there is, but maybe he's right, maybe there is no God. Maybe it's just men and women, war and love, hope and despair. Maybe that's all there is. Maybe that's all that makes us up.

"I don't want Leonard to die."

A grin spreads across Richard's face. "I don't believe you." He steps closer to me.

I can't hold his gaze again. "I don't," I say again, but I hear it; it's so clear in my words.

"It's okay." Richard reaches me, and I focus on his chest. He takes hold of my chin and raises my head. "It's okay." He repeats before pressing a soft kiss to my lips.

CHAPTER TWENTY-THREE

O'REAGAN
AN CHLANN

RICHARD

Killing is an art form that I've learned from a very young age. Leonard will be my masterpiece. Claire still trembles under me from her confession and from coming all over my fingers. My cock is throbbing painfully, with a want I won't satisfy right now. She needed to allow herself to let go.

"I don't know why I'm confessing this to you." She frowns. Even her frown is beautiful.

She won't look at me. "It's a talent I have." I hide the grin that wants to make an appearance. "People confess their deepest secrets to me." Mostly by force or by some form of torture. Nonetheless, they confess.

This time when she looks up at me, with flushed cheeks and troubled eyes, I remind myself that Leonard will die slowly for what he has done to her. Killing a woman or child is something that you can't come back from. Putting your hand on a woman is also something that I don't give in to. To think Leonard broke her legs so she couldn't save her parents. Leonard's actions were a new kind of evil.

I cup her cheek and love when she leans into me. The fear that normally wraps itself around her is gone, and seeing her more comfortable makes me more determined to keep it that way. I want her trust. I don't want her to fear me anymore.

I won't put her back in the box.

I need her more than she needs me, and when I pull her into my chest, she doesn't protest. I plant another kiss on the top of her head, her smell intoxicating and turning my cock to steel.

I release Claire. "I have to go."

Shay and I agreed to meet to discuss the future of the O' Reagans. Anyone else I would cancel on, but not him.

She nods and bites her lip that I had bitten. She hisses and releases her lip as fresh blood blossoms along the cut. She's killing me here. My control is slowly slipping. I step away at the sight of the blood.

"You have free rein of the house. I'm sure you saw all the security, and Davy will be here." I don't want to say there is no escape, but I see the knowledge that she is being watched constantly flash behind her crystal blue eyes that widen.

"I don't have to go back into the box?" Her chest rises and falls, and she looks fucking perfect in my t-shirt.

"No. I'll have clothes arranged for you." I'd have Mario do that while I'm gone.

She half-smiles, and if I don't leave right now, I never will.

The moment I leave the pool, a crushing sensation tightens my chest. Taking out my phone distracts me as I send a text to Shay to tell him I'm on my way.

Davy intercepts me in the hallway. "Have Mario do some clothes shopping for Claire. Get her measurements."

Davy doesn't look pleased. He pushes up his glasses. "Where are you off to?"

"I'm meeting Shay." I put the phone back in my pocket. "Claire is allowed around the house. Let her spend some time with Connor, too."

Davy tilts his head, and the look of defiance on his face has me stopping. "Is there a problem?" The warning in my voice has Davy smirking.

"No problem, boss."

Smart fucker. He never calls me boss. I don't have time to find out what is wrong with him.

"I won't be late." I look back at the corridor that leads down to the pool and wonder if she's still in there. Placing my fingers in my mouth, I taste her as I walk to the garage. Her juices are sweet, and my cock starts to harden all over again.

MAFIA GAMES

Shay is alone at the bar, nursing a pint. Some hurling match has captured his attention on the small TV screen. He doesn't look away from the television as I pull up a stool beside him. "I honestly didn't think you would show."

The bartender wipes the counter a few feet away. Once his head rises, and he sees me, he walks over. "What can I get you?"

"Whatever he's drinking," I say.

"A pint of lager it is."

I'm not a lager kind of man, but I would manage it on this occasion. "Out of all the places to meet, you picked this place?" I ask.

"Are you here to kill me?" Shay looks at me this time; there is no fear in his eyes.

The bartender arrives back with the pint. Taking out my wallet, I slide him a twenty and sit back down. "No. I'm here to talk." I take a sip of the cold pint.

The bartender arrives back with my change before returning to wiping down tables. I pivot on the stool, so I'm facing Shay.

Shay takes out a cigarette box and lights up.

"You can't smoke in here." The bartender stops his cleaning and walks towards us. I sit back and see how Shay will handle this.

"Why don't you make yourself busy and shut the pub down." Shay takes another drag while the bartender laughs.

"Look here, sunshine, you might have a pretty face, but that's not going to happen. Put out the smoke." The bartender fills a glass with some water and slides it down to Shay to put out his cigarette.

I have never heard anyone refer to Shay as pretty. He always looks ready to chew someone's face off.

"How much do you want?" Shay offers.

The bartender looks at us a bit differently, and I'm tempted to say our names. We are in Kells. Everyone here knows who we are.

"Five grand." The bartender throws out the figure.

Shay grins. "You are one greedy cunt. You'll get two."

Two is two too many. Once again, I don't interfere.

"Two?" The bartender questions.

"That's what I said." Shay flicks his ashes in the glass of water. There's no one else in the bar, so giving him two grand is overkill. "He's paying." Shay points at me and grins.

This time when I look up at the bartender, I nod. "You'll have your money. We O' Reagan's always pay up."

Color leaves his face, and he moves promptly from behind the bar. He scurries out of the room to close the main doors.

"You could have said your name; this would have been free and a lot quicker," I say.

"I hate the fucking name." Shay fires back.

"You hate what it stands for, and that's what I want to change. It can stand for so much more."

"Does your da have a hit on me?" Shay throws the cigarette into the glass.

"Of course he does. You disrespected him."

"He killed my fucking brother." Anger twists Shay's features.

"Lucian Sheahan ordered the kill. My father carried out his orders."

"Never liked him." Shay takes a drink.

"I'll help you kill Lucian Sheahan." I offer.

"I can do it myself."

Maybe he could, but I am trying to offer an olive branch here, and killing the leader of the RA wouldn't go unnoticed.

"Will you help me kill your da?" Shay asks.

"Would you help me kill yours?"

A warning flashes in Shay's eyes.

"I'm not going to kill your father, Shay. But don't expect me to kill mine." My father had to be removed from the Irish Mafia by killing him, and I didn't think I could do that.

"He will be removed. You have my word. If you don't start to trust me, this won't work." Shay doesn't trust me. I don't blame him, but it's a leap of faith that he will have to take. "I'm going to bring Jack in on everything."

Shay sneers. "I'm sorry, but he put a gun to my head."

I grin and pick up my drink. "He was protecting his father. We leave our fathers out of this."

"So don't tell Jack that we are going to clip your da?" Shay's angry, I get that, but the idea of him shooting my father isn't working for me. I take a drink and don't break eye contact.

"I hope you will work with me on this, Shay." I push the pint away from me and stand up. Disappointment has me pausing. "Killing my father won't bring back your brother."

I'm ready to walk away when Shay speaks.

"He has to die, Richard."

I tighten my fists. "Why do you have to say that?" I'm turning back as Shay slides off the stool.

"If he's removed, you think he will retire? Drag a blanket across his knees and suck on sweets at night? It will hang over our heads, every night, every day." Shay steps closer to me. "Everyone we love will be a possible target. The only way to end this is...." He doesn't finish his sentence. But I hear it. The only way to end this is by killing my father. How do I say yes to that? He's right. I have no idea what to do with my father once I force him to step down.

"Maybe we will blackmail him." I run my hands across my face before sitting back down. "He asked me to kill Finn."

Shay's laughter continues as he also sits back down. "Finn?"

It's an odd look on Shay, but the surprise is there: it bleeds into disgust.

"Yes. He also knows how Cian died."

Shay withdraws, and his features close down. My father having that knowledge about Cian, meant he has something on Shay too. The words hang between us. I don't need to say them.

"Shane is his right-hand man. What would he think?"

Shay is watching me, not saying anything, and I regret bringing up Cian. But we are going to build this on honesty.

"I don't give a shit that you took part in Cian's death. I know it was Maeve. We could just use Finn as a way to blackmail him."

"When he asked you to kill Finn, what did you say?"

The weight of his question is heavy. I could lie, but isn't that what I'm trying to stop here? Yet giving him the truth will make it harder to convince Shay to work with me.

"I said yes."

He shakes his head. "He's your uncle."

"You wanted the truth. There it is."

Shay nods and sits back. "Blackmailing your father won't be enough," Shay admits, and he's right. I'm happy he's starting to really think about this.

"We could kill Finn and pin it on my father," I say and take a drink.

"What the fuck?" Shay stops as I laugh. "You're joking." Shay sounds surprised, and I suppose we never let our guards down around each other.

I'm staring at the top row of spirits. "I want this to work." I side-eye him. "Really work."

He's coming around. I can see it in his gaze. He holds his drink up to me, and I turn to face him while clinking my glass against his.

"You double-cross me, and I will kill you like I killed Carlos."

"I won't. You better not cross me, either." I grin, but my threat is serious.

We drink our drinks to seal the deal.

"We take down Sheahan first," Shay growls. This is the problem with emotions: we never see things clearly. He's out for blood, and I need to make Shay spill it very fucking slowly, or we will bring the whole RA down on our heads.

"Killing Sheahan will have to be tactfully dealt with."

"Are you saying I'm not tactful?"

"You're a bulldozer."

Shay's laughter has me relaxing further. "We need someone on the inside. Someone who would double-cross him."

"How the fuck do we find someone like that?" Shay asks.

"I don't know. But you know Sheahan."

Shay shakes his head. "No, but I know someone who does. My da."

My father knew him too, but that was not a road I would go down. "We talk to your father."

Shay is already shaking his head. "You think I'm a bulldozer, my da...." He shakes his head. Pain refills his eyes.

"Okay." I touch Shay's shoulder, and he tenses under my hand. "We will find a way. We take down Lucian and then my father."

Shay finishes his drink and lights up another cigarette. "When do you bring Jack up to speed on all this?"

"I'll talk to him soon."

I get up, happy with how this went.

"Don't forget to pay the bartender," Shay says.

The weight I felt arriving here has lifted slightly. I leave the bar and find the bartender sitting on a bench inside the door. His head snaps up, and he stands.

"You can re-open. I'll have someone deliver your money."

"No, there's no need." He shuffles nervously. "Shane O'Reagan owns this pub."

That isn't knowledge I am aware of, but the idea of Shane knowing that Shay and I had met could be a problem. I'm staring too long at the bartender.

His Adam's apple bobbles. "I didn't see you." Fear has his words low.

I curse. Why the fuck did he just say that? I didn't want to kill him. Did Shay know Shane owned this pub? Is that why he picked it?

I grip the door and leave the bartender alive. Shane's bartender, I remind myself. I can only hope Shay didn't fuck me over, but the coincidence that we met at this bar has my hope dwindling.

CHAPTER TWENTY-FOUR

O'REAGAN
AN CHLANN

RICHARD

Days pass, and I'm not sure what I'm waiting for, an army to crash through the front doors, led by my father? I'm waiting for Shay's betrayal to come to the surface. Our meeting at one of Shane's pubs is still playing on my mind, I just can't figure out what angle Shay is coming from. I'm slowly losing hope of ever finding loyalty in anyone.

I keep waiting, and nothing happens. That leaves me more unsettled. My mind forgets my worries as Claire comes into view again. She's outside with Connor. I watch her play chase with the dog. I can't help thinking again about how it was the best decision I made in regard to keeping him.

As she runs through the garden, she looks like she's always belonged here by my side. She's leaving me unsettled, too. Having her here and seeing her smile more with each passing day makes me afraid of losing her.

"Jack rang earlier looking for you," Davy speaks from the doorway. I glance at him over my shoulder before turning back to Claire.

"I know. I have a phone." I'd seen all the missed calls but cutting myself off and just existing here with Claire is all I want to do. The more I learn about her growing up, the more I want to know her. She's the strongest person I've ever met; after all she suffered at Leonard's hands. He will be the reason I leave this house soon. Killing him will be a true joy. Claire turns like she can feel my eyes on her, and I love how her cheeks flush. I haven't touched her since the pool, and it's all I want to do each time I look at her.

"He keeps ringing." Davy continues.

I exhale and turn to him, holding back my irritation at being disturbed. "Did he say what he wanted?"

Davy steps into the room. "He wants you to ring him." Davy's gaze travels past me and out the window. "She's settling in well." Sarcasm drips from each word.

"She's none of your concern."

"I never interfere, Richard, with your personal life, but..."

I hold up a hand, cutting off Davy. "You don't interfere in any part of my life, Davy, because I pay you to do what I need you to do. That's it. Right now, I don't care for your opinion or advice."

His jaw tightens. I hate having to put him in his place, but he's getting a little too lippy for my likings. He takes a final look at Claire, much to my annoyance, before facing me again. "I've given you my servitude without question."

I take a step toward Davy. "Yes, you have. I pay you well, and I appreciate it. So before you go a step further, I advise you to end this conversation."

He won't answer me with words. His eyes are angry, narrowed slightly, and it's taken a whole army to keep him from voicing his words. I can appreciate that, so before he loses control, I speak.

"You are dismissed, Davy."

He marches from the room, and I run my hand across my face before returning to the window. My stomach twists painfully as my gaze darts around the garden. I can't see Claire. I'm ready to race outside when she steps out from behind a tree laughing. Connor races after her as she hides behind another tree.

She does this with him several times, and as much as I love watching her, I know I'll have to face the world again soon. When people like Davy start to question me, what are other people doing? The sharks are surely starting to circle my home. Hiding behind my walls is a sign of weakness, one that will not just put me in danger but Claire, too. I pause before moving away from the window when Claire looks directly at me. She's happy. She gives me a little wave like she's not sure what to do.

I give her a half-smile that I try to bury, but with Claire, it's hard not to smile around her. She walks back to the house, and I leave the room and meet her at the back door.

"You've been out there all morning," I say.

There is a shyness in her eyes that has grown considerably over the last few days. "I love spending time with Connor." She rubs behind Connor's ear.

"I was starting to think you were avoiding me."

Her smile is sweet as she pats Connor on the head before straightening up. "No, why would I do that?"

Yes, she is avoiding me.

"Would you like to go for a swim?" I ask.

Her face blazes, and it's exactly what I wanted. I want her to remember my hands on her. I want her to remember how I had made her cum. I can't stop thinking about how sweet she was.

"I don't have a swimsuit."

"Yes, you do. I had Mario pick you up one. It's in your room." Her having her own room isn't exactly something I am happy with, but giving her space seems to relax her.

I'm waiting for her to make up another excuse.

She bites her lip. "Okay. I'll just put Connor in the garage."

"I can do that." I didn't want her to change her mind.

She hesitates, but when I reach for Connor, she goes into the house. I lock him in the garage, and a buzz has my steps quicken as I make my way to the pool. I want to be there before her so I can see her in the red bikini that I got her.

I strip down fully and dive into the pool. Ten lengths later, Claire arrives with a white towel wrapped around her bust. I swim backward so I can watch her.

"It's nice and warm."

She's nervous, and if I swim away, she might get in quicker, but I'm a bastard and enjoy her nervous gaze and hunched shoulders.

She holds the towel with one hand while walking to the steps that lead down into the water. She's staring at them like she's considering the best way into the pool. Her gaze dances across the water before her eyes land on me.

I grin. "Whenever you're ready."

Boldness fires in her blue eyes, and she unclenches her fist and drops the towel. I straighten in the pool and wipe any excess water off my face. My cock skips all the first stages of hardening and becomes a rod of steel. The red bikini against her skin has every male part of me come alive. She's fucking perfect. She doesn't turn around but instead dives into the water quickly. But I've seen enough to make me want to ravish her. I dunk my head under the water to see her swimming towards me; I don't want to miss a second. Blonde hair flows around her like a halo, and I break the surface at the same time she does.

She's pushing hair and water out of her face, and my plan was to swim for a while, but I lose all semblance of control and reach for the beauty. She startles at my touch as I help her push the hair off her face. Claire's eyes widen at the sudden closeness. I devour her lips in the most unapologetic manner. I suck, nip, and taste her. Her hands are pressed against my chest but soon slide up to my neck, and she matches my kiss heartily.

I move both of us to the side of the pool to help support me as I greedily push my tongue into her mouth. She's perfect against my body, her breasts swell against my chest, and I open my eyes and break the kiss. She appears startled; her breaths brush heavily against my lips. She's trapped between me and the edge of the pool, and I slip one hand down and let my fingertips dance against the fabric that covers her pussy. I'm testing the waters, and when she does nothing, I continue touching her. I keep watching her as I slip my fingers under her pants. Her breaths grow more frantic, and I hope she's thinking about the last time she came on my fingers. I haven't stopped thinking about her juices coating my fingers; all I want to do is fuck her hard.

I push a finger inside her pussy. Her head falls back, and her eyes close. I keep moving my finger in and out, dragging it up to her clit that I circle slowly. She squirms and whimpers between each painfully slow stroke. My finger's still inside her, and a look of almost panic has me elated at how much she wants this. Her hands tighten on my neck, and she pushes down on my fingers.

"You want to cum?" I ask her.

She nods her head eagerly.

I grin. "Tell me you want to cum."

She blinks a few times before speaking. "I want you to make me cum."

I remove my hand from her pussy and run it up her side, grazing the side of her breast that I want to taste.

I let my thumb glide across the fabric that covers her breast, her nipples are pebbled, and I take my time running my finger across them. Claire bites her lip, drawing my attention to the small cut on her lip. It's nearly healed, and I think about opening it up again, about tasting her again. But what I really want to do with her, we can't do in the pool. My intentions alter from wanting to make her cum to wanting to fuck her hard.

I guide her to the opposite side of the pool, and she doesn't question me. Once I reach the edge, I pull myself out, water cascades down my body. Her gasp has me grinning as I stand up naked. My arousal has captured every ounce of her attention. I reach down and stroke my cock. She startles at the movement, her innocence widening her eyes.

"Have you ever watched a man make himself cum?" I ask.

She shakes her head and swallows.

I kneel down and hold out my hand for her. She's looking at my open palm like it's a choice that will change her life. I'm not sure what I'll do if she doesn't take my hand. Dragging her out of the pool seems like the only option at this stage. Her small hand fits perfectly in mine as she takes it, and I pull her out of the pool. She's light, and once she's standing beside me,

I resist the urge to take her here and now. Instead, I press a soft kiss to her lips and take her hand, walking her back to where she dropped her towel. Picking it up, I place the towel around her shoulders, covering up most of her body. I don't want any of my men to look at her. The thought alone has my jaw clenching. Her eyes are dull, and she looks almost pained like I'm rejecting her. I don't explain what we are doing as I take a robe that hangs on a row of hooks off and cover myself up with it.

"I want to show you something."

"Okay." Her voice wavers, and she chews the inside of her cheek. Once again, I hold out my hand for her to take, and once again, she stalls before her hand slips into mine.

Her hand remains in mine as I lead her through the hallways and up the stairs.

I glance at her a few times, and she won't look at me. Instead, she focuses on the floor. Her hand grips the towel in a death grip.

I bring her to my bedroom door and pause before entering. "I want you. But I want you my way," I say before pushing the door open. I release her hand and take her face, making her look at me. I kiss her, and it's not gentle; nothing about fucking for me is. I want her to know that when we go into my room, I won't hold back.

She appears pure, but she matches my kiss with her own ferocity, and I push the door to the room open fully, leading her inside. I pause one more time, breaking the kiss giving her the opportunity to stop this, but she's still standing in front of me as I close the door behind us.

CHAPTER TWENTY-FIVE

O'REAGAN
AN CHLANN

CLAIRE

I don't know if I'm ready to bolt or fall down. Richard removes the robe from his sculpted body, and I'd be a liar if I said I didn't want him. The more I'm around him, the more I crave him. The last few days, my attraction towards him has grown tenfold.

The attraction right now is all hormones and lust. His gaze teases me as I stand, holding the towel tightly in my hand. I want to be as bold as I was in the pool, but knowing why we are here, makes being braver so much harder. A cool breeze along my neck stirs all the hairs on my body, and when I finally get the courage to drop the towel, the air presses against every inch of flesh. Richard's eyes roam my body, and I burn up with how he looks at me. He's pleased with what he is seeing, and I notice that same primal glint in his eye that I saw in the pool. I take the time to study him. Small white scars decorate his lower abdomen. Some look fresh, and I take a wobbly step towards him.

Be brave.

The chant I say in my head has me reaching him, and my fingers flutter across the scars. He doesn't stop me. The muscles bunch and twitch under my touch. My gaze keeps sliding down to his very large cock, and everything inside me swells and tightens. My breasts push heavily against my bikini top. Richard's hand reaches out and takes mine before he removes my hand from his stomach. I think the story behind the scars must be traumatic. I want to know everything about him. I take a peek at him, but he guides me toward the very large bed. He spins me, so I'm facing him, and I swallow as his large hands clamp down on my shoulders; he presses until I'm sitting on the edge of the bed, and he's towering over me.

His cock is in my face, and I'm chanting to myself to be brave, and touch it when he slowly descends to the floor, and he's kneeling at my feet. Something in his eyes makes me feel like a woman who has a King at her feet. He's bigger than life, and when his hand presses against my stomach, I lie back at the command in his touch. My heartbeat is wild and erratic. Closing my eyes, I wait. The air is bitterly cold against my bare skin. I don't know what he's doing, but I hear a drawer open, and I'm thinking he must be getting a condom.

Be brave.

"Open your eyes." Richard's voice is close to me, and I do as he commands.

The blood turns cold in my veins as I stare at the knife in his hand. I'm trying to sit up and shuffle away from him, but his free hand grips my hip tightly, and his body presses close to mine. I'm ready to protest when he pushes the knife into my hand, and my confusion deepens. My fingers are loose around the knife, and Richard tightens my fingers around the handle, one at a time.

"I don't understand," I say.

Richard stands back up, leaving me bewildered, lying on his bed with a knife in my hand. I'm ready to drop it when the tip of his fingers pushes my legs apart. My heart trips over itself as he drags me quickly to the edge of the mattress. His huge cock sits at my opening. He leans over me, and once we are face to face, he presses a kiss to my jawline, leaving a trail until he reaches my ear. "I want you to cut me."

I swallow saliva and confusion. "No."

He leans out so he can see me. His eyes are black like a starless night, a warning not to proceed any further with this game. He looks possessed as he takes my hand that holds the knife and brings it to his torso.

"I want you to." He pushes the blade a little harder, and I try to pull back. Richards's body moves closer, and his cock is heavy against my opening. The knife nicks his flesh, and blood swells. He hisses, and I'm ready to apologize as blood drips down his torso, but the grin and pleasure that feeds the smile on his face is heavy with ecstasy.

He reaches down and runs a finger along the cut. I'm transfixed as he brings it to his lips. His tongue flicks out, and he tastes the blood before leaning closer to me. I'm still holding the knife, still wondering what is going on, when he presses his bloody finger against my lips.

His gaze is asking me to take part in this. Take part in something he clearly enjoys. My heart rages, and my lips part as he pushes his finger into my mouth, and his cock hardens even further against me. The metallic taste is instant on my tongue and on the back of my throat. I hold the knife away from his body but don't drop the weapon as he kisses me, plunging his tongue that's coated in blood into my mouth. My core tightens.

Richard's hand leaves my skin as he reaches up and takes the knife from my hand, peeling each finger back slowly. The cold steel against my flesh has my heart thrashing in warning of the impending danger. A danger that I want to be a part of. I have no idea where Richard is taking me, but I am willing to go with him. The blade splits the skin on my chest, and the pain has me hissing. His warm wet lips press against the open flesh before he drags his lips up to my neck, leaving a trail of blood in its wake. His lips hover over mine, and I reach up and drag his face to me. His hand reaches down and separates my legs, giving his large frame more room to press against me. His body is warm against mine, but it's brief before he pulls me up into a sitting position and gets off the bed. My gaze is snagged on the red liquid that drips from his torso. He's watching me as I touch the blood and drag it down closer to his cock.

Be brave.

The head of his cock is swollen, and I press a bloody finger to the tip. His cock jumps, and Richard growls low in his throat. His large hands drag my body closer to the edge. Black eyes swallow me whole as he rips my bikini bottoms aside and pushes his cock into my entrance. The force rocks my body, and I cry out for a moment before the air is cut off from my lungs. Richard tightens a hand around my throat. My instincts kick in, and my hands fly to his to try to stop him, but he squeezes tighter as he pounds into me hard and fast.

"Give into it." His command penetrates the fear that's clouding me.

I'm not sure if he loosens his hold, or maybe I could always take in small swallows of air, but I try to relax and release the hold I have on his hand. The pressure on my throat has me craning my neck back, but as he pushes his cock into me, the pleasure takes me above the pain and panic. For a moment, that's all I am, pleasure and pain. No air, no words. There is no sense to this act, only Richard.

His body plows into me, and he moves closer, his head dips, and his teeth dig into the cut on my chest. The pain flares, and panic rears its head, only to vanish like some phantom as he licks the damaged skin before plunging his tongue in my mouth and his cock into my pussy.

His pounds grow more frantic, and his hand tightens on my throat until this time there is no air. Stars dance, and I can't stop my reaction of trying to pull his hands away from my throat.

"Give in to it, Claire." Richards's words brush my ear as he moves erratically inside me.

I feel like I'm ready to snap in two. His cock plows into me, and he takes me to a new height. Everything mingles together, the burning of the cut on my chest, the sting of his bite mark, the pleasure of his cock inside me, the pressure on my esophagus. It all mingles, and when it finally crashes together, the impact rocks my body, and I cum hard and fast, but it's soundless. My core tightens and throbs around his cock. His hand leaves my throat, and I gasp for air. My vision is dark but returns slowly as I continue to cum and watch Richard's powerful body thrust inside me. Each stroke is hard and fast. He's loud as he empties himself inside me, and we both come down slowly together.

CHAPTER TWENTY-SIX

O'REAGAN
AN CHLANN

RICHARD

I never understood peace, what it looked like or how peace felt. Nothing on this earth could bring us peace; that's what I used to believe. Looking at Claire's sleeping form gives me a sense of peace that I didn't know existed.

The navy bed sheets are tangled around her naked body. Having her every night in my bed and exploring her body slowly allows me to really enjoy the perfection that makes her up. She stirs, and I remain still until her breathing evens out and she falls back into a deep sleep.

Taking my suit jacket off the back of the vanity chair, I leave the room. Closing the door, the peace she had given me seconds ago dissolves with each step I take down the stairs.

Another week has passed since the meeting with Shay, since Jack's persistent ringing, since my sister had messaged me wanting to talk. Everyone wants to talk. I don't think anyone listened. I am not leaving the house to talk to them. I will soon, but first I have to do something else.

I have to kill Leonard. Letting him breathe air is a sin. A sin that I will eradicate in the next coming hours.

Downstairs I search for Davy, but no one seems to know where he is. I've been avoiding him. Maybe now he's avoiding me.

I know if he doesn't show soon, I will have to track him down, and I don't like having to track anyone down, especially not my fucking staff.

"Marcus, if Davy returns, tell him to call me straight away." I pause beside Marcus.

"No problem."

I don't walk away from Marcus immediately. He's close to Davy, as close as Eamon once was. "If you know of his whereabouts, I advise you to speak up now. You don't want to end up like Eamon, do you?"

"I don't know where Davy is."

I hold Marcus's stare. The truth of his words shines in his eyes, and I release him with a nod of my head before leaving the house.

The asylum rises in front of me, and I hope it's the last time I have to make an appearance here. This time when I enter, they know I'm coming. The arrangements I made before arriving cost me a decent penny, but no price is too great to end Leonard's life. Killing him is no longer about me. Killing him is for Claire. I'm thinking of something slow and extremely painful.

I'll enjoy this. I enter the reception and double-check that the cameras are dead. The lights are off, and when I push the door to the left of the empty reception desk, it opens. The lock that keeps the door sealed has been disabled.

My footfalls bounce around the empty corridors, and I like to think if anyone sees me that they'll scurry away, knowing I mean business. Room two hundred and twenty is the room number I'm looking for. That's where he is locked up. I'm ready to take a left down a corridor when a camera blinks to life. I keep walking and try to check out the other cameras subtly. They all appear to be switched off. Room two hundred and ten appears, and I count the room numbers as I continue to walk. I'm at room number two hundred and eighteen when I notice another camera is on. I pause outside Leonard's door. Why am I being watched? Who is watching me? I reach for the door handle, the code box devoid of light telling me it has been disabled. I open the door, and the empty room is like a laugh in the face or a fucking kick in the teeth. I step back on high alert. The gun in the waistband of my trousers I don't extract, but the heaviness of the gun against my shirt gives me a calm that I shouldn't be feeling right now.

I take a step back from the door and turn fully to the camera over my shoulder. I wait a few beats for something to happen, but nothing does. Leaving the hallway, I hear the buzz of electricity as all systems return. I make it to the door that leads into the reception area. The palm of my hand burns from the impact that makes no difference as the door remains closed.

I'm trapped.

The fear starts to grow along with my anger, and this time I take my gun out and raise it toward the camera over my head.

"Open the fucking door." I keep the gun pointed at the camera, and whoever is watching me better open the door. The pause is too long, and hope dwindles fast. I will claw my way out of this place. I will take down every one of them before I'm placed in a glass room again.

The door buzzes, and I reach out and grip the handle, opening the door. I take one final look at the camera. With the door half-open, I know it's my way out. I know I can leave. I'm no longer trapped, but I can't leave without spilling Leonard's blood.

"Where is he?" I speak toward the camera again. Nothing happens, and I wait a few beats. Footsteps are ahead of me, and I drag the door open wider.

"He escaped." The director speaks.

I keep my hand on the door while raising my gun toward the director.

"Bullshit," I say straight away and step into the reception area where he stands, alone and unarmed. It doesn't make me lower the gun. The director being alone doesn't ease my uncertainty about this situation.

"You'll get your money back." The Director says.

The door creaks behind me before it closes. I'm looking left and right as I walk towards him. I'm waiting for an ambush. These are slimy fuckers, ones that I don't trust. "I don't want my money. I want Leonard."

The director keeps his hands raised. "Richard, he isn't here. He escaped."

I walk to him and press the barrel of the gun in between his eyes. "That's not possible. I've tried. There is no way out of this place. Do you think I'm a fucking moron?" I push the gun harder against his head. "Do you think I won't pull this fucking trigger?"

Panic shows on his old wrinkly face for the first time. "He had help. But I swear I knew nothing of it."

"Help from whom?" I ask.

"I don't know, Richard. Please take the gun away from my head."

His gaze is drawn to the gun that I keep pressed to his head. "You will find out who helped him and give me their names."

He's shaking his head. "I can't do that."

I pull the gun back before slamming it into his temple. His knees give way under the force, and he cries out on the ground. I keep the gun pointed at his head. Blood trickles down the side of his face as he looks up at me. "I'll find out."

I don't threaten him any further. Instead, I take one final sweep of the area before leaving through the front door.

I don't feel settled as I drive to the Lough Leigh mountains, where Jack and Shay want to meet. Once again, the fact I'm being dragged to a place that my father and his brothers have a stake in isn't lost on me. My father and his brothers bought a lot of land and property in the Kingscourt area in their youth.

I glance down at my phone that's resting in its portal and ring Davy. His phone rings out, and I curse him again for not answering. I need him to find out Leonard's whereabouts. I didn't fear for Claire. Leonard had no idea where I lived, and even if he somehow got that information, he wouldn't get past the front gates.

The road grows rocky, and I start to feel the bumps as I drive up toward the side of the mountain. Shay's green Range Rover is here, but I don't see Jack's black one, and no other vehicles are around. My BMW is low to the ground, and I curse each pothole in the so-called car park.

So far, I can't see anyone. I get out of my car and take off my suit jacket, throwing it on the passenger seat. I untuck my shirt, so it covers the gun in the waistband of my trousers, and lock the car. I walk up the side of the mountain, following the marked path. Small bushes are sporadically placed on either side of the barren landscape.

I can smell the smoke before Shay comes into view. He's sitting on the edge of a large rock that's embedded in the side of the mountain. How easy it would be to stand behind him and push him off the edge. I climb up to the rock and look over the drop. Yeah, the fall would kill you.

"I wonder how many bodies are down there." Shay muses.

It's like he knows my thoughts. Like he can see I want to push him over the side of the mountain. That is if he has betrayed me. I focus on him and not on the edge. "I don't see any."

He looks at me through a cloud of smoke and grins. "That's because our Da's buried them good and deep."

"Yeah, I've heard this area was their own personal dumping ground." My father and his brothers were no strangers to killing people and making them disappear forever. It is a gift I think all O' Reagan's possess. One day someone would find their mass graves. I'm sure my father and his brothers will be long gone by the time that happens.

"Did you know my granda had another son?" Shay asks and flicks the cigarette over the edge.

I glance back down the mountain, watching for Jack. He should be here by now. "No."

"Yeah. He had my da with your nan. When your nan died, he had another son."

I look at Shay. His father, Connor, is my father's half-brother. That's why my father hates Connor. He is less in my father's eyes and not just that. My grandmother had really played the field with both brothers. So add another family into the mix, and that shit is fit for some soap opera.

"His name was Bernard, and he's buried down there." Shay gets up and points over the drop.

He has my attention.

"Shane and some other guy killed him. Bernard would have been the leader of the RA today," Shay says.

"Shane killed your father's brother, who would have led the Republican Army?" I ask. Making sure we are on the same page.

Shay nods. "My da told me this. He was trying to explain how dangerous it was up here for us Northerners."

"I didn't know," I say honestly.

Shay nods. "No one knows about it. They buried the truth along with Bernard's body." Shay steps off the rock and joins me on safer ground. "The pub we met up in, Shane owns it. He bought it after he killed Bernard there."

The blow of his words, I hope, doesn't show on my face. "Why meet me there, then? You know that word will get back to Shane."

Shay nods again. "Exactly. I want Shane to know that Connor and Liam's sons are meeting."

I take a step toward Shay. "I don't."

"I don't care, Richard." He points over the edge again. "All I care about is taking down Lucian Sheahan, and your father, for killing my brother. And the way to do that is at the bottom of this mountain."

"You want us to dig up a fucking body that's been rotting away for what, thirty-odd years?"

Shay grins. "That's exactly what we do. Can you imagine the panic when the body of a RA leader comes to light?" Shay's eyes shine. He's almost giddy. "Can you imagine the fear in Shane's heart? Can you imagine the war that Lucian will unleash on the west?"

I hear each word Shay is saying, but I don't feel the giddiness he feels. Frankly, I think Bernard should be left in the ground. That secret should die here.

"I hate to poke holes in your future plans, but taking down Shane has never been part of this, and that's all it would achieve."

"Your da will kill Lucian before he allows him to kill Shane. It solves our problem with Lucian, and the RA will take care of your da."

I'm looking into a set of wild eyes, and for the first time, I wonder how unhinged Shay really is. Yet, he's right. My father always protects Shane, no matter the cost.

"So we dig up a body, call it in, and sit back?" I say to Shay.

He claps his hand like he's reached the end of the race or the joke. "Those cunts won't know what's hit them."

I'm grinning now because it's pretty perfect, and also, it tells me that Shay never betrayed me. This could really work.

I hear the crunch of the stones and turn as Jack appears around the corner. All my earlier excitement dwindles away. I want Jack beside us, so he isn't in the path of all this destruction. I just hope he will come over to the winning side.

CHAPTER TWENTY-SEVEN

O'REAGAN
AN CHLANN

CLAIRE

I woke up this morning, the mattress beside me cold. The fear that clutches my throat isn't because Richard is no longer in our bed. It isn't all the things that should stir fear in my heart. It isn't the idea that I was kidnapped; it isn't because I witnessed someone dying. Fear tightens its fingers around my throat because, for one tiny second, I thought I was back in my own bed. I thought I was back in my own apartment. I thought I was back in my old life.

I thought by Richard placing me in the glass box that he had placed me in a cage. He hadn't. He freed me from a cage that had no walls. My life had been filled with nothing but uncertainty and fear. For the first time in my life, I understand freedom.

I take a shower, my body still humming with last night's escapades. Richard is an unselfish lover, always wanting to please me first before himself. The ache between my legs is subtle, but it still throbs in the background. Turning off the water, I get out and wrap myself in a large white towel. Moving to the mirror, I wipe the steam away. I meet a pair of large blue eyes, blue eyes that are clear for the first time. When I think of Richard, I smile and quickly cut it off with a bite to my lips. I'm falling hard for him. Everything that is wrong about him is what makes him right for me. He's lethal, and falling for a man like him is dangerous. I look away from the mirror and finish brushing my teeth before getting dressed in a pair of cream linen trousers and a red blouse.

Brushing my hair out, I tidy the room before walking downstairs barefoot. I don't expect to see anyone in the kitchen apart from Mario, who greets me every morning with a warm smile. This morning there is a much nicer surprise waiting for me in the kitchen.

Richard sits at the breakfast bar. His phone in his hand, his brows drawn as he focuses on the device. A black suit jacket is strewn across the back of a second stool. He isn't aware of my presence, and I take a moment to appreciate him. The white shirt he wears is stretched across his wide frame.

I'm smiling again. All the sharp angles of his face are defined as he concentrates.

"A cup of tea?" Mario asks, breaking the spell.

Richard doesn't look up but lowers the phone to the counter, and his brows relax as he picks up his own cup of tea.

MAFIA GAMES

"Thank you, Mario." I smile at him before turning to Richard, who's watching me. The look in his dark gaze sends shivers down my spine. I want to ask what's bothering him.

"How did you sleep?" He asks.

My face blazes as I think of last night. I dip my head as I walk to the breakfast counter. Richard pulls out the stool beside him for me to sit on.

"I slept well," I answer as I slide in. The smell of his cologne circles me. My stomach tightens.

Mario places a cup of tea in front of me. "Thank you." I take a sip of the tea. "How did you sleep?" I ask Richard, without looking at him.

"Like a baby." His words are whispered, and when I glance at Richard, his eyes are a soft brown, he's smiling, and my core tightens.

"Good," I say as my heart hammers.

His smile dissolves into a grin. "Good." He repeats.

My heart pitter-patters, and the smile takes over not just my lips, but I feel it like a balm to my soul. My smile turns into laughter. "Good." I have no idea why I'm saying the word again, but when he continues to smile, I'd say 'good' on repeat all day every day just to keep that glorious smile on his face.

"I want to show you something." He gets up from the breakfast bar. Stretching around, he brushes his hard chest against my back. The warmth circles me as he picks up my cup of tea. The moment he steps away, I feel the loss of his body against mine.

I follow him out of the kitchen and down the hallway that leads to the swimming pool. I wouldn't object to a swim with him. I'm already picturing his tanned chest, strong, toned legs, and his experienced hands. His shoulders move up and down, the white material almost a sin. He should never cover up. My mind leaves the gutter as he takes a left. The disappointment is short-lived that we aren't going to the pool, as he pauses outside a room that I've never been in. In fact, only a few days ago, I tried to see into this room, but the door was locked.

He turns the handle, and he pushes the door open and stands back, allowing me to go in first. I step into a space that leaves my body light. The white room has empty frames covering three of the walls, the fourth wall is made of glass overlooking the garden. I step deeper into the room, my throat tightening as I take in everything, including the large easel that holds a blank sheet of paper. It's to the right of the room, facing the wall of glass.

Richard passes me, and I can't move. A workstation is filled with every shape and size of papers, brushes, and the more I look, I see every shade of paint in small tubes. The shaggy rug under my feet is the bluest I have ever seen; it complements the white-walled room.

"What is this?" My voice doesn't sound like my own. I know what I'm looking at. The most exquisite art room I could have ever imagined.

"This is for you." Richard's voice is different. I glance at him. He still holds my small cup of tea, that looks tiny in his huge hands.

I want to ask why?

He walks to all the empty frames. "You can fill all these. You might even draw me again."

My throat and eyes burn, and I turn away from him and face one of the walls filled with empty frames. I don't want him to see me cry. "That is a lot of frames." My voice wobbles. I blink, and tears fall, so I wipe them away quickly.

"You have a lot of time."

Time. "Do I?" *Or are my days numbered here?* I turn to Richard, who's standing in front of me.

"I don't want you to leave," he says.

A lump in my throat keeps my words down. I don't want to leave. My hand trembles as I wipe my lip like I can stop the shake that's started to take over my body. It rattles my soul, and this room is so much more than a kind gesture. This room is a future I'm craving.

Richard towers over me, waiting for me to say something, but I can't. All the words I should be saying aren't there. If I bring them to the surface, they will sound as hollow and untruthful as they feel. I should be saying I want to go home. *I don't.* I should be saying you're a monster. *He's not.*

He holds out the small cup of tea. I take it and try not to spill any. I spin away from him again and try to settle the conflict that tears through me by walking around the room.

"You did this for me?" I ask, stopping at the station that holds all the different colored paints. Every shade of every color fills the space. Hundreds of colors, all new, all sealed, all ready to be brought to life on a canvas.

"Yes." Movement outside has me looking at the wall of glass. Connor races around the garden; so fast it's hard to track him. I want to add, is he for me too? Is that why he kept Connor?

It's too much.

Hands caress my arms, and the blouse is no barrier for how his touch feels on me. "If you don't like it, you don't have to paint, Claire." His voice holds a hint of disappointment.

I tighten my fingers around the mug. They are itching to start painting. "I like it," I whisper.

Lowering the cup to the sideboard, I turn in his arms. "I've spent most of my life afraid." I can't hold his gaze as I speak. "Afraid of Leonard," I admit. "Afraid of my own shadow." I'm thinking about how I turned off every appliance before going to bed, afraid of fire. Or making sure I thought before I spoke, as I was afraid of offending someone. Afraid, afraid, afraid.

Be brave.

A laugh jolts my pain. "You took me from a cage." I look back up at Richard and blink. Tears spill. "I'm not afraid anymore." I don't think my words will mean much to him, but to me, not being afraid anymore frees my soul.

Richard's large hands encase my face, and I close my eyes against the warmth and security they provide. "Nothing will ever hurt you again."

I turn my face and press a kiss into his palm. "I don't want to leave," I admit.

Opening my eyes, I look into his face. He dips his head and presses a kiss to my lips that heals me a little bit more.

His kiss isn't enough. My hands fumble with the buttons of his shirt; I want to touch his flesh. His hands dig into my wet hair before he helps me with his shirt. He lifts me up, and I'm sitting on the edge of the sideboard. I have a second thought of telling him not to mess up all the paints that are perfectly lined. All words fail me as he pushes his rock-hard cock against me. My fingers skim tanned skin. His pecs move under my touch. I drag a nail across his nipple, and he hisses in pain. The kiss is broken, and his eyes drink me up with darkness.

"You want to play dirty?" he asks.

My core throbs. "With you? Yes."

His lips move to my neck, his tongue flicks out and wets the skin before his teeth drag across the sensitive flesh. I drag my nails heavier along his nipples as he presses down on my neck. Red marks are left along his chest. He stands back and unbuckles his trousers, and pushes them down along with his boxers to the ground. His cock springs free and the excitement of having him inside me has me opening the buttons of my shirt. I pause and take a peek at the large open window. Anyone could be watching us.

Richard steps closer and opens the button of my shirt. "Are you worried about someone watching?" He asks.

"No." The answer surprises me. The thoughts of someone watching us turns me on. My red blouse flutters to the ground, and I push Richard back so I can follow the blouse down to the floor. My knees press into the shaggy blue rug, and I look back up at Richard as I take his large cock in my hand. I'm still watching him as I run my tongue along the side of his shaft before taking his cock into my mouth. I gag as the head hits the back of my throat. Dragging my lips back up, I stroke his shaft before running my tongue along the head; his cock twitches in my mouth, and his hands land heavily on my head, pushing me deeper towards his cock. His balls are heavy as I take them in my fingers and squeeze them before dipping under and taking them one at a time in my mouth. The growl from his lips satisfies me, and I lick and suck his balls while stroking his cock. I lean out and look up at Richard. I'm off my feet in a second as he drags me up and pulls the string on my linen trousers open. His fingers flutter along my core, and he doesn't dip them in. I want him to, so badly. He lifts me up, and I wrap my legs around his waist, ready to accept his cock that he plunges inside me. He carries me to the nearest wall, and my back impacts with a frame that sways and crashes to the floor.

The frame shatters, the glass cracks, but we don't stop. Richard continues to plow himself into me. My nails drag across his shoulders, and when he hisses and uses his pain as a driving force behind his thrusts, I dig my nails deeper. He plows into me deeper. His mouth is hot on my neck, and I'm preparing myself for the pain. His tongue licks the sensitive skin, and the pain comes hard and fast. There is a moment where I want to end this as the agony is too much. My body temperature soars, and Richard's thrusts grow more frantic. Each thrust takes me back to the pleasure I had felt only seconds ago. I cling to him as his teeth break the skin on my neck. The warmth of my blood trickles, and he growls before his tongue darts back out. His mouth moves to mine, and I look into his black eyes before I suck his tongue that's coated in my blood.

"Fuck." His growl has him burying his head in my neck again, his tongue moving in fast circles around the cut. I dig my nails into his shoulders. My back slams repeatedly against the wall, and my cries grow louder as the pleasure and pain continue to build. His teeth graze the cut, and the burn takes me over the edge as my body spasms. He fills me with his seed and the room with his ecstasy, and we both come down together.

CHAPTER TWENTY-EIGHT

O'REAGAN
AN CHLANN

RICHARD

I leave Claire to do some painting. She's happy and carefree as I take one final look at her from the door. She said she'd stay here. If she had said no, I wouldn't have let her go, but I'm glad she made the choice herself.

My phone vibrates again, and I pull the door nearly closed as I open the message from Dana. She wants to meet me in Dun Na Ri park. Her messages today are worrying, and I can't ignore them any longer.

I'm on my way.

It's been some time since I spoke properly to my sister. Since I have been home, I haven't seen her, and now over the last few days, she keeps texting, saying she needs to talk. On top of that, Jack is quiet after our meeting with Shay. I'm not sure what he made of everything Shay and I had to say. My father wasn't on my doorstep, so that told me that Jack was at least listening to what we had to say. We had discussed other bodies that might be buried along with Bernard's. We have no idea whose, but Connor has given Shay another location where they dumped bodies; we could only hope most of them were in the other location and not at the foot of the mountain. More bodies turning up is a risk we were willing to take.

I pull up at Dun Na Ri park, where Dana wants to meet. I hate leaving Claire in the house, but I remind myself that she is content painting. Her neck looks a bit battered, but I like to think I left my mark on her.

I lock my car and make my way into the park. Not many vehicles are around. I walk to the picnic area; I don't see Dana, so I continue until I reach the open lawns. My childhood wants my attention. This place holds too many memories. I see Dana, she's speed walking across the lawn toward me.

My stomach tightens as she drags large sunglasses off her face. She looks so much like mother; it's frightening. Her eyes are red and puffy, and she keeps looking around us. She's making me jumpy.

"What's wrong?" I ask the moment she reaches me.

She shakes her head. "Nothing. Why?"

Looking for the threat that Dana is making me believe is out here, I glance around, but it's just trees and wildlife. I relax. "Why are you acting all shifty?"

I take her arm, and she jumps slightly before forcing a smile. "I'm not. You are. Why are you looking around?"

Clearly, there is something wrong. I lower my head, so my sister is looking at me. "What's wrong?" I keep my voice low but force a warning into my tone.

Her lip wobbles, and she bites it. "I don't know what to do." Her tears are unexpected, and she's getting loud, like a hysterical woman.

I don't want anyone to hear her. This place is a spot for joggers. I pull her into my arms. "Okay. Calm down."

When she gathers herself a bit more, she leaves my arms and wraps her hands around her waist.

"When was the last time you slept?" I ask. Dark circles are painted under her eyes. The longer I'm standing here, the more worry worms its way through my system.

"I don't know." She answers honestly and starts scratching her arm.

I've never seen my sister like this. She is always so happy, and emotions aren't something she displays much, especially not to me.

I have no idea why she has called me here. Jack is the brother who fixes problems, not me. That alone is scaring the shit out of me.

"Did someone hurt you?" I ask.

She shakes her head. Her blue eyes fill with a look of pure devastation, and her shoulders drop forward as if the weight of the world is on her shoulders. "A friend of mine killed someone." Her words give me relief, and I'm about to smile, but Dana bursts into tears.

I have to console her again and pull her into my arms. "It's okay."

"No, it's not." Warmth spreads across my shirt from her tears.

"It wasn't just her." Dana's tears stop, and something enters her voice.

I have to lean out so I can see my sister. "Just tell me what happened. I swear we will fix it."

She's shaking her head, and I can only imagine how this must seem to her. She must think it's the end of the world. It's at moments like these that I wish my sister knew what we did. So she wouldn't worry or panic. "It will be okay," I repeat.

She's nodding, but I can see in her eyes that she doesn't believe me. "My friend Maeve...." Dana swallows.

"Jack's Maeve?" I question. Trepidation triples as Dana continues to stare up into my eyes.

"She killed Cian."

Fuck.

"Let's talk in my car." I try to steer Dana in the direction of my car, but she yanks her arm out of mine.

"Jack knows." Her voice grows louder.

I'm glancing around the area. "We can talk about it in my car," I repeat and try not to growl at her.

"Shay shot him in the head." Her words are getting hysterical.

I grip her arm and shake her. "Calm down."

She blinks rapidly as tears pour from her eyes. "They killed a person. They killed our cousin." She hiccups on a sob, and this time when I lead her to my car, she doesn't resist.

I help her into the passenger side and walk around to the driver's side. I quickly fire a text to Shay and Jack to get here ASAP. I climb in, but the sounds of her sobs make me want to get back out.

"You're okay." I pat her leg.

"They killed someone. Maeve said that Cian was trying to hurt her. It was an accident; she pushed him over the railing at Jack's house."

"Did you tell anyone?"

My question has her tears stopping. "What?"

"Did you tell anyone?" I repeat and turn in my seat, so I'm facing her.

"You're not shocked? You already knew." She recoils away from me.

"Dana, focus. Did you tell anyone?"

She shakes her head, but I know she's still looking at me like she doesn't know me. *She doesn't.*

"What about a friend or Mother or Father?"

"No." Fear shakes her words.

"Anyone. A fucking dog?" I need to know that this went no further.

"I don't have a fucking dog!" She screams. "What is this? They killed someone, Richard." Her hysteria tears through her short-lived composure. She covers her face with her hands and sobs. "I can't do anything. Poor Una and Shane." She looks at me through splayed fingers. "Poor Cian. His neck..." Dana touches her neck. "The fall broke his neck."

Jack had a lot of fucking explaining to do, letting his woman mouth off like this, especially to Dana.

I nod. "It's terrible."

My words cut off her sobs again, and she looks at me like I'm a stranger. "Did you know?"

There is no point in lying. "Yes."

She quickly looks away and covers her mouth before looking back at me. Any color that had been in her cheeks moments ago is gone. "We have to go to the Gardaí." She's staring out the window shield.

"If you were going to go to the Gardaí, you'd have already gone," I state the obvious.

Dana starts to cry. "You remember coming here when we were kids?"

I nod and keep an eye out for Jack and Shay. We had to contain this. I just wasn't sure how.

"Jack was always so cruel. Hurting younger kids, taking their stuff."

Father had made Jack do that to them. It was part of his training. I don't share that knowledge with Dana, but it seems like that is really the only way forward. She needs to know who we are.

"You always seemed so vacant. Just watching us."

"It's going to be okay." I reassure her.

"No, it's not." She sobs for a while. She continues to reminisce about how cruel Jack always was. Like he is some kind of monster. When she finds out what we all do, she will see each of us for what we really are.

"Maeve, she was always so kind." Dana shakes her head in bewilderment.

Jack's Range Rover pulls into the car park. Shay sits in the front.

Dana's words fall silent. "Why are they here?" Her eyes widen as she stares at me. "You told them?"

I reach across, but Dana swipes my hand away. She's frozen in the front seat, and the look of betrayal on her face turns to anger. Her hand connects with my face, and she goes into a frenzy, hitting me. I cover my face as she lashes out. The car door opens.

"Dana." Jack grips her, and I'm about to warn him not to when she drags her nails down his face. She must spot Shay as she kicks out at the door and tries to slip from the car.

"Calm down." I grab her and restrain her arms, dragging her back towards me.

"Fuck sake." Jack's holding his face as he turns away from my car.

Shay lights up a cigarette and bends over to look into the car. "You okay, love?" he asks Dana.

Dana grows still in my arms. Jack turns, still holding his cheek that bleeds. "What the fuck, Dana?"

To save us all the aggro, I explain what's happening. "Dana knows that Maeve killed Cian, and you both played your part."

It's funny to watch everyone's features transform. For Shay, it was amusement, and now I see the glint in his eyes, the want to silence the threat. Jack has gone from angry to a look of oh-shit.

"Yeah. You need to put a muzzle on your woman."

Jack flashes me a warning. "Don't you fucking dare." He tightens his hands into fists.

Shay squats down and takes a drag of his cigarette. "What did she tell you?"

I loosen my hold on Dana, and when she doesn't try to hurt me, I release her. She sits back up in her seat. "What you did. You shot him." Tears trickle down Dana's face.

"Where is Maeve?" I ask Jack.

He clenches his jaw. "Don't go fucking near her."

"Who else has she told?" I ask.

"Only me," Dana whispers.

"I'm sorry, but I'm not exactly believing that."

I don't like how Shay is staring at Dana like she's a complication that we can just get rid of.

"Jack, why?" Dana sounds devastated.

Jack really looks at Dana now. "I'm sorry. He was going to hurt her. It was an accident."

As sweet as this is, explaining what happened didn't solve our problem. "Dana needs to know."

Jack straightens. "What, you think this isn't enough for her?"

"Know what?" Dana sounds terrified.

"She's a risk now, Jack. Are you going to spend the rest of your life looking over your shoulder?"

"I won't tell anyone," Dana mumbles quickly.

We all ignore her.

"Telling her will gain nothing," Jack says.

I shake my head. "Keeping her in the dark has gained us nothing. If we want to move forward, we need to tell her."

"Tell me what?" Dana asks again.

"We are Kings of the Irish Mafia." Shay grins as he tells her.

Jack looks from me to Shay. "You have both lost your minds."

I grip the steering wheel as I stare at Jack. "No. It's only a matter of time before she tells someone. What will Shane do? He will rip your fucking heart out. What do you think he'll do to Maeve?"

"Mafia?" Dana mumbles.

"Yeah, love." Shay confirms.

"We need time." I'm glaring at Jack. He has to know that if we stick to our plan of digging up Bernard's body, Shane will no longer be in the picture. So it won't matter. In the meantime, we need to keep Dana quiet.

"You're Mafia?" Dana asks me, facing me, demanding my attention.

"Father is the head of the Irish Mafia." I confirm.

Dana scratches her arm and glances from Jack to Shay and back to me. "Mafia. Like the Godfather?" Her brows drag down, and I see it; she's ready to have another breakdown.

"She needs to be kept safe while we deal with all our other problems." I address Jack.

"Safe or quiet?" Jack fires back like I'm being unfucking reasonable.

"If your woman had fucking sense." I start.

Jack's marching to my door, and I don't give a fuck.

"Boys, this won't help." Shay stands up.

Jack opens my door. "One more word about Maeve." He threatens.

I can't help myself. "She's a fucking liability."

His punch has some serious force behind it. My head whips back, and blood pools in my mouth.

Dana's screams tear through my anger, and I turn to her.

"Get away from him." She's screaming at Jack, who stumbles back. "Don't you hurt him!" She's half-covering me like she could possibly protect me.

Jack kicks the side of my car. I see it in his eyes. If she knew the things I had done, she would be scrambling out of the car.

"Calm down," I tell Dana for what seems like the millionth time.

"Don't touch him." Her screams have retired themselves to shouts.

"It's okay, Dana." I pat her arm this time, and she looks at my hand before sitting back up. She's in shock. Her eyes are wild, and she doesn't look like my sister.

"I know someone who might be able to help us with this." Shay speaks up, and we all focus on him.

Jack moves away from my car.

"You'll pay for the damage." I call after Jack as I rub my aching jaw.

"Who?" I ask Shay. "Remember, this is my sister."

"She's my cousin." Shay fires back.

"Yeah, just like Cian was." I sneer.

Dana starts to look frazzled again, and I don't want her starting. "Who?" I ask seriously.

"Cillian O'Hara."

"Have you fucking lost your mind?" Jack speaks up.

"I agree with Jack." I wouldn't let Cillian O'Hara near my baby sister.

"Who's Cillian? And what's he going to do to me?"

Dana's starting to panic. "He'll take care of you, love." Shay's words are meant to relax Dana; only they send her into a frenzy.

"Kill me." She's looking at me with wild eyes.

"He's kind of like a bodyguard." I try to explain Cillian's role. He was more than that, but he had stepped away from the Republican Army at a young age. Some shit about his sister going missing had driven him away. He's a bit older than Jack and me, but his skills are next to none.

"No one will ever find you." Shay continues, and he isn't helping.

"She's not going to Cillian," Jack protests.

"We need to keep her quiet, Jack," I growl.

"I'm not going anywhere," Dana speaks up like she has a choice. When she looks at me, her eyes narrow with anger. "I came to you for help." She shakes her head.

"You have a better idea, Jack?" I ask.

He looks horrified as he rises. "No. I don't."

Dana starts to cry. "Please don't do this. I don't want to go away."

Shay crunches the cigarette under his boot as he waits for an answer. Who else would I trust with my baby sister? There is no one, and she needs to keep quiet. I look at Dana as fresh tears pour down her face.

"Please, Richard. I won't tell anyone." Her words ring true to me. But tomorrow, when she's feeling better, or in a week's time when she's at a party and had too much to drink, her moral compass will switch on. I can't risk that happening.

I glance at Shay and nod my head for him to make the call.

CHAPTER TWENTY-NINE

O'REAGAN
AN CHLANN

CLAIRE

The brush glides across the canvas. I'm almost finished when Mario arrives with sandwiches and some tea on a large silver tray.

"I'm sure you're hungry." He always carries a smile with his words. I like Mario.

"Starving," I say as he sets the tray down on the sideboard. I stand back and take in the picture I've been painting the last few hours. My mother's blue eyes stare back at me. Her blonde hair is swept over her shoulder.

"She's beautiful." Mario compliments the painting from behind me.

"She was." I have the urge to touch her face. My fingers tighten around the paintbrush. Some days my mother would pass the day away in the kitchen baking bread and cakes for us. The classical music would float out the window, accompanied by the smell of warm bread. Stepping in the back door, I often thought how beautiful she was, with her flushed cheeks, messy appearance and her smile. She was happy. We were happy.

"Did she pass away?" Mario asks.

I turn away from the agony I'm feeling while looking at the picture and face Mario, tucking all my emotions neatly away in their box. "Three years ago."

"I'm sorry for your loss." His head dips as he gives me his condolences. The look in Mario's eyes I've seen before, he's waiting for the explanations of how she died or how her death made me feel.

"Thank you." I return my attention to the painting, ending our conversation. Mario leaves me. I hold the brush to her cheek and brush a little more pink. She looks happy, she almost looks real. I hate it.

My fingers itch to remove the canvas, but my thoughts won't go away if I do. It's like I'll be stuck in reverse if I don't keep pushing forward. So, I select a smaller and finer paint brush and dip the bristles into a dark gray, and do something that isn't true to her memory. I give my mother a pair of earrings. She never wore them. I can't recall one time I saw a pair in her ears. My soul lifts as I paint, and I get lost in the motions of the brush. My thoughts cease, and all there is is the color that bleeds across the pages as I give her a red cardigan instead of the beige one she truly loved and wore daily. I hadn't planned to paint my mother, yet here she is coming to life on the page, only now with my small changes I don't really recognize her.

The lies we tell ourselves. It's her eyes. Nothing could ever take away from her eyes. I resist touching her again. It's only paper, I remind myself as I step away. Her eyes follow me, and I feel the full weight of them. Her gaze is too heavy on me, so I put the paint brush down and turn my back on my mother.

The tea is ready to be poured, and I make myself a cup and bring it with me to the window to see if Connor is close to the garage where his food dish often is. I glance out the large window, but I don't see him. He's been racing around the backyard most of the morning, and seeing him might ease my nerves, but I don't see him as I walk the full length of the window.

There are moments in life, and they can be tiny, so very tiny. Some are unforgiving that they bleed into our memories, painting one moment red.

Red moments often break us, like I consider the moment when my parents died one. But really, the red moments are in the before. It was in the strike of Leonard's match that is the tiny, unforgiving moment.

As I continue to scan the garden for Connor, a tiny moment happens again. Only this time, it's the creak of the door. I turn, and before I even see him, I know something isn't right. That everything is wrong.

The cup falls from my fingertips. It makes no sound as it shatters across the floor. The roar of my blood is all I hear. Nothing else as Leonard steps into the room. Liquid scorches my leg, and the sounds come crashing back. My stomach lurches as he looks around the room.

He can't really be here. He passes the picture of Mother, and his face hardens before he picks it up.

It's still wet. She's still flushed. He is hurting her all over again. "Please don't." I find my voice.

He turns to me, and with nothing but death in his eyes, he tears it in two.

"Leonard." I plead as the image floats to the floor. I'm not sure what I'm pleading for, the painting or my life.

"So this is where you have been hiding." He takes a step closer to me.

I've never felt so small as I shake my head. "Please," I beg.

His fingers dig into my face as he reaches for me. "Please what, Claire? My sister."

My face aches from the tightness of his hands.

"You're a whore." He shoves me back, and I stumble toward the glass window.

His words burn not just my cheeks but my soul. He looks around the room. "So this is what it costs to sleep with my sister."

"Stop it!" I bark.

Leonard's eyes swing toward me. His gaze makes me shiver, and his face turns stoic as his gaze lands on my neck. "He's been hurting you."

I shiver as he returns to me and yanks my neck to the side painfully. The bite mark from Richard is still very much visible. I try to cover it. "It's nothing."

My fingers are pried away. "What the fuck. The sick mother fucker." He releases my neck.

How did you find me? What are you doing here? How did you get out of the asylum? They are all the questions that race through my mind. Yet, I say nothing, only watch him as he continues to move around the room. His fingers run along the sideboard, and he knocks over my paint brushes. Paper flutters to the floor and is accompanied by pots of paint. His destruction makes no sense.

"You don't seem happy to see me," he says. He picks up a tube of red paint and opens it. As he walks to me, he squeezes the bottle onto the window and draws a long red line.

He stops when he reaches me. "What was the name of our fish?"

The question throws me off. Leonard holds up the tube of paint and squirts the remainder down the front of my red blouse. A blob falls off my top and lands on the floor. Everything in me quivers. "Leonard." Fear keeps the volume of my voice low.

"Answer me!" His roar makes me jump.

"Oscar." I clutch my blouse like I might be able to keep myself standing.

"Oscar." Leonard laughs and turns away from me.

My body sags, and as I blink, tears fall. I need to get away from him.

"How many minutes?"

The air halts in my lungs as he picks up a handful of paint brushes off the floor. They are only paintbrushes, but they seem deadly in his hands. "How many minutes did Oscar live?"

"Fifty-one minutes." It was a stupid goldfish. They don't have long life spans, anyway. But Leonard had me sit and watch for fifty-one minutes. Oscar had flapped, and his small mouth had opened and closed for air. At moments I had thought he was dead, but the small fish would gasp again. Leonard had sat with me, enjoying each twisted second. I was glad when the fish finally died.

Leonard waggles his fingers at me. My focus still snagged on the paintbrushes. "Stupid fucking creatures. They really have no purpose."

At least they aren't cruel. They had more purpose than Leonard will ever have. I curl in on myself as he hurls a paintbrush at me. The impact I feel, but the paintbrush will do nothing more than leave a bruise. I turn to the side as he continues to throw them at me.

"You left me," he finally says.

He has no more brushes to throw because they are all at my feet.

"You left me in there to rot." He's in my face; his fingers squeeze my cheek. "You're a sorry excuse for a sister." He pushes me, and my head collides with the wall behind me.

"I'm sorry."

"Why are you lying?" His hand rams into my shoulder, sending me back into the wall again. "I hate a fucking liar."

"I'm not lying. I was kidnapped."

Leonard's laugh is maniacal. "You don't look like you have it too bad." Leonard becomes transfixed by the red paint on the window. He runs his fingers through it before returning to me. He presses his fingers across my cheek; the feel of the paint on my face has me turning away from him.

"Did he touch you?"

The question has bile crawling up my throat. There is no right answer to this. Leonard has never touched me, but it's in his eyes a sickness that I try to run from.

His hand tightens on my wrist, and he slams me back against the wall. His fingers squeeze on my arm. The wound along my wrist is healed, but he must feel the slightly raised skin on my wrists as he yanks my sleeve up.

Surprise isn't something I've ever seen in Leonard's eyes before. "You did this?"

I yank my arm back, feeling a bit braver. "Yes."

"What about me?" Real sorrow fills his eyes.

He's sick. Twisted.

"What about you?" I fire back. "You burnt our parents alive." My heart races in my chest. I said it. I finally said what he did.

"You are still yapping on about that."

My throat burns, but so does the blood in my veins at the injustice of his words. "That? You murdered our parents!"

He shrugs. "I was sick of them."

He's truly twisted. He needs help.

"I can't believe you were going to leave me here alone." He waves his free hand around the room before his fingers run along the scar. There is nothing caring about his touch, and I try to pull my arm back with no success.

His hand tightens, and he takes a knife out of his pocket.

"Leonard." I plead and start to pull out of his hold.

"We could go together."

I'm shaking my head, pleading with my eyes and words. "I don't want to go. I'm happy here." I blink, and more tears spill.

"You don't look happy to me." Leonard tilts his head.

There is nothing, nothing in his eyes, nothing expressed on his face. All I sense is a burn, like the heat of the fire the day my parents died. Warm liquid splashes on my barefoot, and I blink, my brain refusing to register what's happening. Leonard releases my arm, and the pain increases. I know I'm bleeding. There's so much blood. The room tilts, and I slide down the wall.

"No." I swallow the darkness and grip my arm.

Leonard meets me on the floor and pushes the hair out of my face. "Shhh. It will be okay."

I'm looking into blue eyes that are not like mine or my mother's. They are too cruel, too harsh, too menacing to be anything like my mother.

"I hate you." I manage to say as I tighten my hand on my arm. "You disgust me."

His lips curl back, and he's shaking his head. "You're confused. Don't say those things." He's rubbing my hair.

"You're disgusting." I sob.

He drags me to his chest while stroking my hair. "Stop." He keeps repeating. The air grows too thin, and I reach for his hand that holds the knife. He's too caught up in comforting me to even consider me getting the knife. I pull it from his loose fingers, and surprise has him jumping back.

I roar, the adrenaline pumping fast around my body as I lash out, and the sinking feeling churns my stomach as the knife cuts through flesh and embeds itself into his side.

Shock widens his eyes. I barrel past him and hold my arm as I run from the room.

"Help me!" Each doorway I pass is empty. I blink as the world tilts again, and I hit the ground hard. Where is everyone? "Mario!" I scream and get back up. Looking over my shoulder, Leonard has exited the art room. He pulls the knife out of his side. I'm scrambling off the ground. If I don't get up, I'll die. I half run, half hobble until I reach the kitchen. The floor is slick with blood. My bare feet can't find traction in the pool of blood and they are ripped out from under me. I hit the tiled floor hard. The air leaves my lungs. I'm expecting to see Mario or a security man dead on the floor, but it's neither. It's Connor. My dog is still, on his side; he's unmoving.

Leonard appears over me, but no air enters my lungs. I'm staring at Connor's still form, searching for a flicker of life that I don't see. A foot lands on my chest, and my hands automatically grip Leonard's boot. I didn't want to die like this.

Air slowly filters in, my chest protests in pain, and I sputter as I look up at my brother.

I want to beg him not to do this, but words fail me as air becomes my number one priority. Oxygen slowly starts to trickle in, and I manage to squeeze out a word. "Please."

His foot leaves my chest as he grips his side. He's looking at his hands, which are coated in blood, before his gaze swings back to me. His blue eyes build with a storm, and his foot rises. I could close my eyes, but I don't. His foot doesn't slam into my face like I'm expecting. It hovers above me.

"Killing her isn't part of the plan yet."

Leonard's foot touches the floor. My scalp burns as he stands on my hair. I know that voice. I'm rolling my head, trying to see behind me. The bald man, Davy, steps into the kitchen. That's how Leonard got into Richard's home. That's why no other security is around.

Davy's gaze skims me as he takes a step towards Connor.

"What the fuck did you do to the dog?" Davy's more outraged about the dog than me, but I'm trying to get up. Leonard's heavy boot lands on my chest again, stopping me from rising. The room spins. I've lost too much blood. The pool under me is a mix of mine and Connor's. I tilt my head, so I can see Davy, who is kneeling next to Connor.

"Is he alive?" I ask, closing my eyes to fight off the wave of dizziness.

I open my eyes when he doesn't answer. He's no longer beside Connor but standing next to Leonard. "Killing the fucking dog wasn't part of the plan."

Leonard removes his foot from my chest, and I drag in more air.

"What are you going to do?" Leonard sneers and steps up to Davy.

Connor is dead. My heart cracks, and the loss feels physical. They continue to argue about the plan, and Leonard pushes Davy, sending him sprawling onto the floor. I turn on my belly, and the hallway appears before me. I drag my body. The pain in my arm is nearly mind-numbing, but I need to get out of here. Davy has taken Leonard to the ground, and as they fight, I manage to get to the door frame and use it to pull myself up. My arm is still bleeding, and the weakness in my body scares me. I try to push the fear aside and keep moving. The walls keep moving, they keep shifting, and each time they smack into me, I bite my lip, so I don't cry out in pain. The front door is growing closer with each tiny step, and I force my body to move faster. The wall hits me harder each time, but I know staying upright is all that matters now. If I fall again, I don't think I'll ever get back up. I glance over my shoulder to see Leonard and Davy still in the thick of their fistfight. Neither of them has noticed I'm missing.

I face forward, my legs still, and whatever was keeping me up no longer exists as hope and freedom disappear, and in its place stands Liam.

Richard's Father.

The noise of the altercation behind me ceases, and footfalls sound behind me, but I don't look away from Liam.

"It's unfortunate it has to end this way, Claire." His monotone terrifies me. "Pick her up."

Hands touch my arms. Davy and Leonard drag me to my feet.

"You nearly cost me my son." Liam takes a step towards me. "Don't worry, Claire. This will be all over soon."

His smile shakes me to my core. It's the smile of death.

A scream pours from my lips as fingers dig into my arm, freeing more warm liquid, and the world turns red with my blood and terror.

CHAPTER THIRTY

O'REAGAN
AN CHLANN

RICHARD

Jack hasn't spoken since we left our sister in Shay's hands. He's staring out the window of my car as I drive him home. We gave Jack's Range Rover to Shay to take Dana straight to Cillian, who agreed to keep her safe. One of the conditions was that Shay would follow Cillian's directions, no questions asked. It's terrifying to put my sister in someone else's hands, but until this whole mess with Lucian Sheahan and my father is resolved, there is no safe place for Dana.

When the shit hits the fan, everyone we love will become a pawn, so the fewer pawns lying around, the fewer people we risk losing. It brings my mind back to Claire. She isn't safe from this either. My house is like a fortress, but if my father gets wind of our plans, an army won't hold him back.

I take another look at Jack. His jaw is clenched as he stares out the window. "You've been quiet lately." I want to say you have been quiet since the meeting at the Loch Leigh Mountains.

"Have I?" Jack sits up, and something is really bothering him, but I zero in on Maeve. She is a problem.

There is so much I want to say. Each time I open my mouth to speak, I close it. My jaw still aches from Jack's left hook, and if I speak my mind, I'm sure he'll hit me again. So, I go to softer ground.

"How is Maeve?" I ask.

"Don't start with me, Richard." Jack bites.

So the topic of Maeve in any capacity will cause a problem. I bite the bullet. "I know you don't want to hear it, but we have to discuss the possibility that she has told someone else."

"She hasn't." Jack barely contains himself.

"Did you know she told Dana?" I ask.

He glares at me. "Of course not."

"So, how can you be so sure she hasn't told someone else?"

"She wouldn't." Jack grinds out.

Once again, I want to ask how he can be so sure. This time, I do stay quiet. It's his neck, and Shay's on the line. He has got to know that. Maeve has dragged our sister into this mess.

"She's been struggling with Cian's death." Jack looks at me. "I can't have anyone hurt her."

I'm ready to protest and say I wouldn't, but my sister would take priority if it came down to Dana and Maeve.

"You wouldn't understand. You don't care for anyone." Jack pipes up.

We reach his house, and I pull up at the gates. "I actually have someone at home."

Jack quirks an eyebrow. "Really?" Jack doesn't believe me.

"Yes, right now, she's painting a picture of me." That's what I like to think anyway.

Jack opens the door. "Why can't you take anything seriously?"

"I am."

Jack gets out but holds the door open. "Do you really trust Shay?"

Did I?

"I trust him just as much as I trust you," I admit.

"That's fucking brilliant." Jack sneers. He slams the door and storms off.

So much for telling the truth. I drive home, wondering if Claire has drawn a picture of me like I had asked. The memory of what we did in the art room has me driving faster. I don't live too far from Jack's and pull up to the gates that open. I hit the remote as I roll up the driveway. The garage door rises, and when I reach the entrance, I drive in and turn off the engine.

I remove the gun from my waistband and put it in the glove compartment before getting out of the car. The garage doors close down, and the light slips away. My phone vibrates in my pocket, and I pull the device out. My father's name flashes across the screen. I hit the mute button and enter the kitchen and place the phone on the counter.

My brain registers the blood, the overturned furniture, the dead dog. I reach for my gun in the waistband of my trousers. Only I remember my gun is in the glove compartment of my car. I'm listening while I slide the drawer open beside me and take out a sharp steak knife. Entering the hall, my gaze zeroes in on the trail of blood marks on the wall. They lead me in the opposite direction of the art room. I try not to allow my mind to process that part; the art room was the last place that Claire was. I stop at a hall table and reach under it. The gun holder is empty. The revolver has been removed.

I keep moving, following the trail of blood that stops at the door to the basement. Before entering, I open the closet to the left and reach in for a gun that's always stashed under a stack of towels. Once again, my hands come up empty. There is only one person who knows where all the weapons are stashed in the house.

Davy.

Betrayal is a funny thing. After being betrayed by the people you trust the most, you would think that it would make the betrayal less painful, but it doesn't. Each step I take down the stairs has my stomach sinking further. There is blood on every step. The basement is lit up as I clear the last step. I stop at the glass box. The door is open, blood trails the whole way to the bed where Claire lies under the duvet. She isn't moving, and that alone has me racing to her. Forgetting everything else, I stuff the knife into my pocket as I drag the blanket aside. Blood has soaked into the duvet, and as I grip the blanket, I pull it back. I'm spinning away from the pillows that have been laid out to appear like a body when the door to the box slams shut.

"Open the door." I march towards my father. "Where is Claire?" I ask the question that has the fear of God in me. "What did you do to her?"

My father doesn't flinch as I slam both fists into the glass wall. I expect the glass to tremble under my wrath, but the glass doesn't budge, a testament to the wall's stability.

"This is quite impressive, I must admit." My father waves his hand toward the box. "Genius." He moves along the perimeter.

I match him step for step. "Where is she?"

"Davy told me of the purpose behind this box. To torture your enemy by taking away someone they loved. I'm happy to hear some of my lessons stuck. I really was starting to question if you ever listened to me at all."

My fists collide with the glass again, and my father stops walking. We are face to face. "Where is she?"

"Claire is upstairs," he says.

"Is she alive?"

"That clearly depends on you." My father doesn't smile or give an evil laugh. He's the same man who stood at my bedroom door and said goodnight, or the one who placed a gun in my hand for the first time. He's the man who wears only one face. He's Liam O' Reagan, my father. The head of the Irish Mafia. He didn't get there by being kind. He didn't place me here for fun. Everything he did and said had a purpose.

"What do you want?" I ask the question he really wants me to ask.

"You are going to tell me what you and Shay are up to. I hear you have been meeting behind my back."

"I'm trying to convince him to return as a King. We need him," I say.

"We never need people, Richard. Jack, you and me. We are enough."

I step away from the wall, my gaze darts to the blood-soaked bed. "Is she dead? Is that her blood?" Words pump out of me, and I see the disappointment in my father's eyes that I can't keep my emotions under control. My panic is unraveling quicker than I expected, but each glance at the blood-soaked blankets makes my stomach curl in on itself.

"Forget about her for a moment." My father starts.

My fists slam into the glass. "No!"

"I will leave you down here to rot. Three years in your own cage seems like a fitting sentence for lying to me." My father's threat is real.

I built this cage. I know there is no way out. I try to push down my fear for Claire and focus on getting out of here.

"That's better." My father says as I reel in my anger. "Final time. What are you and Shay up to? Davy informed me of your secret meetings."

I push Davy's betrayal aside. I'll have my revenge.

"Shay knows you bought the uncharted ground up the North. He knows you are behind his brother's death. He wants revenge. He wants your head."

My father doesn't look surprised. "Yet, my head is still on my shoulders. Are you telling me that it is because of you?"

"No. It's because he isn't stupid. I want to be a King; I want to rule the Irish Mafia. I never betrayed our purpose. I only tried to convince Shay to return as a King."

My father glares at me, and when he nods his head, something close to hope of getting out of the box blossoms in my chest.

"Shay is very much like Connor. They bury the hatchet in your back and not the ground."

My father starts to move around the perimeter, and I move with him.

"I always expected Shay's betrayal. Not yours, Richard." My father stops walking. "Jack's loyalty, on the other hand, that honestly was completely unexpected."

My stomach sours at his words.

I see the glee in my father's eyes.

What have you done, Jack?

"You had your chance to tell me, Richard. To tell me how you and Shay tried to convince Jack to dig up Bernard's body. At first, I have to say, I was very impressed with your thinking."

Everything I had worked for crumbles around me—Jack, Davy, and now my father. The betrayal and disloyalty will never stop with our family.

"If it's any consolation, Jack was conflicted when he confessed to me what you have been up to. He also seemed very concerned about your mental state."

"It's no consolation," I growl. "What do you want?" he isn't telling me all this for nothing.

My father's hand hits the glass. His anger is unexpected. I'm not able to hide my reaction from him. I flinch.

"I want a son who won't plot my death. I want a leader we can follow. All I get is you, a disappointment. You and Shay plotting my death is your demise and his."

My father turns away, but I see the look in his eyes. He's torn. He's never torn. I still have time to convince him to release me and let Claire live.

"I never plotted your death," I admit. "I never would have let you die."

"You will say anything to get out of that box, but it's too late, Richard." My father looks me dead in the eye.

"You will die in this box, your own creation. Right now, Shay is driving, and I have a hit on him. He won't be alive much longer."

Each word has the blood draining from me. I'm shaking my head.

"You left me no choice." My father tries to defend his actions.

"Shay isn't alone."

My father starts to walk away, ignoring my words. Leaving me here to die. "Dana is with Shay." I roar.

My father stops and glances at me.

"Dana is with Shay, you take that kill shot, and you're risking Dana, too."

My father isn't convinced, but he hasn't left. He takes a phone out of his pocket and makes a call.

My heart beats too fast as I wait.

"You have your eyes on the target?" My father's words aren't quick enough for me. "Is there anyone else in the vehicle?"

My father walks back to me and holds the phone away from his ear. "Where is he taking my daughter?"

I don't answer. "Abort." My father speaks into the phone. "You heard me. Do not take that shot."

"Where is he taking my daughter?" My father asks again.

"I want to see Claire."

My father shakes his head. "This is not the time for bargaining. Your sister is at risk."

I nod my head in agreement. "She is. She's in a lot of trouble, and I can't imagine how Mother will feel."

My father grinds his teeth, and I'm surprised when he makes another call. "Bring her down."

He stuffs the phone back into his pocket. "When you see Claire, then you tell me where he's taking Dana."

Footsteps on the stairs have me wanting to race to the door, but I don't move. Davy is the first to enter, and he has the audacity to meet my eyes. I can't wait to kill him.

When Davy steps to the side, it's not Claire I'm looking at, but Leonard, and in his arms is Claire. She isn't alert, her head is bent back, and she's pale, her complexion frightening.

"She needs a doctor," I speak in a low voice, my body ready to snap.

"You have seen her. Now, where is Shay taking your sister?"

I tighten my fists. "Is she dead?" I need to know. Claire doesn't look alive.

Leonard rattles her, her head snaps back and forth, but she stirs. He grins at me. The longer I stare at him, I notice he's not looking too healthy himself.

"I want to see for myself," I say.

"I suppose you want us to let you out." My father sneers with little to no patience.

"Bring her in here to me."

My father doesn't answer.

"What difference does it make? You said I'm going to die here. I want her with me," I say.

"She's not going in there," Leonard speaks up.

"I'll tell you where Dana is going," I speak to my father.

My father nods at Davy.

"Give her to me," Davy orders Leonard, but he won't release Claire.

"This isn't part of the deal." Leonard starts, his hold tightens on Claire.

"This is the final warning, Leonard. I have an important matter about my daughter that I need to resolve. So hand over Claire."

"No. You said…" His words get cut off as Davy raises a gun to his head. I want to roar at Davy, 'that's my kill,' but he pulls the trigger.

The noise bounces off the walls, and I'm reaching as Leonard's dead body hits the ground with Claire still in his arms. Davy drags Claire away from Leonard by the arms. He dumps her on the ground and points the gun to her head. "Tell your father what he needs to know."

"I saw you as a friend." I start.

He cocks the gun, and I don't look away from Davy. He will pull the trigger.

"Dana found out that Maeve, Jack, and Shay killed Cian. She came to me for help."

"So you gave her to Shay?"

When I look at my father, I see how the effect of losing Dana is slowly robbing him of his mask from his normally stoic face.

"She knows what we do. We told her. He's taking her somewhere safe until she comes to terms with who we are. It was the best choice we had."

My father doesn't look happy at all. "Where has he taken my daughter?"

"I don't know," I answer honestly. I want to look at Davy again. He still holds a gun to Claire's head, but I focus on the man in charge.

"Richard." I hear the warning clearly in my father's voice.

"I know who he is taking her to."

My father blinks in shock. "Who?"

"Cillian O'Hara."

"You gave your sister to Cillian O'Hara?" He asks.

"Yes. I didn't know what else to do."

My father's earlier emotions are erased from his face. "Put away the gun, Davy."

I glance at Davy, and my relief is short-lived as he puts the gun away. Something troubling has taken hold of Davy's features. There is that instinct to ask Davy what's wrong but all I can think about is getting to Claire. My father isn't going to just let this go.

My father takes out his phone and makes another call. "Have you still got eyes on Shay?" He steps away from me. "What do you mean, you lost him?"

I take a peek at Davy, who's watching me still wearing a troubling look. "You're going to die," I promise him.

He doesn't respond but pushes up his glasses and turns to my father like he didn't hear me.

"Something wrong?" I ask my father when he ends the call.

"Shay knew my men were following him and managed to lose them."

This is why I picked Shay to take her to safety. He would go to any lengths to get the job done. He is a man I want to rule with.

I should have let him take my father's life.

My father turns to leave.

"Don't leave me here."

My father stops walking. "You will die in this box, Richard. Because you can't be trusted."

"Get her to a hospital. She's innocent."

My father smiles, and it chills me to the bone. "No one is innocent. She's nearly dead. You can watch her take her final breath. Consider it a parting gift to you," My father turns to Davy. "Let's go."

"Davy, don't. Don't do this." My words fall on deaf ears as they leave me to watch Claire die.

CHAPTER THIRTY-ONE

O'REAGAN
AN CHLANN

CLAIRE

"*I lay my body down to sleep....*" *My father stops mid-sentence and tucks the blankets around me.* "*You have to say your prayers with me.*" *His smile is wide, and I smell toothpaste off his breath as he leans in and brushes a kiss to my cheek before we finish the prayer together. His voice fades.*

"Claire."

Bang! Bang! Bang! My head hurts. I wish whoever is making the noise would stop so I can sleep.

Bang! Bang! Bang!

"Claire!"

I blink, the light burns my eyes, and I close them again. My lips part and all I can think of is water and why am I so thirsty?

"Claire." The banging continues, and I lift my head. I'm outside the glass box. I can't keep my head up. I'm tired.

"Don't you lie down. You look at me!"

The command in Richard's voice has me peeling my eyes open once again.

Funny, he's in the box. Why is he in the box? He slides down the glass, and he's closer to me. His features soften, and his eyes are swollen with devastation. "You have got to stay awake, sweetheart."

I want to smile at the endearment, but my mouth doesn't move. I'm tired.

"Claire." Richard's voice has risen.

I want to ask why he's in the box. Why am I out here? My arm aches, and I try to turn my head to look at it, but I'm too tired.

"Claire." Richard's voice fades.

I close my eyes. I just want to sleep.

The loud banging will not allow me to sleep. I want to tell Richard to stop making noise.

His roar rips through my body and forces my eyes open. He's beating his fists against the glass wall. His hands are a bloody mess from plummeting the glass.

Stop, you're hurting yourself.

The words don't form as he slams his fists repeatedly into the glass wall. He pauses, and his gaze meets mine. He falls to his knees.

"You have to stay awake. I'll get us out of this." He pushes his hand against the glass like he can touch me. I remember what his touch feels like, and I want to move and touch him too, but my body won't obey the command. My brain keeps misfiring, and I can't move.

A coldness seeps into my toes and soon floods my body.

Leonard.

I remember Leonard attacking me, cutting my arm open. I try to turn my head but can't. My vision wavers as the memories pour in: Connor's dead body; Davy's betrayal; and Liam, Richard's father, who had orchestrated all of this.

"Richard." I manage to squeeze his name out as sheer terror takes over. I want to scream for him to run, that it's all a trap. I blink, and he's still kneeling on the floor, his hand still pressed against the glass.

A cold sweat has me shaking, and Richard starts to rise.

Don't leave me.

His fists hit the wall faster and harder, and all I see is blood before my vision fails me and the world turns dark and cold.

"Richard," I say his name again as my body starts to tremble. Or maybe the world is shaking.

The distinctive noise of someone coming downstairs reaches my ears. Footsteps pound too close to me. Had Richard gotten out of the box? Had he gone upstairs and come back down? None of it makes sense to me.

Silence follows, and I'm floating in an abyss of darkness. I must have imagined the sound.

Richard. Richard. Richard.

His name circles my mind. I'm dying. That's what this feels like. Death. Leaving this earth isn't painful. I'm not clawing or holding on to anything physical. It's the memories I'm holding onto. The faces that have gone before me of my mother and father the face that nearly destroyed me, Leonard, and the one that saved me, Richard.

If I could cry, I would. But tears are tangible, and I think wherever I am, everything is intangible.

"I'm here to help." The voice speaks above me, and I'm being dragged away from the darkness towards the voice. "She's alive." The voice is close to my ear. I don't recognize the person.

"Get away from her!" That's Richard. His voice I would never forget.

"Stand back." The words come from the male.

Bang! Bang! The noise is louder, different. I've heard it before. It's a gunshot. Pain races through me, and I wonder if someone shot me. The pain is everywhere, but mostly in my arm. I want to hang on, but my mind is spinning, and it's like I'm falling into a tornado of memories and faces.

RICHARD

"Have you come to finish the job?" Anger accelerates through my body, flooding every part of me. The bullets crack the glass, but they don't break it. Jack keeps his gun pointed high. My fists slam into the glass in front of me. "You can't fucking kill me!" My roar is fueled with pure hate and hurt as I look my brother in the eyes.

"I'm trying to help." Jack fires another shot at the glass, and it cracks further, but it still doesn't shatter. Not like how I am shattering as I stare at my brother. "You told him everything." My fist slams into the glass again, wanting it to be my brother's face.

Jack lowers the gun. "I didn't think he'd ever do this to you."

Jack's voice carries his truth, but it doesn't stop what he caused. Claire's body is so still on the floor, and I know my time is running out. I shove down my hatred for my brother. "Fire at the keypad. The glass is the weakest there." That's why I had focused on punching that area, hoping it would crack. I stand back.

Jack fires a round into the keypad. The bullets shattered the wall like I knew they would. The glass tumbles down, giving me enough space to get out. All I want to do is hurt Jack the moment I am released. I slip the knife from my pocket and slam both of us into the wall, holding the knife to his throat.

"What you wanted to do was madness. You and Shay aren't seeing the bigger picture."

I push the knife harder against my brother's throat. My vision wavers at the level of his betrayal. Everyone in my life had failed me, and now my big brother, too. I'm aware he's holding the gun, yet it hangs at his side.

"You betrayed me." I allow every ounce of my pain into my words and release Jack. My want for blood is strong, but my need to save Claire is stronger. I scoop her up off the floor and drag her small frame to my chest. She seems smaller and lighter in my arms.

"Stay with me." I press a kiss against her forehead and take the steps two at a time upstairs. Jack races behind me, and when we reach the hall, he's moving to the front door. "I'll drive."

I shouldn't trust him, but I don't have allies right now, and Claire is getting paler by the second. I get into the back of the Range Rover with Claire in my arms. She's covered in blood; all I see is blood. I pull her closer to my chest as Jack tears down the driveway and to the hospital.

"Stay with me, sweetheart." I press a kiss on her forehead.

I'm not a praying type of guy, but I send up my threat nonetheless. If she dies, I'll wreak havoc on this earth.

That's my prayer. That's my promise.

"I didn't know he would do this. I thought I was protecting you." Jack's words mean nothing right now. "Mario rang me and told me what Davy and Father did."

So it had been Mario who had rung Jack. I had wondered how Jack knew, but my anger wouldn't allow me to ask earlier.

"Davy betrayed me, too." I find myself saying. Davy had fed me the fucking lies that Mario was one of my father's men, that Mario was the one giving my father information. All along, it was Davy.

I feel played. Truly played.

"I'm sorry, Richard."

I meet Jack's gaze in the rear-view mirror. "Shut the fuck up, Jack." I refocus on Claire.

We pull up at the hospital. The vehicle hasn't fully stopped when I push the door open and get out with Claire tucked into my chest. The main doors open, and I rush past the receptionist.

"I need a doctor now!"

"Sir, you can't go back there." The receptionist tries to stop me.

I slam my shoulder into the double doors that have "No Entry" taped onto them.

The emergency room is hectic, but I walk up to the first doctor, who's examining someone's fucking arm.

"Save her."

He takes one look at Claire and starts calling out to another doctor and some nurses who follow him. I'm racing behind them.

"What happened?" He asks.

Two nurses veer up beside me, pushing a gurney.

"A stab wound to her arm."

"Put her down." The doctor says, and it's like the world has paused as they all stand around the gurney waiting for me to lower her.

I can't let her go.

"Let them help her." I hadn't even noticed that Jack had followed me into the hospital. I shrug his hand off my shoulder and release Claire. The moment she's on the gurney, they are running toward another set of white doors, and she disappears from my sight.

Sound resumes. The ringing phones demand attention, voices buzz all at once, shoes squeak along the floor.

A small girl with a pink band tied in her long blonde hair stares up at me. I look down at my blood-soaked shirt and hands. Her mother drags her away and tucks her behind her legs.

"She's in the best place." Jack's comforting words propel me out of the emergency room and outside.

"What Shay and I were doing was trying to stop the disloyalty. I wanted to build something on strength and loyalty." I focus all my anger on him. I can't allow myself to think of Claire.

"Both of you were going too far. I honestly thought Father would just have a talk with you. Removing Father or killing Lucian isn't going to make us better, Richard."

"You should have fucking voiced that, on the hill of the Loch Leigh mountains," I roar.

"You were too far up your arse to see the mess you and Shay would have made."

I launch myself at Jack and slam my fist into his jaw. It's not enough, and I hit him again. The blow sends him back, but he doesn't retaliate. "I didn't think our father would hurt you."

I slam my fist into his jaw again.

Blood spills from his split lip, and he stands taller. The glint in his eyes is what I want to see. He's ready to fight.

"I'm sorry, Richard." His words are gritted at me as he wipes blood from his lip.

They give me pause, and I don't attack. I turn my back on him. "He left me down there to die." My father was a lot of things, but I didn't think he'd kill me off—his own son. No matter what he had done or did, I might try to remove him from his place in the Irish Mafia, but taking his life, that was a place I would never go. I still didn't think I ever would.

"I never thought he would do something like that." Jack's hand lands on my shoulder, and once again, I shrug it off.

"When I got out of the asylum, I swore we couldn't become Father and his brothers. I don't want to be part of something that's built solely on money and for money. I want more." I turn to Jack. "Stay here with Claire." Opening my hands, I take a step back to my brother. "Give me your keys."

He doesn't question me but places his keys in my hand.

I'm ready to walk away, but his hand tightens around mine. "I'll stay here with her until you get back, but don't kill him. We can still bring your vision to life." Jack's hands get tighter. "We just do it the right way."

"What's the right way, Jack?" I think we have all lost the understanding of right and wrong.

"I don't know, but I promise we will figure it out together. Just don't kill Father." Jack releases my hand.

I make no promises as I jog to Jack's vehicle and get in.

While driving, I flip open the glove compartment. I take out the gun and sit it on the passenger seat.

Jack's phone sits in the dock and I scroll through the device until I find Shay's number. I ring him. Shay answers after three rings. I should tell him to run straight away, but I'm being a selfish fucker and want to know about Dana.

"Did she get across safely?" I ask.

"Yeah, he has her now. Cillian said he'd be in touch in a few days, but something was off." Shay trails off.

"What do you mean 'off'?"

"I don't know," Shay answers. "I know him. His word is good."

I'm not convinced, but time is running out. "My father knows everything. You need to run."

"How does he know?" Shay's still driving, his voice is calm, but it's hard to know with Shay just how pissed off he might be.

"One of my men betrayed me. They told my father everything." I can't drop Jack in all of this.

"You ask about Dana first before you tell me this. This is some bullshit, Richard."

"For now, you need to keep your head down until we figure this out." I ignore the comment about Dana.

"You are all some bunch of cunts. I'm always the fucking one running after doing your dirty work." Shay hangs up. The protest on my lips slips away as a string of curses takes its place.

I fling the phone onto the passenger seat. I hate that Shay had to run, hating that he no doubt is feeling every inch of the betrayal that I feel from Jack. If I said it was Jack who told my father, I didn't think Shay would control himself.

My hands still bleed, and the blood that coats my fingers is making the steering wheel slippery. Removing my hands one at a time, I rub them on my trousers before re-gripping the wheel as I power down the road.

Davy's semi-detached house is my destination. I pull up in his driveway. Checking Jack's gun, I make sure it's loaded. I slip it into the waistband of my trousers and get out of the car and walk up to the door. A camera over my head doesn't give me pause. I try the door handle, but it's locked. I walk around the side of the house. The side door is unlocked, and I step into Davy's kitchen. Taking the gun out of the waistband of my trousers, I keep it raised as I move through his home.

Running water upstairs doesn't draw my attention straight away. I do a sweep of the downstairs, and when I don't see Davy, I make my way carefully upstairs. The water stops running, a clear indication of where he is.

Taking a fucking bath.

I push the door open with my foot, my gun trained on his head. He has removed his top but spins, and his gaze flickers to a green army jacket.

"Move, and I pull the trigger," I warn.

Davy slowly raises his hands. "He's helping me find my daughter."

I fire a shot to the left of his head. It tears the tiles off the wall, which explodes into the tub.

Davy's chest rises and falls rapidly as he stares at me.

The silence drags out, and I'm okay with that.

"My daughter is being trafficked."

I fire another shot to the left of him.

"Fuck's sake, Richard. I've always been loyal. Your father promised me my daughter."

I'm moving. His lazy excuse for betraying me has me slamming the gun into his nose. It breaks with a satisfying crunch. His roars fuel me, and I slam my fist into his face. He stumbles back toward the tub.

"I had no choice!" His roar has me pausing.

"There is always a choice."

Davy dives for the gun in my hand. He squeezes the trigger and fires a shot into the wall. My knee hits between his legs, and he falls to the floor. Gripping him by the back of his neck, I drag his traitorous body to the tub.

He knows what I'm about to do. "Richard, I can make it right."

I push his head into the water and hold it under. He's hysterically thrashing and kicking.

I use both hands and force his head deeper. The gun in my hand shimmers, and I know I could be merciful and use it on Davy. Water pours over the side of the tub as he continues to fight for his life. When his legs kick out slower, I know his life is slipping away. I wait until he goes still before releasing his head. It floats to the top of the water.

No matter how many lives I take, it doesn't get easier, especially with people who had become like family. Davy was the closest I'd had to a friend.

I leave his house, still hungry for revenge. Once I get back into Jack's vehicle, I ring the clean-up crew.

I give them the address before giving my instructions, "Burn it to the ground." I inform them. I didn't want any of it standing. His elimination would be a warning to others.

CHAPTER THIRTY-TWO

O'REAGAN
AN CHLANN

CLAIRE

Bleep! Bleep! Bleep!

I part my lips, and a layer of skin tears off. Something heavy is on my finger as I try to lift my hand to my face. Something is lying under my nose, making it difficult to breathe.

"It's okay. You're safe." I blink, but it's too bright, so I close my eyes again. Hand's touch mine and push them away from my face. "You're in the hospital."

I swallow the dryness in my throat that has me begging for water. Richard's hands leave mine, and fear tightens its bony fingers around my throat.

"Don't leave me." I don't recognize the deep voice that cracks on each word.

Something touches my lip. "I'm not leaving. Take a drink."

I allow the straw fully into my mouth and drink deeply. Richard moves away again, and I try to clamp down on the panic I feel. The light in the room fades as the blinds clink together. I slowly open my eyes. My stomach tenses as Richard comes into view.

He takes up so much space, and when he sits down beside me, it doesn't make him smaller. He's still a force that takes my breath away.

He's darkness.

His eyes fill up slowly with unspent anger.

Yet as he touches my hand, I've never felt anything so gentle. My throat tightens at his touch. Everything in me quivers.

"How are you feeling?"

The door opens, and the nurse steps in. She looks at the closed blinds, and I want to explain the light was hurting my eyes, but words fail me, as Richard releases my hand and leans back, giving the nurse some space.

"It's great to see you awake." Her smile is warm as she speaks and looks at the monitor.

I don't look away from Richard. I fear if I do, he'll disappear. I have so much I want to ask him, but I know not to ask in front of the nurse.

"Your recovery is going great." Her words don't drag me away from Richard.

His gaze is a storm, and I want to reach over the edge of the bed and touch his hand. "Are you okay?" I ask him. My voice sounds odd.

"Let the nurse check you," he replies.

The nurse in question is smiling down at me. "I just need to take your blood pressure."

I nod, and she rolls up my sleeve. "How are you feeling?" She asks while she writes down my digits on her clipboard.

"Thirsty."

"That's to be expected. You've been asleep for three days."

Three days?

Three days, that's a long time. The nurse removes the blood pressure band, does a few more checks, and leaves as the silence is making everyone uncomfortable. The moment she leaves, I try to sit up.

"What happened?"

Richard rises and towers over me. "Claire, you need to lie back." He guides me back gently and picks up the water. "I'll talk. You drink."

I allow the straw to enter my mouth as he speaks.

"Do you remember the attack in the house?"

I nod. "Davy was there and your father." I hate saying it, but I don't think I'll ever forget that moment when Liam blocked me from leaving. The memory of his coldness sends shivers racing down my spine.

Richard's jaw clenches. "That's right. Do you remember Leonard?"

I stop drinking as my throat closes. I nod again. "He's dead?" I want him to be dead.

"Yes." Richard doesn't sound happy.

I'm confused.

Maybe he sees my confusion. I'm not exactly sure what prompts him, but he speaks.

"He's dead. I just wish he wasn't so I could kill him slowly."

His words should terrify me, but they don't. I should feel something for my brother, but all I can think about is how he dragged the knife down my arm, how he killed our parents, how most of my childhood memories are tainted by his cruelty.

My fingers touch the bandage that covers most of my arm.

"You lost so much blood." Richard's voice is strained. "I thought I was going to lose you." Fear clouds his eyes.

"I'm still here." My heart starts to dance in my chest. My brain is trying to process everything that has happened.

"Connor?" I already know he's dead.

Richard's eyes light up. "He's alive." A slow smile graces his handsome face.

Thank God.

"He's at home making a full recovery. He misses you." Richard's words heat up my cheeks and my heart.

Home. He called it home.

Richard shifts closer, and when he takes my hand, I lie deeper into the pillows with a sense of contentment.

"I miss him too," I say.

I can sense Richard's gaze on my face, and I look at him.

He smiles. "It's been three very long days." He brings my hand up to his lips and presses a kiss on my fingers. His own hands are tattered and battered. I'm ready to ask what happened, but I remember him in the box, beating the wall.

"How did you end up in the box?" It's ironic that I had once been captured in the box, and that's where he ended up.

"They tricked me. Made it look like you were in the bed."

The hairs rise along my body. "They dragged my arm along the walls leaving a path of blood."

Richard's eyes turn hard, and a coldness seeps into my veins.

"They won't hurt you again." His words are growled.

My heart starts to beat wildly in my chest.

Richard glances at the monitor and leans into me. He brushes the hair off my forehead. "I promise you. I will keep you safe."

I reach up and stroke Richard's face. Touching him is like a salve on my frazzled nerves.

"My brother is dead." I come back full circle as I keep allowing that knowledge to sink in.

Richard's jaw is clenched, but his face relaxes as the room door opens and a guy I have never seen before steps in with a coffee in each hand.

"You're awake." He smiles.

I glance at Richard. "This is my brother Jack. He stayed with you for a while."

I try to give a smile to Jack. I don't see the resemblance, but he's extremely good looking, and I'm very aware of my appearance. I'm tempted to drag the blanket up higher, but I tighten my hands in my lap.

"Thank you for staying with me."

His smile grows wider, and he hands the coffee to Richard. Some silent conversation passes between the brothers, and Richard smiles.

"How do you feel?" Jack asks. He doesn't sit but stands at the foot of my bed. He has an air to him that would make you believe he is someone. Someone you should listen to. Richard possesses that air too.

"Like I've woken up from a dream," I say honestly.

Jack nods his head and sips his coffee. "It will take time, but you're in good hands." Jack's words are said with humor, and he gives Richard a quick glance.

I love the feel of Richard's fingers as he twines them with mine. The intimate act feels strange in front of someone else, but I don't pull away from his touch.

"You are coming home with me?" He asks.

I pretend to consider it, like I had any other option in the world. Jack's gaze is heavy on us, and when I meet his eyes, they've hardened. My stomach twists for all the wrong reasons.

I refocus on the softness of Richard at this moment. "Yes."

One word and it changes the atmosphere in the room. I push away the thought that maybe saying no isn't an option.

"That's good. We've been moving all your stuff into Richard's," Jack says.

"You were that certain I'd say yes?" I ask Richard.

"I was hopeful." His deep voice and dark eyes have me quivering.

When he raises my hand to his lips, I feel the kiss searing all the way down to my soul.

I love you.

The words are there on my lips, but I don't voice those words. The truth of what Richard means to me is deeper than love or lust. What we are is two damaged souls healing each other.

"I'd never say no to you," I find myself saying instead.

His smile warms me all over again, and I know everything will be okay, that we won the war, that I have nothing more to fear, and that I can finally live my life.

Two more days I spend in the hospital before I'm discharged. Going home with Richard is exciting, but there is also that small amount of fear.

He hasn't mentioned anything about his father, and I don't ask. The moment he opens the door, Mario and Connor are there to greet me. Connor walks to me, his movements stiff, but he's alive, just like me. I kneel down and take his face in my hands and rub mine against his.

"Good to see you, boy."

Richard stands patiently, and when I'm ready to get up, he helps me.

"It is great to see you home." Mario's sweet words have me reaching out and gripping his hand. His eyes widen. The bandage on his head tells me he didn't come out of this unscathed.

"Thank you." Richard had told me that Mario called Jack, that's how we got out of the basement. Otherwise, I am pretty sure I would have bled to death.

I release Mario, only to have Richard's fingers intertwine with mine. "I want to show you something."

Mario takes Connor into the kitchen, and Richard leads me down the hall. I'm ready to pull back when he stops at the basement door.

"Trust me." He looks over his shoulder, and when he releases my hand and walks down the steps, I know he's really giving me my freedom.

I do trust him. I follow him into the basement.

"It took a few days, but it's all gone."

I step up beside Richard. The space is clear, with no glass box, no dead bodies. No traces that my prison ever existed.

He doesn't turn to me as we stand shoulder to shoulder. His fingers intertwined with mine. "I'm sorry I ever put you in the box."

His fingers squeeze mine, and when I look up at the side of his face, I smile. He can't see my face as he's staring forward. The apology strains his jaw.

"I'm not, Richard." He looks down at me. "Honestly, I've never felt so free."

His lips are warm on mine, and I want so much of him, but he breaks the kiss, much to my disappointment. He keeps his face close to mine, our breaths mingling together.

"I'm not sorry I took you." He grins.

My stomach squirms and I touch his handsome face. To think how much my life would change in one moment, one single terrifying moment, and it turned into such a defining moment.

It has been a long time since I felt like any place was home, but in Richard's arms, I know I am finally home.

EPILOGUE

O'REAGAN
AN CHLANN

RICHARD

I like to leave the house only when she's asleep. Otherwise, I find myself making excuses of why I should stay. Nothing has been easy since everything went down. Every corner of the house is covered by cameras, and security guards have been doubled. I hate making Claire carry a panic button, but my father is still alive and kicking. The fear that knowledge caused has sparked fear in her eyes and made my stomach twist. I need to protect her.

The sad reality is that my father will always be a threat to us. I know myself or Jack won't actually kill him, but we need to confront him. That's where I am going today. To my parents' home with the backing of Jack, to first call off the hit on Shay and also call a truce for now.

It may be a panel of four Kings, but we would be stupid fuckers to really believe that. The panel is one King, my father, and his three princes. That's how I like to see the situation. It means one of us will become the King, and I personally think any of us are far more fitting than my father.

The gates to Jack's house open, and I pull up outside his door; I don't go in but blow the horn. Minutes pass before the door opens, and Jack steps out of the house. He's wearing a dark suit, just like me. I'm proud of the man he has become, and I hope he's proud of me, too. I've never yearned for anything so badly with how I yearn for this to work, for us to have more than a circle of men who control everything. I want us to be a legacy.

Jack gets into my car and glances back up at the window of his home.

"How is she?" I ask.

He buckles his belt. "She's guilty over Dana. She blames herself."

So she should feel guilty.

"It will all work out," I say.

"Any word from Shay?" Jack asks once we hit the main road.

"No. The last time I spoke, he was pretty pissed, and I've heard nothing from Cillian." That's a serious concern. He could have contacted Shay, but Shay isn't answering me. So our sister is missing.

"Mother has started to ask questions. I don't think she believes Dana is off with friends," Jack says.

I want to laugh. "That's a first. She believed I was on holiday for three years. Dana's only been gone a few days." I can't stop the bitterness that slips into my words.

"Dana and Mother talk every day, that's why. She did question where you were, Richard. We all did."

I didn't want a fucking pity party. I turn to business. "So, how do we play this?"

"Like what we agreed. He has to call the hit off Shay as he's the only one who Cillian will be in contact with."

I nod. We had discussed this. I just hope when the hit is lifted off Shay's head that he will return.

"If Shay doesn't come back?" I say what I fear.

"He will. Shay wants what you want, Richard. He's loyal almost to a fault. He'll come back."

I wish I had the same amount of faith in Shay as Jack does.

We are close to our parents' estate. "Are you sure Mother is not here?" I ask.

"I told you already, she's out. I made sure of it." Jack sounds irritated.

I keep asking the same questions, but I don't want to deal with my mother. I hate lying to her about Dana.

I'm about to ask Jack if he is sure that Father is here. That's what I had him do this morning before we agreed to this meeting or ambush. It depends on how you look at it, to make sure Father was home and Mother was gone.

It's like Jack reads my mind. "Father is there in case you were going to ask."

"I wasn't."

We pull up at the house. I have to roll down my windows and show my face before the gates are opened. I know my father is alerted to our arrival. You can't creep up on him. So fucking annoying.

I don't pull up at the front door but park around the back. Old habits die hard. Getting out, I clock three security guards making a path towards us. I bend back down and look in at Jack, who's checking his gun. I shake my head at him, and he stuffs the weapon in the glove compartment. I straighten as the first security guard reaches me.

"Hands in the air." His gruff voice suits his face. He's a face on him like a butcher's dog.

I raise my hands and cooperate. He removes my gun and two knives. Jack is being patted down across from me. Once we are checked, they stand back.

"Go ahead, Mr. O' Reagan is in his study waiting for you both."

I meet Jack's eye, asking him if he's ready. A curt nod of his head, and he leads us into the kitchen. We walk down the hall and pass four more security men. My father has really upped the security here. I wonder fucking why.

I grin in hopes it's because of me, that I am a threat to him.

Jack knocks, but I turn the handle and step into his office. My father isn't alone. He rises from behind his desk, his face stoic. He's polished like always, but I see the fucking glint in his eyes. He's smiling at us.

"Come in."

The second man turns and faces us from his chair.

"Meet Cillian O'Hara. Cillian, this is my oldest son, Jack."

Cillian gets out of the chair and walks up to Jack, who looks at me like I know what the fuck is happening.

"This is Richard, my youngest son." My father continues the introductions like we knew about this.

"What's going on?" I ask my father as he returns to his desk. I take Cillian's hand and size him up. He's the same height as me, his build is not far off mine, but I'm not sure what would happen in a fight with him.

I still have no idea why Cillian is here. This is what would save Shay. The fucking person who is here. We had nothing to bargain with. I release his hand, but he doesn't stand back. His green eyes are hard, and they dance across my face in what feels like a challenge.

"Where is Dana?" Jack asks, pulling Cillian's gaze from me.

"Everyone sit down." My father points to the three chairs in front of his desk. Cillian returns to his seat, and Jack sits down too.

"I think I'll stand."

"There is no need to be hostile." My father says and waves me off. "Suit yourself." He sits down like he hasn't a care in the world.

"I was working with Cillian's father, helping him to find his daughter who was trafficked."

My father speaks to me, and sitting down seems like a good idea, but I remain standing. My father's words are a case of deja vu. Everything is familiar, and the final conversation I had with Davy springs to mind. Before killing Davy, he had said my father was helping him track down his daughter. I didn't care at that moment, but now I'm thinking I should have asked some questions.

"Eight days ago, we got word that Davy's house was burnt to the ground, with him in it."

"Davy's your father?" I have to clarify what I'm hearing. Davy's second name is Markey, so it made no sense.

Cillian turns toward me, but I catch the look of pure glee in my father's eyes. When Cillian finds out in the next thirty seconds that I killed his father, what would stop him from killing me? All our weapons were removed. I'm starting to bet Cillian's weapons weren't taken from him.

"Yes, he's my father. We didn't have a good relationship." Cillian seems somewhat uncomfortable, but that same hardness is in his eyes. It's a look that a lot of Mafia men carry. I think his weight is a little heavier.

"Cillian uses his mother's maiden name, O'Hara, so I'm not surprised no one made the connection." My father chimes in.

Jack hasn't spoken. His shoulders are stiff. He knows I killed Davy. He knows what this means.

"The Russian's who run the trafficking rings must have found out that Davy was looking for his daughter. He was getting too close to the truth, so they killed him. But I have promised Cillian that he will have his revenge, and I will help him find his sister, and in return, he has agreed to keep Dana safe."

My father is a fucking snake. He's looking at me, daring me to say anything. How easily this could all swing back to me. He was giving me an out right now, and I wasn't stupid enough not to take it.

"Since Shay no longer wants to be a King, I have offered the position to Cillian."

"Shay will return," I state, getting everyone's attention. We can't let someone like Cillian on board with us. He is too tied up with the RA. This is getting messier by the second.

"Can I have a moment with my father?" I ask, staring at my father, who looks too fucking comfortable.

"There will be no secrets among the Kings. Say what you need, son, in front of everyone."

I run my hand along my jaw, wanting to rip it off with the irritation that claws at me. He really screwed us all.

"No offense, Cillian," I say first. "But isn't he tied to the RA?" I direct the second part toward my father.

My father stands up from the desk. "I have always searched for a bridge to help bring the North and the East together. I had thought we had found that in Shay, but I was wrong. Cillian is that bridge now."

I'm looking at Cillian. He isn't afraid or intimated. He sits back, not with arrogance but self-worth. I don't like it. I don't like him.

He's dangerous.

"I don't take part in the RA anymore. But yes, Lucian is like a brother to me. I still work for them. I'm more of a freelancer nowadays." His words carry more weight than he is telling.

Jack turns and meets my eye. Of course, Lucian is like a brother to Cillian, the man we had wanted to take down along with my father, and now my father had thrown everything out the window by bringing Cillian into the mix.

"I like to think of you as a lone ranger, but I hope that day has come to an end, Cillian. We can do great things," my father says.

"So, where is Dana?" Jack asks, and right now, I don't fucking care. All I see is a mess that I'm not sure I can clean up.

"She's safe. Cillian is going to make sure no harm comes to her. I will speak to Dana soon when she calms down."

"Let me talk to her." I find myself saying. I had given the go-ahead to hand her over to Cillian. I should at least make sure she is okay.

"No. I think you and Jack have done enough damage."

My father gets back up and takes out four glasses, along with a bottle of brandy. He pours out each glass and hands it to us. Jack and Cillian get up too and join us for a fucking toast.

"To four Kings."

I pause, wondering if the brandy is poisoned. It looks like everyone is thinking the same thing, and my father grins before taking a drink, and we all follow suit.

"Welcome to the O' Reagans." I click my glass with Cillian, and I hope he reads the warning in my eyes that he better not fuck this up.

I leave the office with more anxiety than I have ever experienced. But with the Irish Mafia, there is always a mess to make and one to clean up. Only this time is different. I get to go home to a woman I love, one I will continue to fight for. For now, it looks like our father will play with his new toy. I just don't think Cillian O'Hara will play along easily.

He might just end up being the one who takes our father down.

THE END

I hope you enjoyed *Mafia Games*.
Mafia Boss is the next book in the Young Irish Rebel Series.
Read Cillian and Dana's story.
You can download by scanning the QR code below:

Or read on for a sneak peek!

MAFIA BOSS

O'REAGAN
AN CHLANN

CHAPTER ONE

I'd like to say I'm broken as I stand in front of my father's grave. I'm pretty sure that's how I should feel—broken. A sense of loss should choke me, a pain that should take me to my knees. The priest looks up from his bible; he gives me a nod like I'm a soldier that has every right to rest or shed a tear.

But I don't. I'm not even close to any of those emotions. I feel nothing.

"Ashes to Ashes." The priest walks around my father's coffin, dipping a golden stick into a pot of holy water and sprinkling the contents over the coffin as he continues his prayer. We had to have a closed casket. My father's bones were charred black from the fire that burnt his home to the ground.

My mother stands tall beside me. She isn't broken either. She isn't a grieving widow. She is simply here to give her once-upon-a-time husband his final goodbye. I'm here as a mark of respect and as support to my mother.

I still lean in and wrap an arm around her, even though she doesn't need my support. The world is watching at our backs, so I will play my part. My mother turns her head, and I'm actually surprised at the level of sadness I see in her green eyes. It's unexpected, and I'm wondering who the sadness is for. It surely can't be for the man who's being lowered into the ground as we stare at each other. He wasn't a good husband or father. I never connected with him, though he tried. His belt was his favorite tool for making me hear his words, but all the beatings did was make me want to be a different kind of man.

One not like him.

"May he rest in peace." The priest draws my attention, and I release my mother as she steps forward and drops a red rose on top of my father's coffin. Her hands are clad in small black leather gloves that she joins in front of her. I do the same, and a line of mourners follows suit until the coffin is coated with red petals.

As they release their roses, they turn to my mother and me and shake our hands. "I'm sorry for your loss" is repeated. The words bounce off me, and a sea of faces morph into one another.

"I'm sorry for your loss." Robert's large hand grips mine tightly. "Thank you."

Robert is unnaturally tall. He towers over everyone else. He's a giant of a man with too much facial hair and not much composure. I'm not sure how he gained his position so high in the ranks of the Jaguars. They controlled parts of the east of Ireland that weren't under the O'Reagans' control.

"We are all here." He pulls me slightly toward him before looking over my head. I follow his line of sight, and there they are—all the members of the Jaguars nod at me. My gut twists. I knew they would arrive. My father was a member, but as I look across from them and meet Liam O'Reagan's intelligent stare, I know everything is about to get very fucking complicated.

Robert addresses me while glaring at Liam O'Reagan. "We aren't afraid of no ghosts."

My mother clears her throat. "There is a time and place for that kind of talk." She speaks out of the corner of her mouth while keeping her voice low.

Robert releases my hand.

"They aren't ghosts," I warn him before he steps up to my mother and takes her hand. Robert isn't foolish enough to believe that the O'Reagans are to be underestimated. I haven't had a chance to tell the Jaguars that I'm now a king with the Irish Mafia. So much has happened in a short space of time.

I continue to shake hands, and when the line starts to dwindle, I'm looking from one side of the mourners to the other. Walking to the O'Reagans first would give a message to the Jaguars that I didn't want delivered. So, I leave my mother talking to the priest and walk over to Robert and the men.

Five of the front runners shake my hand. I grew up with them around our home, but I never joined them. I wasn't a member.

"Davy's death will not be in vain, son." Razor grips my shoulder. "We will have justice for his death."

I nod. "I can take care of it." The moment I say the words, I know they're the wrong ones.

Razor grins, dragging the jagged scar on his cheek higher. "Davy was a brother to me. We don't leave one man to take care of another man's death. We work together. We are strong as a unit."

Razor grips my shoulder tighter. "You are now a member, Cillian. It's your legacy."

"I need to take care of my mother." Movement to the side has me glancing in that direction.

Shit.

Liam, Jack, and Richard are approaching me, and everyone watches them. They have an air about them that demands everyone's attention. They piss me off to no end, but I keep that buried. Razor releases me and glances at them; a snarl twists his face.

"Only ghosts," Robert whispers to Razor.

I turn as Liam steps up to me with either son flanking his sides. He's the godfather, the center of the Irish Mafia, and he's to be feared.

Liam holds out his hand. "Sorry for your loss." I take it, and we shake, but he doesn't release my hand instantly. Instead, he looks at the Jaguars. "Robert, how nice to see you." Liam releases my hand as Jack and Richard give their condolences. Richard glares at me, and I try to ignore him.

"Have you any idea what happened to Davy?" Robert fires out, and I curse him. He's not very tactful.

"A discussion for another day," I interrupt. But Liam isn't taking my subtle interruption kindly.

"I actually do know what happened to Davy." Liam steps up closer to Robert, and I swear Razor snarls.

"We're all listening." Robert's smugness doesn't go unnoticed.

"That information is for Cillian since he is a king with us." Liam is ready to walk away after dropping his bomb. He should have given me time.

Razor zeroes in on me, and there's no point denying that I'm now a king. I nod my head.

"Cillian is also a Jaguar, so that knowledge will be shared with us, Liam."

Liam's lip moves slightly. He doesn't look at me for confirmation. "Like I said, the information will be given to Cillian. After that, it is up to him."

Liam gives me his full attention. "Always use knowledge wisely."

A large black limo pulls up close to the road, and the slick vehicle garners a lot of attention. Robert smirks when he glances at the limo. The smirk remains on his face as his gaze dances between Liam and me.

"Skinner wants a word." Robert is too fucking joyful.

Any other time, meeting Skinner would be a privilege, but not right now.

"We will talk later." Liam makes it sound like a promise, and he starts to walk off with Jack and Richard flanking him. In the distance, I can see Shane O'Reagan as well. He gives me a nod when our eyes meet.

Razor drags me away from the O'Reagans. "Skinner doesn't like to be kept waiting."

I take a final look at my mother, who's still in deep conversation with the priest, and walk away from the Jaguars to the limo.

This felt like a coin toss. Skinner arriving here could be to give his condolences in person or to warn me away from the Jaguars. He never liked me, but he was very fond of my father.

The door opens, and all I see is his hand. The ruby-red ring on his forefinger gleams off the afternoon light. I take a final glance over my shoulder, my gaze drawn to the last place I saw the O'Reagans, but they're no longer there.

I climb in and close the door behind me. Skinner looks the part in his black suit and black shirt, and he even sports a pair of black sunglasses. The dividing window is in the process of rolling up, giving us more privacy.

"Davy was a good man," Skinner starts, but I can't agree.

My silence has Skinner sitting forward. "He was hard on you, Cillian, to make you a better man."

He didn't. He just made me hate the man he was. Once again, I don't voice this.

"Your mother looks broken." His words carry no truth.

"Yeah. She's hurting," I lie.

Skinner removes his sunglasses. It doesn't matter how many times I see his face. The scars and the missing eye still make me want to look away. I hold his stare.

"Your father saved me. When we were young, I nearly died. A group of men decided they wanted my blood spilled across the streets of Cavan. They got as far as removing an eye." He points at the eye as if I haven't noticed it missing. "Your father arrived. They laughed at him." Skinner's smirk twists his grotesque face.

My father was small and thin; he looked non-threatening. So Skinner's story rings true.

"You should have seen their stupid fucking faces when he removed his glasses and pulled off his top." Skinner's deep laugh rumbles as he shuffles closer to the edge of the seat.

"Blood was pissing out of my eye. I started to laugh at them. I remember telling them they were all going down. They turned their back on your father. Big mistake." Skinner sits back, the memory dancing on his lips, tugging them up into a smile.

"He was like a ghost, taking them down one after another. I had a front-row seat."

I'm smiling too, wishing I had seen it. My father was a skilled fighter. His hands were deemed weapons. My own skills, I owed to him.

"You know how you really know you have a good friend?" he asks.

"They give you money," I throw out.

Skinner laughs. "Close. They help you bury a body. He and I, well, we dug lots of holes." Skinner sits back and slips on his glasses. "I hear you are working with the O'Reagans."

There's no point in hiding the fact. "Yes, Liam has offered me a place on his board as a king."

Skinner nods. "Take it."

Irritation claws at me. Like I need his fucking permission. "I already have."

"Good. You know what they say—keep your friends close but your enemies closer."

"Liam O'Reagan is not my enemy," I say plainly.

Skinner smirks like he knows something I don't. "Liam is an enemy of the state. Don't ever forget that. He's everyone's enemy."

Politics and more politics. That's all I grew up listening to. "Thank you for coming to my father's funeral. I'm sure he would have wanted that."

Skinner sneers. "Take care, Cillian."

The door opens, and Skinner faces away from the sunlight as I step out of the limo. Crowds are still gathered around the grave, and I meet my mother's gaze.

The door closes as I step onto the grass, and the limo pulls away.

The O'Reagans, the Jaguars, and even Sheahan, who rules over parts of the north, will pull at me, each having their own agenda. But to me, there is only one: finding my sister.

That's all that matters to me, and If I have to play everyone to get my sister back, I will.

Download and read by scanning the QR code below:

OTHER BOOKS BY VI CARTER

WILD IRISH SERIES
RECKLESS (prequel)
VICIOUS #1
RUTHLESS #2
FEARLESS #3
MERCILESS #4
HEARTLESS #5

THE BOYNE CLUB
DARK #1
DARKER #2
DARKEST #3
PITCH BLACK #4

THE OBSESSED DUET
A DEADLY OBSESSION #1
A CRUEL CONFESSION #2

THE CELLS OF KALASHOV

THE SIXTH (NOVELLA)

THE COLLECTOR #1

THE HANDLER #2

THE YOUNG IRISH REBELS

MAFIA PRINCE #1

MAFIA KING #2

MAFIA GAMES #3

MAFIA BOSS #4

BROKEN PEOPLE

DECEIVE ME #1

SAVE ME #2

ABOUT THE AUTHOR

Vi Carter - the queen of **DARK ROMANCE**, the mistress of suspense, and the high priestess of *PLOT TWISTS*!

When she's not busy crafting tales of the **MAFIA** that'll leave you on the edge of your seat, you can find her baking up a storm, exploring the gorgeous Irish countryside, or spending time with her three little girls.

Vi's Young Irish Rebels series has been praised by readers and can be found in English, Dutch, German, Audible and soon will be available in French.

And let's not forget her two greatest loves: ***coffee and chocolate***. If you ever need to bribe her, just offer up a mug of coffee and a slab of chocolate, and she'll be putty in your hands.

So, if you're ready to join Vi on a wild journey with the mafia, sign up for her newsletter and score a free book! Just be warned - her stories are so **ADDICTIVE**, you might not be able to put them down.

WHAT READERS ARE SAYING

Editorial Reviews

"Vi Carter has once again blown my mind with another outstanding story. She never fails to create a masterpiece with memorable characters that leap off the page. This book is complete perfection."- USA Today Bestselling Author Khardine Gray

Vi is one of those authors who never disappoints. She weaves **LOVE** & **DANGER** effortlessly. ★★★★★ stars

I definitely recommend this book. It is **SUSPENSEFUL** and exciting. I enjoy reading Vi Carter's book. ★★★★★ stars

HOW TO KEEP IN TOUCH WITH VI CARTER

Visit Vi's website:
Join her newsletter: t.ly/yZWbX
Or scan the QR code:

MAFIA GAMES

On Facebook, Instagram, TikTok and Youtube @darkauthorvicarter and on Twitter @authorvicarter
Or scan the QR code:

ACKNOWLEDGEMENTS

I'm very lucky to have such amazing readers and Beta Readers. I want to thank the following people who worked with me on this book.

Editor: Sherry Schafer

Proofreader: Michele Rolfe

Blurb was written by: Tami Thomason

<u>Beta Readers</u>

Amanda Sheridan

Lucy Korth

Tami Thomason

Laura Williams

www.ingramcontent.com/pod-product-compliance
Lightning Source LLC
Chambersburg PA
CBHW021146040525
26150CB00010B/174